CATCH A GHOST

HELL or HIGH WATER: BOOK 1

SE JAKES

Riptide Publishing
PO Box 1537
Burnsville, NC 28714
www.riptidepublishing.com

Cover art: Victoria Colotta, www.vmc-artdesign.com/vmc
Editor: Sarah Frantz
Layout: L.C. Chase, lcchase.com/design.htm

ISBN: 978-1-62649-039-0

First edition
September, 2013

Also available in ebook:
ISBN: 978-1-62649-038-3

CATCH A GHOST

HELL or HIGH WATER: BOOK 1

SE JAKES

For JH, because it all started with you.

You don't know what you're alive for until you know what you would die for.

—Martin Luther King, Jr.

Every saint has a past and every sinner has a future.

—Oscar Wilde

TABLE OF CONTENTS

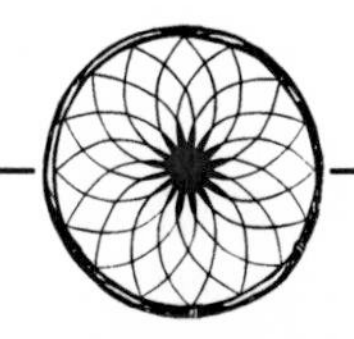

PROLOGUE

The encrypted email had been sent to Tom Boudreaux's private email address. He couldn't trace its origins, but after watching the video attachment, he was betting it hadn't come from either of the men who held the starring roles.

The footage was dated a decade ago. The quality was grainy and slightly dark, but steady, most likely shot from a mounted camera fixed at a slightly downward angle to capture what appeared to be an interrogation of a military prisoner.

The opening shot showed a small room, cut in half by a table. Two men sat across from one another. The first man's face was shadowed—purposely so, perhaps—and he was dressed in battle fatigues. Directly across from him sat a younger man, his face in plain view, his wrists handcuffed, the chain passed through a metal ring attached to the table in front of him.

His hair was blond and spiked with sweat and blood. His nose looked broken; his eyes were already bruised underneath. His chest was bare except for his dog tags and some tape wrapped around his ribs. There were enough bruises on his body to fell most men.

But not this one.

He didn't shift in his seat or look uncomfortable or scared. Instead, he listened to the interrogator's questions silently, with what might've actually been a trace of amusement.

"Why were you on the border?"

"Who sent you?"

"Are you a spy?"

At some point, the prisoner began a continuous sort of half humming, half singing under his breath, words to a tune that Tom couldn't quite place.

Interrogation was all about the mindfuck. But this guy—who looked maybe nineteen if he was a day—was better doing the fucking than being fucked, and that made the interrogator angry. He banged the table, repeating the questions, and the young guy kept his singing/humming routine going. This time, Tom caught a few of the words—*world* and *alive*—and realized that both men were American.

Maybe this is just a training session? Tom knew they could get brutal, especially for Special Forces operators.

The interrogator spoke, a low, short burst—Tom couldn't catch it no matter how closely he listened, no matter how many times he rewound—before he reached across the table and ripped the tags off the young man, hard enough to jerk his body forward before the chain broke.

"We know you killed an innocent man. No one's coming to help you."

The interrogator threw the tags across the room. Tom couldn't see where they landed, but he heard the ominous clank when they did.

Tom's blood ran cold as something in the young man's eyes changed. It had nothing to do with the interrogator's words. No, it happened when the tags were thrown away.

The next moves took mere moments. The young man managed to pick the table up with his wrists still chained to it, knocked his interrogator to the ground, and pinned him there by his neck with a table leg. The camera was blocked for a few seconds as other men rushed into the room, all yelling.

When the men cleared the camera space, Tom saw the young man refusing to move, even with guns pointed at his head. His knees were on the table, and he was balanced just well enough so the interrogator could breathe. But if he leaned forward, even a little . . .

None of the men were rushing him, probably afraid he'd move and break the interrogator's neck. The young man turned his head toward the camera, teeth bared in a feral snarl, and then the video cut off abruptly.

CHAPTER ONE

One month later.

Prophet didn't like sitting still, found it nearly impossible to do so unless it was a life-or-death situation—and that had to be literally life or death and not some bullshit *sit still or I'll kill you* type of non-threat.

Right now, he was supposed to be playing good little office boy. Doing paperwork, which sucked anyway, but more so because he was wearing not one, but two casts. Goddamn it. He looked mutinously down at the blue encasements that covered his hands and forearms to just below his elbows, and fought the urge to slam them against the desk. He'd done that once before—it'd cracked in half, but it'd been a different kind of cast. These he could fucking take a grenade to and they wouldn't open, thanks to Doc's tricks.

There were a few marks on one from where he'd tried to saw it with his KA-BAR, but that had just made the ends a little sharper and the whole thing more annoying than it had been, which was already pretty damned annoying. Although still not as annoying as the paperwork.

He planned on rectifying that situation as soon as the office emptied out a little—with a match, a garbage can, and a disabled smoke alarm—

The phone rang. He stared at it like that would make it stop. Desk duty wasn't his forte, and this was some serious desk duty. It was partially because of his injuries—although he'd played hurt before—but mainly because of what he considered a minor infraction on his last trip out.

Obviously, his boss disagreed that storming a building protected by twenty guards and a state-of-the-art alarm system, without waiting for backup, and with a thief who hadn't technically, as of that mission, been an Extreme Escapes employee, was a minor infraction (although he'd like to point out that all the good guys had lived, thank you very much), but hell, Phil Butler had known him long enough to realize that nothing with him ever went by the book.

Since the damned phone wouldn't shut up, he finally answered with, "Yeah," and then someone was yelling in his ear. Oh, hell no, he didn't do that. He hung up and it started to ring again almost immediately. He muted the volume and began to draw on his cast, highlighting the number he'd gotten at the bar last night, before Phil walked into Prophet's office—unannounced and without knocking—and slammed files down on his desk.

"Ah, come on, man." Prophet flipped through them. "I finished these."

"Not completely."

"I thought the benefit of working here was not having to do this shit," he groused, but Phil just smiled. Because Phil was grooming him, he knew, to take over EE. But the old man wasn't all that old, and he wasn't going anywhere for a while.

Plus, Prophet guessed he should be grateful he could still do shit like paperwork.

"Finish it and I'll buy you lunch," Phil said.

Prophet started to nod, then pushed back in his chair, which went flying, stopped only by the wall. "What do you want?"

"You're all so suspicious."

Prophet pointed a finger at him. "Because you only buy lunch when you're up to shit. Dinner's reserved for someone who's dying."

Phil pressed his lips together, pinched a thumb and forefinger to the bridge of his nose—the classic *I'm trying to hold it together so I don't kill Prophet* signal—and said, "You're getting a partner."

"What?"

Phil spoke louder. "You're getting a—"

"I heard you. It's the eyes, not the ears."

"Hey, you made a joke."

Prophet couldn't even begin to curse the man for that. He was too distraught over the partner thing. "Why now? It's been a year."

"I know. You're not the easiest man to partner up."

"So why try?" Prophet ground out.

"Because these are my rules."

"You own this place—you can change the rules anytime you want."

"True." Phil rubbed his chin with two fingers as he contemplated Prophet's words, then smiled. "Try this new rule on for size—you can't order office supplies."

"This isn't going to work."

"It has to."

"This isn't another one of your jail charity cases, is it?" he asked, and Phil shrugged. "Ah, come on. Who is he? Some prick fresh from Special Forces, thinking he's the shit?"

"And that would differentiate him from you, how?"

Prophet pointed at him. "Nice one, Phil. Come on, answer the damned question."

Phil conceded, leaning a hip on desk as he said, "Most recently, he was a deputy in one of the parishes of New Orleans. He's former FBI, too."

Prophet groaned, put his forehead on the desk and slammed it lightly several times. "I don't know which is worse—the Cajun part or the Fed part. Don't we have anyone applying here who's a career criminal? I could at least learn something useful."

"Just Blue—and he's already partnered up," Phil pointed out. "And we're being a bit dramatic, no?"

"No," Prophet deadpanned. "Look, I'll do a job with him, but this permanent partner thing..."

"You know why I'm doing it."

Prophet straightened. "So what? This guy's going to be like my Seeing Eye dog? Because I could just get a real dog, you know. Would save everyone a lot of time and money."

"Yes, that would work out so well jumping out of planes."

"I'm fine for now, Phil. I wouldn't be accepting missions if I wasn't."

"I know. I get your doctor reports."

"And when I'm not—"

"I prepare for any and all eventualities," Phil said, echoing what Prophet told him on a daily basis. "And I'm not losing you. This partner thing is final."

Prophet knew better than to continue arguing. He rubbed his cheeks with his fingertips, realized he needed a shave badly. He looked down at the sweats and ripped T-shirt he wore because he'd come here straight from training, without bothering with things like a shower. Or shoes. "Fine," he mumbled. "But don't expect me to like him."

Phil handed him another file he'd had tucked under his arm. "New mission intel. And I never know what the hell to expect from you anyway. He'll be here soon."

"Soon, like soon?"

Again, Phil did the nose pinching thing and walked away, cursing to himself under his breath. Prophet had that effect on everyone, he supposed.

No time to shower or change. But hell, he wasn't looking to impress. Maybe the guy would think he looked like a crazy homeless person and demand another partner.

He gave his most put-upon sigh and left his office with the new op file to go raid the supply closet in the common area looking for his favorite pencils. Because when he was forced to ride a desk, he wanted his favorite supplies. Was keeping them in stock too much to ask?

Apparently so. And now he couldn't even order them.

He grabbed a box of paper clips instead so he could try to fix the communal copy machine. He pulled open one of the panels that held the ink supply, brushed the hair out of his eyes impatiently. Too long for most jobs, maybe even longer than he really liked it, but he wore it this way because he could. A daily reminder of his freedom from the bullshit bureaucracy that had hampered him in the past. But the thing of it was, he couldn't escape the future hurtling toward him like a meteor delivering a death blow.

Going blind doesn't have to be a death sentence.

For him, he wondered if it would be.

No one knew, except Phil. Prophet had told him in the hopes that Phil wouldn't want him for EE, that he'd stop courting him and just go away.

That hadn't happened, obviously. Phil had made sure that no one else at EE knew, except for Doc, and he'd made sure Prophet's insurance at EE covered the specialist he now saw.

It would be up to Prophet when and if to tell anyone else at EE, and he wouldn't ever do it. Didn't need anyone treating him differently. Especially a new partner.

He thought about heading out to lunch, but he wanted to see if the guy was punctual. If he wasn't, Prophet would yell at him. And if he was, it'd prove that he was some kind of kiss-ass to Phil.

A sense of dull foreboding overtook him and he tried to shake it, but couldn't. Another glance at the clock, and he looked down in time to see Phil usher a man into his corner office.

Right on time.

Asshole.

To distract himself, he leaned against the copy machine and paged through the new mission file Phil had given him. He and his new, annoying partner were set to fly to Eritrea. EE kept a second base of operations there. Most of the time, it was strictly recon, which meant you'd wait for something to happen, check in twice a day, and then maybe, if you were lucky—or unlucky—be sent out to do something.

Still, Prophet always managed to find some trouble there. It was hot. Corrupt. And he'd need plenty of weapons and cash for payoffs. T-shirts and candy for the kids. And knives. Maybe another machete because last time he was in-country, he'd broken his. A hell of a trip, his souvenir was an elbow that ached when it rained, and a scar on the back of his neck from the guy who had tried to cut his head off.

With Prophet's own machete. So maybe scratch the machete.

Elliot was in the Eritrea office, had been for the past three months while he'd healed from a bullet wound. Prophet assumed he was being sent there to heal as well, and probably to bond with his new partner.

Son of a bitch.

He glanced up at the man who walked out of Phil's office. The guy was almost as tall as Doc, which put him in the six-foot-five range. And he was broad, with dark hair, but man, the chip on his shoulder was visible from the fucking moon.

Prophet stared down at his casts and sighed. Picked at the edges of them. Wondered if he went into an ER and complained about pain whether they'd take them off for him, then remembered he was banned from the two closest ERs. He pulled his phone from his pocket and Googled ERs over twenty miles away, flagging a few viable options, until a shadow fell across him.

No doubt the gargantuan man. He took his time looking up, and when he did, he stuck out one of his casted hands. "I'm Prophet."

"Seriously?"

"Why? What's your name? Jesus?"

The guy didn't crack a smile. One of his eyes was green, the other mostly brown, and it gave him a slightly unbalanced look, like a German shorthaired pointer Prophet'd once owned. But man, could that dog track.

"I'm Tom Boudreaux." He ignored the casted hand, and Prophet pulled it back. Saw Phil hovering a few feet away. What did Phil think he'd do, punch him out in the middle of the office?

"Nice to meet you, Tommy," he said, smiling, and the guy rolled his eyes at him and wasn't this going to be fun? Prophet rubbed his fingers along the back of his neck. Getting his head cut off with a machete would be more fun than this, but he forced himself to be semi-human. "What's your background?"

"I don't tell people things like that unless they buy me dinner first." The drawl sounded deep Cajun. The drawn-out words and the lilting, easy roll of his voice made Prophet want to throw a chair at him, mainly because it had always been an accent he'd found irresistible. On anyone but this guy.

Okay, a little on this guy. Fucking bayou asshole.

But I'll bet he can definitely track.

"Dude, what's your area of expertise?" Prophet tried again.

"What's yours?"

"Look, I'm not getting into a pissing contest with you."

Tommy narrowed his eyes at him. "Didn't want a partner?"

"Never."

"Awesome. Glad we got that out of the way. Because neither did I."

"Got it, Tommy."

"Tom," the man said evenly.

"What I said."

"This is going to go well," Phil said, more to himself than to them. "Look, assholes, everyone here works with a partner. Don't fuck this up or I will fuck you up. Both of you."

Prophet didn't doubt it—the former Marine wasn't even six feet, but he was stout and muscled. And Prophet had learned a long time ago that bigger didn't always equal winning, which was good for him.

Not that he was small, but six foot two was a midget among this land of six foot four–plus giants.

"I've got shit to do," he told Tommy, turned away from him and toward the copy machine. The paper tray wouldn't even open, so he banged his casts on it a few times, and the damned thing started working for the first time in days. "I should get some kind of bonus for that," he told Phil.

"I've got a bonus for you, all right," Phil shot back.

"You're not talking about him, right?" Prophet pointed at Tommy. "Because no."

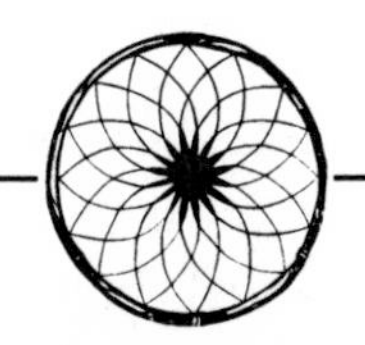

CHAPTER TWO

Meeting the man from the video shouldn't have been so goddamned unexpected.

You've really lost your touch, Boudreaux. You're off your game.

Tom hoped he'd get it all back soon. Like riding a bike. Although he felt more like he'd just fallen off one and gotten run over in the process.

Why the hell someone had sent him that video of his new partner—how anyone knew Prophet would be his new partner a month ago—was the most pressing question.

Not telling Prophet about it at all was the best course of action until he discovered the answer. He already had the proof that Prophet was a maniac—a lethal one, both things perhaps born from necessity.

Or maybe he was just born that way.

He was a couple of inches shorter than Tom, and lankier. And there was no mistaking the fact that the man had war in his eyes. Tom didn't know if the general population could see it, or if they'd stop at the rugged handsomeness, the way he looked as though he'd just literally rolled out of bed . . . and hadn't been sleeping.

But if you watched closely, you'd see that his gaze swallowed whole areas, that he stalked as opposed to simply moved. That he missed nothing.

The man was trouble. Those eyes had him locked and loaded, and Tom would've felt less conspicuous naked on a float in the middle of Mardi Gras. He didn't scare easily, but this could easily become the most trouble he'd had in his life, and that was saying something.

As he watched Prophet walk away, Tom rubbed a hand across the back of his neck, then cursed because he was mirroring the man.

"That went well," Phil said as he escorted Tom into a large office across from his.

"Is this the part where you tell me he'll come around?"

"Hell, no."

At least Phil Butler was an honest man. Five minutes before he'd met Prophet, Phil had told him, "We're more of a discover-on-your-own type of company. I don't have time to hand-hold you through a partner or a mission."

All Tom had been able to get out of Phil was his partner's age—thirty-one to Tom's thirty-six—and the fact that Prophet was probably one of the best operatives Phil had ever seen, hands down. He'd used words like *highly skilled*, *capable*, and *lots of field experience*.

EE had a reputation for providing their operatives with everything they needed, including what Phil liked to call creative freedom. They'd also given him a lot of training the past month. He'd had his ass kicked by several operatives to get him up to speed on everything from new techniques in hand-to-hand and weaponry, to demolitions and explosives. It was a crash course, one Phil told him would continue in between his missions.

"What else do I need to know about Prophet?" Tom asked him now. "Real name, maybe?"

But Phil ignored his question, telling him instead, "You can work here or at home. Most operatives rarely come in unless there's a meeting. Just know your intel for your first mission. Details are in your secured email." Phil pointed to the laptop on an empty desk before he left the room.

Email. Right. He opened the brand new computer and found that his first name popped up, along with a list of passwords for him to reset. He did so quickly, anxious to check that he could get his secured emails, knowing he'd read them when he was out of this place and away from the maniac. He'd figured if he could deal with the Cajuns, he could deal with anything. He might've been seriously wrong.

Someone knocked briefly on the still-open door. He turned to see the woman he'd met earlier—Natasha, from support systems—and motioned for her to come in. She was tall and slim, and he had a feeling her body type belied her capabilities. Phil had told him that even the support staff knew how to kick ass.

Natasha would run the computers when they were on missions. Get them supplies. And right now, she might be his best friend here, because she asked, "What do you want to know?" with a small smile playing on her lips.

"Anything."

She looked behind her and moved closer, rather than shutting the door. Whispered conspiratorially, "He's been working here for years. I think he was Phil's very first recruit when he started EE, but his file's nowhere to be found. New partners always ask for it. He's also former Special Forces—SEALs, I think."

"Ah, fuck."

"Right. And I think he was in the CIA, too."

Worse. So much worse. He wanted to bang his head against the desk, and she seemed to sense that. "He's really not *that* bad, Tom."

Yeah, okay. "What's his real name?"

Natasha smiled broadly this time. "Why don't you ask him?"

Because I don't really care. "I will." He paused. "Wait—you don't know yourself, right?"

Natasha shrugged. "I've given you more than you'll get from him in a year."

It still didn't stop him from asking the question he of all people had no right to ask. "Why can't he keep a partner?"

"If it helps, they all want to keep him. He's the one who disengages."

Now *that* was interesting. "He'd kill you for giving this away."

"I know. But he messed up my supply order twice. I warned him."

Tom couldn't help but laugh as she slipped out the door. Maybe there was hope for this place yet.

It was only when he went to shut the door that he realized that the thing on the other side of the fairly large room was a desk. Covered with a tarp of some sort.

Prophet kicked the door open seconds later, which explained the black scuff marks on both sides. He was carrying a can of Coke and a box of donuts balanced precariously on files. All of it got dumped on Tom's desk.

"We're sharing an office?"

"Technically, you're sharing my office," Prophet pointed out.

"Are you going to be a dick the entire time we're working together?"

Prophet smirked. "I'm what they label 'not good with authority,' Tommy."

"Great. And it's Tom."

"But you're not an authority figure, so as long as *you* don't act like a dick, we shouldn't have a problem, right?"

"Seriously, I'm going to kill you," Tom told him, then muttered, "If I can't hide the body well enough, it will be so worth it going to jail."

"I heard that," Prophet called over his shoulder as he left the room with the donuts.

"I meant you to."

So he was stuck with an asshole who happened to be former Special Forces—and a possible POW, according to the mystery video—and CIA to crazy-assed mercenary who'd been allowed to roam the earth shooting things and amassing destruction in his wake.

And he rescues people too. Helps those who can't help themselves, Tom reminded himself. Because this job paid well, sure, but the missions weren't frivolous, and they were never against the interests of the United States.

Yeah, so the bastard is a walking paradox.

He'd partner with the guy for this job, prove himself to Butler, and then he'd ask to work with someone new. For all he knew, Prophet the Great would do the same thing.

How bad could it possibly be?

He opened the one email he found and stared at the ticket that popped up, revealing his first trip.

To Eritrea.

With Prophet.

In a small office.

For three months.

So yeah, it was bad. Really, really goddamned, motherfucking horribly bad.

Then he saw the actual email, which started, "Prophet will share the mission plans with you."

Yeah, right.

Because Prophet, of course, was nowhere to be found.

There was nothing else of any help to him but a "what to pack for the extended trip" missive and a "don't bring your own weapons" clause. He slammed down the lid of the computer, grabbed the cord, and walked out of the EE offices to his Harley. Maybe a long-assed ride would make everything better.

He had to move forward, because there was nothing to go back to. Sometimes, having no choice made every decision, no matter how bad it seemed, easier.

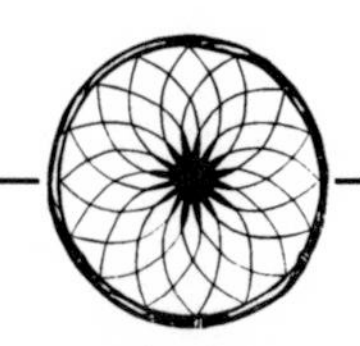

CHAPTER THREE

No weapons his ass. Prophet never went on a trip without a little something of his own, didn't give a shit that the Eritrea office had enough C-4 to blow up the country and then some. He liked something on his own person at all times, and the ceramic knife would pass muster easily enough. His go bag was always packed, one at home and one here at the office. Now he locked away some of the weapons he wouldn't risk, and prepared to do nothing but prep until takeoff. Which should've been tonight, as far as he was concerned, but there were always reasons.

His new partner had gone home. Emailed him and said he'd meet him on the plane, as if Prophet gave a shit. Asked for the mission plans, which Prophet reluctantly had Natasha deliver to him. They didn't send shit by email when they didn't have to, no matter how secure. Messenger and then burning the evidence was the way Phil had learned to do things, and it was still the man's preference.

It was also his preference to have EE tucked away from the busier cities. That's why EE's main office was a large house located several hours outside of Manhattan. Moderate weather for a good portion of the year, easy access to both the small local airports and the major international ones too. Ten support staff worked the day shift on a rotating basis—same with the night staff—and on any given day there were a couple of operatives wandering through the halls. And, he supposed, Phil Butler was ever present.

The office also had a twenty-four-hour on-call support staff in case they needed backup. EE was a twenty-four-seven job, and everyone who worked here treated it as seriously as if they were an operative in the field. Because the operatives in the field depended on those men and women behind the desks.

Phil had a real hard-on about the buddy system lately. Yeah, it was safer for most, but Prophet had left that team shit behind. Didn't mind being anyone's backup on and off, but he'd be damned if he'd rely on someone like that.

Have to start relying on someone soon enough, as Phil liked to remind him.

Instead of going home, he hung out in one of the bedrooms on the upper floors of the office building. He'd gone over the file four times. Didn't need the map to tell him shit about the area, not like the fucking new guy, and as much as Prophet wanted back in the field, he could think of a zillion other places he'd rather go.

He paced the floor like an angry lion, tugging alternately at the casts. Felt like they each weighed a thousand pounds, and Doc had refused to take them off for the mission.

"You can shoot with casts—use both hands. Or use a knife. Or *let your partner* cover you," was all Doc had said. And dammit all to hell, he knew Prophet didn't need a partner, could do a proper job of hand-to-hand and wetwork with the casts by himself, a skill learned by necessity. And when Prophet had told him so in his most disgruntled tone, Doc had responded easily, "So you don't really need the casts off, do you?"

"So what, this is like a life lesson? Because I don't like those," Prophet had told him, and Doc'd merely grunted.

Around one in the morning, he showered with plastic bags on his hands and arms, which was a pain in the ass for washing anything, grabbed the well-worn *Shogun* paperback from his desk to tuck into his bag along with his computer, thought about going out for a drink, and decided on the diner for food instead. Ordered enough to put him into a comfortable food coma, and flirted with the waitress who was forty years older and kept squeezing his cheek.

He opened his laptop, logged in using his phone's secure Wi-Fi, and then entered the surveillance code into the private program that allowed him to check on his apartment. It had been wired six months earlier so he could monitor it without ever having to set foot in there. His was a second-floor walk-up with open loft space. It had once been an industrial building, and he'd bought the top two floors. The bottom two belonged to an international financier, which Prophet assumed meant spy. And Prophet assumed the guy, named Cillian—and yeah, he'd made fun of his name already—knew what he was too. They looked out for one another and the building, but they'd never actually met face to face.

He hadn't even known Cillian had wired the damned place until he got the guy's IM late one night.

Hope you don't mind, but I took several security measures you hadn't considered. Here's the link to your alarms and cams.

Usually, you ask if someone would mind before you do shit like that, he'd IM'd back.

Better to ask forgiveness than permission. I've heard that's your motto.

It's a good motto when I'm the one doing things I'm not supposed to. Good alarms, though, Prophet had conceded.

From there, they'd checked in often enough. Flirted, really. Prophet had even considered IM sex once, when he'd been bored out of his mind in Eritrea, but there had been a bombing outside his door just when things had gotten hot. Kind of ruined the whole moment.

This time, Cillian had been gone a week, according to his last message. There was nothing out of place except he'd stolen his lamp back.

Prophet had never actually seen Cillian without his buttoned-up businessman disguise. Knew the guy was dark haired and clean-cut. Former SAS, judging by the way he carried himself.

It was a very distinctive stance.

He typed, *You took the lamp.*

After a few seconds, Cillian IM'd back, *I imagine you sound indignant as you're saying that.*

You broke into my place.

Several times. And are we having a bit of selective memory that you broke into my place to steal it first?

Life runs more smoothly on selective memory. He decided against telling Cillian that the couch would be his next acquisition. *I'm leaving for a while.*

New case?

New case. New partner. Why he'd typed that, he didn't know.

Cillian was too sharp to let it pass. *You've never mentioned a partner before.*

I've had several.

I'd imagine.

Work partners, Cill. Mind out of the gutter.

It's more fun there. You and I both know it.

Prophet grinned at the truth in that.

So, you've had several partners but never mentioned any of them before. What is it about him?

Fuck, he'd gone this far. *Might be a permanent pairing. That's what's being threatened anyway.*

And how is he?

Pain in the ass.

Can't imagine he's not saying the same thing about you. There was a long pause and then, *Must run. Someone just tried to kill me.*

Can't imagine why.

Prophet clicked off to have the last word and continued eating.

His cell rang a little after two. He juggled three phones: EE's, a private one Phil didn't know about and therefore couldn't trace, and a third that only one other person in the entire world had the number to. A person who tied Prophet to his past so thoroughly that the yoke could choke him if he thought about it hard enough.

But tonight Prophet noted that it was quiet on that front. As it should be. As it needed to be. He didn't want any ghosts coming out of the woodwork.

This was the EE phone, the ring set specifically for Butler—Nazareth's *Hair of the Dog*—and he picked it up on the first ring.

"Mission's changed."

"To what?"

Phil paused. "I didn't want to tell you over the phone, but I'm on my way cross-country and didn't want to sit on this. I've got some bad news. It's about Christopher Morse."

"Is he hurt?"

"He's dead, Proph." Prophet closed his eyes as Phil's words hit him like a physical punch. As if Phil knew, he paused momentarily before continuing. "The police found his body in a dumpster a few days ago, but there was no ID. They had to use dental records, so he's already been autopsied."

If he'd been autopsied, they suspected foul play. "How was he killed?"

"You'll have to get that intel from the coroner's report. He's rushing it for me now that he's got a positive ID."

Fuck. Prophet fisted his hands, as best he could, on the diner's table and thought about the old scars under his casts, made with barbed wire wrapped around his arms and hands, ankles and feet, scars that always reminded him of what—who—got left behind.

Not your fault, Proph, his team had said. But he'd never believe it.

Phil cleared his throat. "You do want to check this out, right? Or should I send someone else?"

"I'll go," Prophet said, well aware of how hollow his voice sounded.

"Take Tom."

"I can do this one alone."

"You shouldn't have to. Do whatever you needs to be done to give Christopher's parents some peace. I'll give Mick the other case. Natasha will drop the file to you any minute. She knows where to find you."

Because Phil insisted on GPS chips in all their phones and other devices. And Phil could turn them on remotely if an operative decided to turn them off. "Okay."

"And Prophet?"

"Yeah?"

"Keep those fucking casts on."

Phil hung up, but Prophet cursed him up and down under his breath anyway. Five minutes later, he had the file from Natasha, along with new plane tickets for five that morning.

He thought seriously about not calling his new partner and just going alone, but he didn't need to hear Phil's shit about it. Besides, once Tommy fucked up, Prophet would have the excuse to get rid of him.

The phone rang in the middle of Tom's dream about a phone call and Prophet. He grabbed for his cell as he checked the time.

Three in the morning.

"Forget the file." Prophet's voice, rough but not from sleep. How Tom knew the difference—from watching the video about thirty times since this afternoon—and why he cared was another matter entirely. "We've been reassigned. Coming to get you in twenty."

He hung up. Tom didn't question how the man knew where he lived or his private cell number. With Prophet as a partner, he supposed privacy was a thing of the past.

With that in mind, he made sure his computer password was set, and he locked it down tight.

He was already packed, so he used his precious time to set coffee to brew, and then jumped in the shower with mostly cold water to keep him awake. Sleep had been interrupted by his inability to shake the video images of Prophet from his mind.

As an agent, he used to get mysterious, often classified intel on a regular basis. But that was years ago. Before getting the video of Prophet, the most important email he'd gotten was an invite to the firemen's annual gumbo cook-off.

He'd saved a copy of the video file on a thumb drive, and hid the original among his computer files, along with the original email. Maybe EE had ways to trace it that he didn't know about. A lot had changed in the five years he'd been out of the FBI. At first he'd attempted to stay up to speed, but trying to keep a hand in the world he was trying to quit hadn't worked. He'd eventually broken ties completely and gone back to his old ways, which included more backdoor hacking and do-it-yourself fixes than protocol had ever allowed.

The FBI didn't want him back. The parish didn't want him as their sheriff.

But Phil Butler had come in and offered him a chance. A chance with a fucking maniac for a partner. Prophet was impulsive. Reckless. Lethal. And sure, in the video he'd been under what might've been POW circumstances, but having met him in a non-life-threatening situation hadn't changed Tom's opinion. The guy could pull Tom into trouble far too easily, or at least not be able to pull Tom back from his own special brand of impulsiveness.

Tom knew he had to be on his best goddamned behavior, whether Phil came out and said so or not. Phil was testing him, and rightly so. But more than that, this was also about him and his own personal demons, and his ability to conquer them. If he was really going to get back in, he had to hold himself tight and not get lulled by a partner whose style included building a bomb in his office.

What had Phil been thinking with this match?

When Tom finished with his shower, he toweled off as he walked into the kitchen. Poured his coffee. Stilled with the cup halfway to his mouth, and said, "I still have twelve minutes."

"Twenty was the cap," Prophet offered.

Tom turned toward the dark living room and saw his new partner sitting in the room's single chair, one leg swung over the side. He wore a green bandana wrapped around his head, covering his hair completely, and jeans that looked like they'd seen better days. "How did you bypass the alarm?"

"Not telling my secrets. Why do you live like a transient?"

His apartment was half of an old Victorian. An elderly woman owned the house and lived on the other side. She had round-the-clock aides, and her estate took care of the rentals. Phil had set it up, and Tom had been grateful. The place was old but spotless. Heat. A/C. A working kitchen, and wired for cable. A garage for his motorcycle now, and for the car he'd buy when they returned for the winter months in upstate New York.

He had two suitcases, ten boxes, and his Harley. That was his life.

"Where's the rest of your shit?"

"Trying to minimize my carbon footprint."

Prophet rolled his eyes. "Cajun hippie."

"And I just got here."

"Been two weeks."

How did Prophet know that? And what else did he know?

You asked about him—what makes you think he didn't do the same?

Tom refused to show weakness. A man like Prophet could sense it. "Why do you have such a hard-on for me?" he demanded.

"It's my job. What's yours?"

"Being your partner."

"That all, Cajun? Because I'm thinking starting out lying to me is a bad thing."

It probably was, and he was pissed at Phil for putting him in the middle. "I was told to keep you safe."

Prophet nodded slowly in the dark. "I knew Phil would feed you some bullshit like that. You were told to keep me out of trouble—there's a big difference between trouble and safe."

"With you, I doubt it."

Tom didn't know why he'd said that, like he already had some sort of familiarity with the man. Prophet caught it too, stilled. But all he said was, "You don't know a damned thing about me. You gonna haul ass or what?"

Tom knew several damned things, some just from pure observation—like the fact that Prophet could have a career as a thief and that he was a general, all-purpose pain in the ass—but he shrugged and drank his coffee on the way to his bedroom to dress. It was odd to no longer have a uniform of any kind. He supposed dressing like a civilian was a uniform in and of itself, since he was officially undercover.

If Phil told you to keep Prophet out of trouble, what did he tell Prophet about you?

He didn't think he wanted to know. Instead of focusing on it, he grabbed his gear, but stopped cold when he heard Prophet doing that singing/humming thing. The same tune from the video—it was so clear he couldn't have mistaken it. He listened for a few minutes. Thought about telling the man what he'd been sent.

Then he dumped his coffee instead, flicked the machine off, and followed Prophet, who offered to do the alarm.

Tom let him.

Prophet drove an older-model Blazer that rode like it had something extra under the hood. The interior was fastidiously maintained—the only things out of place were the dog tags on the floor under Prophet's feet. There were two cups of to-go coffee in the cup holders, plus a bag of fast food crap that Tom wasn't above eating to wake himself up.

"Where are we going?"

"The morgue."

"We had to get up at 3 a.m. and pack to do that?" Tom asked around a mouthful of breakfast sandwich as Prophet tore along the highway.

"In Texas."

"You know how long of a drive that is?"

Prophet sighed. "We're taking a plane. You can read the files on the flight."

Tom finished the sandwich and crumpled the wrapper as he eyed the speedometer. "Does this happen often—the case changing?"

Prophet turned to face him with a smile. "And here I thought you'd be able to roll with anything, Cajun."

Never, he wanted to say. But instead, he pointed to Prophet's casts. "What happened there? Did you punch your last partner?"

Prophet had turned his attention back to the road. "Funny, Cajun."

"So why *does* Butler have a hard-on for partners?" he asked, because the hating partners thing—along with hating each other—was something they actually had in common.

Prophet sighed, like Tom was the most annoying person on the planet. "He thinks that EE should be like other agencies in that regard, that partnering keeps operatives from going over the edge, going rogue, going crazy. That kind of shit." He waved a casted arm for emphasis, barely hanging onto the wheel with the fingers on his other hand as the Blazer edged toward 90 mph. "EE doesn't have the same rules as the CIA or the FBI or even the military, which I'm sure you already know, but Phil's a stickler for this partner shit. No getting around it. Not for long, anyway."

Tom wasn't sure why he'd asked about partners. He *definitely* didn't want to talk about his past partners in particular. That subject always made his gut ache, so he nodded and dropped it.

He'd agreed to work at EE, Ltd. because he'd assumed that a private contracting company would want people who were independent. Able and willing to work solo. He'd been wrong about that, but he'd also been immediately impressed with Phil Butler. And he was willing to do anything to get back into the game.

"What exactly do you do?" Prophet glanced over at him, his gray eyes the color of an impending storm. "I can't partner with someone unless I know their deal. We have to be able to work together effectively."

"You don't even want a partner, so who are you kidding?"

"We're stuck with one another. You have my life in your hands. And vice versa. It's time for cooperation."

Tom knew this would be a one-way street, but it didn't matter—he wouldn't have Prophet's life on his conscience. "I left the FBI five years ago. I was a field agent, not a desk jockey."

But Prophet only focused on one thing. "Left?"

"Was asked to take leave. A big fuck-up on a case. I resigned instead."

"Let me guess—it was all a mistake. Not your fault."

"It was all my fault."

Prophet looked at him with something akin to respect. If admitting failure was all it took, well, hell, Tom had a chance.

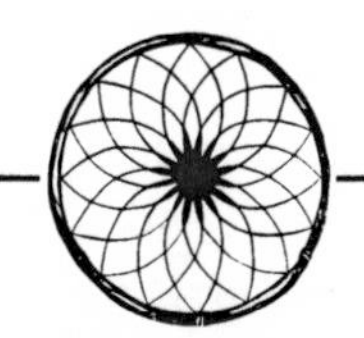

CHAPTER FOUR

Whenever there was a ruckus at security, it was usually Prophet's fault, so it was odd to see one already in progress as he walked toward the area with a soda as big as his head. And he was going through with the damned drink. Somehow.

"What's going on?" he asked the TSA agent, who shrugged, checked his ID, and let him through. It was an odd time for a flight, so the airport terminal was quiet. Except for Tom, who waved his arms as he talked to security.

Prophet heard Tom's choice curses in what Prophet assumed was Cajun French, and walked over to rescue his partner.

Who was actually supposed to be keeping Prophet out of trouble.

He wanted to video this and send it to Phil. Better yet, put it up on YouTube. But by the time he'd gotten close—because he'd argued about keeping the soda with the second agent, telling her about hypoglycemia and the fact that it was only three ounces of soda and a lot of ice, and lost, and goddammit, someone owed him—Tom had disappeared.

He pulled the Air Marshal badge he'd gotten for emergencies like this one—and also because he was more than qualified to help out if there was any trouble on a flight—and asked the female guard, "That guy's with me. What's the problem?"

"He was randomly chosen for a pat-down. We found his piercings, and now he's putting himself through the X-ray machine," she said wearily, like she'd seen it all before. And Prophet could only shrug in sympathy as they watched Tom climbing onto the conveyor belt and lying down flat on his back.

She motioned for Prophet to follow her. As Tom's X-ray came through the machine, Prophet almost bit off his tongue. Clear nipple piercings and slightly more blurry cock piercings. Jesus, he hadn't expected that.

He swallowed hard, and a second agent sputtered, "Holy shit." And then Tom was out, smirking at Prophet and the agents.

"I told you they're attached," Tom said, starting to unzip his jeans. "Want me to show you?"

Prophet wasn't sure which one of them he was talking to, but he assumed it was security. To her credit, the female guard merely said, "Actually, yes, sir. I won't be the lucky one today, but you're still going to need a full body search."

Tom rolled his eyes, said, "Of course I am," under his breath.

"The ladies like that?" a male agent asked Tommy.

"Men like it more," Tom told him, which confirmed to Prophet that the physical yank he'd felt toward the man hadn't been his imagination. Fucking accent.

"To each his own," the male agent said, while Prophet ground through his teeth, "Why didn't you just take the damned things out?"

"Why don't you just fuck off?" Tom bit out, and oh yeah, this was going well and they weren't even on the plane yet. As Prophet put his bag through security and walked through the metal detector, Tom went into a private room with two male guards and came out five minutes later, the men shaking their heads and Tommy still angry at the world.

"You with him?" one of them asked, and Prophet nodded. "Good luck with that."

One of the female TSA agents slid something into Tommy's back jeans pocket, despite Tom's earlier statement. And then she smiled.

Ignoring Tom and his bitching, Prophet led the way across the airport and onto the plane that was nearly finished boarding. It was still coach, which always sucked. But Texas coach was way better than Africa coach.

"Sweetheart, please, some caffeine," Prophet said to one of the flight attendants as he passed the small room that housed the beverage carts. "Coke would be fine. Several of them. Full cans, not the bullshit little glasses."

He was handed two full cans as soon as he sat. He downed one immediately and opened the other. Found Tommy staring at him. "Guess you're not a morning person."

"I don't count four in the morning as morning," Tom said crankily, and stretched his long body as much as he could so his shirt came up a little. He hadn't bothered to tuck anything in after the strip search, and he looked disheveled and way different than he had at the office yesterday afternoon. And cramped in the small space. "I'm going to sleep."

Maybe Tom wanted to, but the guy was way too twitchy for that. Not angry any longer. More like distracted. "Scared of flying?" Prophet asked.

"Yeah, sure," Tom said, barely listening to him as he plugged in headphones. Prophet shrugged and gave up.

The flight was pretty crowded, but their middle seat person didn't show. Once the doors closed and the plane was moving toward the runway, Prophet took the opportunity to stretch his legs across the space. Tom was shifting in his seat, unable to settle in. He had his eyes closed and Bose noise-canceling headphones on, probably hoping they could cancel out his partner.

Good luck with that. Phil always said Prophet could push Mother Teresa to her limits. "I'd take it as a personal challenge," Prophet had told him, and Phil had done the pinching the bridge of his nose while muttering thing.

The announcement from the captain broke into his thoughts. Delay on the tarmac . . . back-up on the runway, third in line, or some shit like that. Other people groaned and the plane powered down a bit, even as the pilot reassured them that it wouldn't be long.

He thought about heading to the cockpit to check things out—half the time, he ended up knowing the pilot or found out they had someone in common—but decided against it. Mainly because he was still playing Air Marshal, but also because Tommy was still decidedly nervous.

He prepared to relax, maybe grab some sleep, when his internal warning radar went off. He'd always had more situational awareness than most, but the training he'd received brought it to levels that sometimes drove him nuts.

He was turning in his seat casually, trying to assess what the hell was happening, when Tom opened his eyes, took off the headphones and said, "Something's wrong."

"Folks, we're up next. Flight attendants, please prepare for takeoff."

Tom had been prepared for Prophet, at the very least, to give him some kind of smart remark. But the man stared straight at him and said, "Danger, or something else?"

It was maybe the first time a partner had ever asked him that, ever actually took him fucking seriously, and he didn't know what to do with that. So he said, "Something else," and Prophet stood and glanced over the passengers who were getting settled again, coming down the aisles from the bathrooms, being shepherded into submission by the flight attendants.

"How far out do your instincts usually run?" Prophet asked, half-kneeling, half-standing in his seat, holding the headrest as he focused on the passengers around him. "Because I'm guessing we don't want to be up in the air for whatever's about to happen."

"No," Tom managed, still stunned at Prophet's reaction.

The flight attendants were headed over, and Prophet said something about distracting them while Tom did his thing. He knew his time was limited, so he started walking, like he was some kind of human divining rod, because sometimes that worked.

He stopped alongside a row of three seats in the emergency exit aisle. In the seat closest to him sat a big guy with a big belly.

Heart attack. But not him.

His gaze shifted to the right, to the thin woman in the window seat who was sleeping, her phone ready to slip out of her hand. She was young, but . . .

"Her?" Prophet asked loudly from behind him as an alarm went off somewhere on the plane, causing flight attendants to scurry away, and the phone fell from the woman's hand to the floor.

"Her," Tom said as her face paled. He moved to get in front of her while Prophet yelled for the stewardess and a doctor.

"She's sleeping," Big Belly said.

"Since when?" Tom demanded as he put his fingers on the pulse of her neck.

Big Belly shrugged. "We were talking. She nodded off. Figured she was sending out an *I'm not that into you* message. And it wasn't very convincing," he added.

"Not everything's about you," Prophet said, as Tommy tried to gently rouse the young woman.

She was maybe twenty-eight, a little pale, but it was the sudden lack of color around her lips that alarmed him.

"I need O2," he told Prophet quietly. "And go through her bag—need her name."

"It's Kelly," Big Belly offered. "Is she dead?"

"And you wonder why no one's into you," Prophet said as Tommy tried to wake her a little more forcefully, calling her name and shaking her a little until she opened her eyes.

Prophet handed him the oxygen mask he'd requested—the flight attendant turned the portable tank on—but before Tom put it on her, he asked, "Do you have a heart condition?"

"Yes," she whispered. "Pills in my bag."

Prophet, of course, had already dumped it out and was searching for the nitroglycerin tablets as Tom let her breathe deeply into the mask.

"You're going to be fine. The EMTs are on the way," Tom told her. "Does this happen a lot?"

"Lately, yes," she said.

"Here." Prophet handed him the bottle and Tom read the prescription, shook out a pill, and helped Kelly put it under her tongue.

"How fast do those things work?" Prophet asked.

"Pretty fast," Tom said, without taking his eyes off Kelly. She'd grabbed for his hand at some point, and he squeezed it reassuringly now as the color began to return to her cheeks.

Prophet reached in between them, handing her the phone she'd dropped.

"Thanks," she said through the mask. "I want to call my dad." She let go of Tom's hand and began dialing. A few seconds later she was talking to someone and saying, "Yes, I don't think I can stay on the plane. Can you send someone for me?"

"The paramedics are here," the stewardess told Tom, and he stood and moved across the aisle where Prophet already was. "I'm so glad you were onboard to help. Are you a doctor?"

"A medic," Prophet said before Tom could say no, and then he heard the loud clank of the paramedics and their equipment behind him. They had their bags and a stretcher designed to fit down the aisle, and he and Prophet switched places with them to allow them access to the patient.

"We wait around much longer and we'll be dealing with press and police," Prophet murmured in his ear under the cover of the medic's questions.

"Why?"

"The name on the pill bottle—she's Senator Greenley's kid," Prophet said, and Tom stifled a groan, even as she hung up the phone, turned, and motioned for him.

"You okay?" Tom asked.

"Now I am. But how did you know?" she asked as Big Belly called out, "Hey, you guys are heroes."

"Gotta go," Prophet mouthed. He was on the phone, talking to someone, and motioning at the same time for Tom to grab their bags.

Tom edged away from the workers and the woman, with a smile and a shake of his head at the hero thing. He moved down the aisle, ignoring passengers who were trying to talk to him because of his newly minted hero status, and went to grab his and Prophet's bags. They'd have to get out before the emergency workers carried her out or their exit would be cut off.

He turned with their bags and made it to first class before he was stopped.

"I'm sorry, sir, but we can't let you off the plane," the flight attendant told Tom.

"You're going to let her off the plane," Prophet protested, coming up the aisle behind him.

She looked at him like he had five heads and a mental deficit, which Tom was pretty convinced he did, and said, "Because she almost had a heart attack."

"I think I am too. Ouch," he said seriously, a hand over his heart.

"Sir, I don't believe you."

"Why would you call me sir? Now this guy, he's way older than me." Prophet pointed to Tom, then said ouch a few more times. "Find my pills."

"I think you forgot them," Tom supplied. "We really need to get him off this plane."

Another fire alarm began ringing. And then another. People began jumping up, and the flight attendant who'd been arguing with them was forced to focus on the passengers who were anxious about the possibility that something was wrong with the plane. The doors were already open from the paramedics, and Prophet pushed Tom out and down the stairs as the pilot's voice came over the loudspeaker, calling for everyone to remain seated.

"Your handiwork?" Tom asked as they rounded the other side of the plane, his ears still ringing from the alarms.

"Thank me later."

They were on the tarmac, and Prophet took the lead, walking behind the ambulance and luggage cars toward where the private planes were parked. Tom followed, well aware he was probably being led to do something completely illegal.

Prophet grabbed him and yanked him into a holding bay that was half-full of luggage. Tom ended up pressed against the man, who simply held him in place with a strong arm across his back and told him to be quiet.

He lifted his head and found himself inches away from Prophet's face. His pulse raced, and it wasn't from the great escape they'd just made. He was too damned close to Prophet and his body was threatening to respond in a way that added yet another reason to the list of why this guy might be dangerous for him. Thankfully, the sirens racing by distracted him, because Prophet wasn't letting go. "I'm not going to run out onto the tarmac."

"Can't be sure of anything after that scene you made at security."

"Fuck off." He bent his head so he was staring at Prophet's neck. "Does this kind of shit just happen around you?"

"Sometimes."

Prophet grunted something that sounded like *Cajun voodoo shit*, and Tom didn't bother to tell him how close to the truth he was. "You have these premonitions often?"

"They're not . . . premonitions exactly."

"That's a shame. I was thinking of renting you out and making some extra money."

Tom pressed his lips together and didn't say anything, the all-too-familiar dread that he'd been found out settling in his gut. And Jesus, it'd come early this time.

"So if they're not premonitions, what the hell are they?"

"I never named them."

"And this happens to you all the time?"

"What if I say yes?"

Prophet leaned in closer, if that were possible. "I'd say you'd better make sure to give me plenty of lead time when your gut starts screaming. Because you held back today for ten minutes before you opened your mouth."

His head shot up, almost knocking Prophet in the chin, and he stared into those gray eyes to make sure the man was serious.

"You feel me, partner?"

Oh yeah. He nodded instead of saying that, then asked, "How the hell are we getting out of here?"

He heard Prophet's phone dialing. When Natasha picked up, she said, "What did you do now?"

"Ah, don't be like that, Natasha. It wasn't my fault a woman nearly had a heart attack."

"Never is."

Tom waited for Prophet to sell him out, but that didn't happen. Instead, pressed against his new partner in the dark, hoping not to be arrested, he realized that maybe this could work.

Maybe.

"You gonna make a scene again with security?" Prophet asked when he'd hung up with Natasha, sliding his phone back in his pocket, the small space making it impossible not to touch Tom somehow.

"You keep mentioning it. Must've liked what you saw."

Prophet huffed a laugh. "Whatever you say, Cajun."

"You realize your hand's in my pocket, right?"

No, he hadn't. Damned casts. But he left his hand where it was, just to see if it annoyed Tom . . . or if it really bothered him.

Tom's body was all hard angles against his. In the tight space, Prophet got the answer he was looking for. Tom had been comfortable being pressed against a man like that and yet uncomfortable enough that Prophet knew the zing of attraction was mutual. He'd known it from the second he'd heard Tom's drawl and had forced himself to act the opposite way, figuring if he pretended he couldn't stand the guy that his body would decide to agree with his brain.

As usual, his dick had other ideas.

Screwing a partner is never a good idea.

Having a partner wasn't either, though.

He pulled his hand away and put the phone in his own pocket this time. Hopefully.

The most interesting thing he'd just learned about his partner though, apart from the attraction and the psychic stuff, was the fact that he'd been right. This man was a born tracker. Even standing completely still, he was taking stock of everything around them. Prophet was doing the same thing, but wasn't nearly as still. He caught himself jiggling his foot a few times. Tapped his fingers against the wall behind them. None of it would get them caught, but stillness wasn't his forte, not like Tom, who he was sure was born to it. For Prophet, it was born from necessity in the military.

And he was pretty sure Tom would notice and mention it in three, two . . .

"Do you ever sit still?" Tom asked, his jaw clenched in a way Prophet recognized. Most people who dealt with him at one time or another wore that look. He didn't need to be psychic to know that the nose pinching would come next.

He started whistling "I Shot the Sheriff," which earned him a dirty look. "I think we're clear to go, Cajun."

"You're really going to keep calling me that?" Tom asked. "Granted, I guess it's better than Voodoo."

"I'll find a way to combine the two," he reassured Tommy, who merely grunted as he pushed away and then disappeared like a ghost.

Nice move, partner.

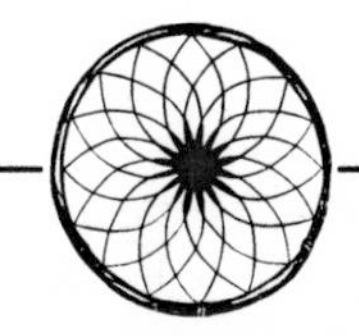

CHAPTER FIVE

Twelve hours after they'd started the trip, they were in a Houston coroner's office. Prophet was sitting calmly in the waiting room, head back against the wall, eyes closed.

Tom didn't know how, because he'd watched him work his way through an entire bag of red Twizzlers in the last hour. He'd figured Prophet would be all jacked up because of the candy. The man had already been increasingly on edge the closer they'd gotten to the morgue, and any progress they'd made between them had quickly disintegrated.

Prophet had only glanced at the photos and the coroner's report before he'd announced to anyone who would listen, "This is worthless to me—I need to see the body."

Tom had taken the file back. "Figured you'd say that."

"Well, let's label you Psychic Hotline and be done with it."

Tom had nearly bit his tongue off trying not to goad Prophet into further insults, which probably annoyed Prophet more than anything. Tom couldn't figure out if the guy was doing it to purposely bug the shit out of him, or if this was simply how he operated on a day-to-day basis. It was like trying to balance in quicksand—in the end, it was easier to give up and let yourself get pulled under.

He glanced through the coroner's report now, silently agreeing with Prophet that it was worthless. It listed the cause of death of the twenty-four-year-old Caucasian male named Christopher Morse as massive cerebral contusions consistent with a skull fracture, which meant it was being treated as an active homicide. The pictures detailed the various bruises the victim had received, but there was little speculation as to whether they were made pre- or post-mortem, or if some of them had been caused by being thrown into the nearly empty dumpster. Whether the coroner was incompetent or had treated this like a street kid's death he hadn't thought anyone would pay particular interest to, Tom didn't know, but when he came out, he looked both apologetic and nervous.

"I understand you're private investigators, hired by the family," he said to Tom and Prophet.

"Your report's incomplete," were Prophet's first words to him.

"We'd like to see the body, sir," Tom said quickly, shooting Prophet a look as they both pulled their PI badges to show the coroner, who was now glaring at Prophet. Phil had prepared them well for any and all eventualities, and lying for the greater good went hand in hand with this job.

"If you don't believe that, you'll never last here," Phil had warned Tom.

They followed the coroner down the hall and into a room with metal shelving along the far wall. The coroner pulled out a drawer near the middle and uncovered the body. He moved aside because Prophet crowded him, giving him no choice.

Tom moved to the other side of the body as Prophet stared down at the guy with the toe tag and swallowed hard. Put a hand on his cheek and murmured something in a language Tom didn't recognize, but he got the gist of it. Prophet knew this guy. So this whole thing was personal.

Even with the massive facial bruising, it was obvious Christopher Morse had been a handsome young man. His blond hair was shaggy and would have hung below his ears. He was listed as six feet one inch and two hundred pounds, most of that appearing to be solid muscle.

His bruising looked consistent with having been beaten by fists, especially along his rib cage.

"He's got a skull fracture along the right side of his head," the coroner pointed out. "The majority of the bruising was made before he died. A few are consistent with being dumped."

"Maybe you could put that in the fucking report." Prophet's voice was a dangerous growl that had the coroner taking a step back.

Tom took the opportunity to look at the victim's hands. They'd been wiped clean of blood, but there were bruises and cuts on the knuckles.

"Were they taped?" he asked the coroner.

"We found some residue, yes, across the knuckles and inside the palm. But no tape itself." Tom looked over to Prophet, but the man wasn't listening.

Instead, Prophet touched the boy's forehead and whispered something as he glanced between the body and the report, and Tom stared at him until Prophet said, "If you want to find your own ride to the hotel, keep staring," before stalking out of the room.

Tom sighed, asked the coroner a few more questions before handing back his file and taking the copies the secretary had made for him. Prophet wasn't in the outer waiting area. Tom found him in the driver's seat of the rental car, the music jacked up to an earsplitting level.

He turned it down after closing the door, then slammed sideways as Prophet took the corner on what could've easily been two wheels. "He was fighting before he died."

"Really," Prophet said in what was probably his best *duh* voice.

"He was wearing tape on his hands, but judging by how badly they were bruised, he didn't wear boxing gloves. The taping is consistent with the kind of illegal cage fighting that's popular in this area of the country. The rings started in Texas and spread to Louisiana pretty quickly. Christopher's injuries are also consistent with it."

Prophet flicked him a glance, like he was surprised Tom had used his name. Surprised—and appreciative. "Chris is dead—how's that consistent?"

"I've seen kids get killed fighting like this before—the injuries match up. The biggest up-and-coming ring is over in the Fifth Ward. Guys who ran the fights used to dump the kids who were killed into the bayou." He pulled a blue card out of his pocket and held it out to Prophet, who took it and turned it over. "I pulled it out of the evidence bag after you left. The coroner said it was in the back pocket of his jeans. No one thought to run it."

"Because it's blank."

"No. Just printed in invisible ink. It's an invite." He pulled up the links to the forums on his phone, which explained the cards and their color-coding for each league, and for fighters versus audience members, and read it to Prophet as he drove.

"Okay, so it's the right color for this league and for a fighter."

"The coroner said he had multiple healed fractures, and that most of them were recent, but when I pressed him, he admitted that he'd found others that went back years. He said it looked like Christopher had been fighting for a long time. And you need to tell me what the hell's going on with this case."

Tom's words came out more forcefully than he'd intended. It must've impressed Prophet enough, because he pulled over into a McDonald's parking lot instead of getting on the parkway. He drummed his hands on the steering wheel, keeping time with some beat inside his head before speaking.

"Yes, I knew Christopher. Yes, that's why we ended up on this case." Prophet spoke evenly, despite looking like he could explode at any second.

"Who is he?"

"I know his family. I served with his brother." He paused. "John didn't come home. Christopher was twelve at the time—took it hard at first, then went off the deep end a few years later. Got suspended, then expelled, and had to be home-schooled. Saw shrinks, took meds, but nothing helped. When he was sixteen, he just ran. If what you're saying pans out, maybe he threw himself into illegal cage fighting as a way to get out his aggression. And I don't expect you to understand that."

Tom did, more than Prophet could've known. But all he did was nod, tell his new partner, "If you don't tell me shit like that, then I don't know what's driving you. Like you said earlier, I can't partner with someone unless I know their deal."

"And now you know. So we're good to move ahead?"

Tom bit back sarcasm, but only because of Prophet's personal connection to Christopher. "Yes. Since you know the family, do you think any of the broken bones could've been from child abuse?"

Prophet shook his head. "Nah. I would've known. This family—they were perfect."

"No one's perfect, Prophet. No matter what, we need to talk to Christopher's parents."

"No. They don't know anything. I'm not going to drag them through shit again."

"I will, then."

Prophet barely moved, but Tom found himself pressed against the seat, Prophet half on him, his casted arm across Tom's throat. "You will not bother this family. They've been through hell."

He blinked, stared into the man's eyes. They were close enough for him to see a few flecks of blue peppered among the gray, threatening to break through the storm. His body was heavy against Tom's, and Tom flashed to the younger Prophet from the video with that crazed look in his eyes.

But the man holding his throat was in total control, and his eyes were almost serene.

"I'd think they'd want to do whatever it takes to find who killed Christopher," he managed, voice strangled, attempting to mimic a calm he didn't feel.

"His parents haven't seen or heard from him in years."

"You talked to them?"

"Not recently."

"Then I don't buy they don't know anything."

"I do."

"That's your conscience talking."

"You want to compare consciences, Voodoo?" Prophet growled.

"Not really. But I can obviously spot a guilty one a mile away. Now get the fuck off me."

Prophet hissed and released him with a shove back. Tom felt shaky but remained staring straight ahead, like everything was fine. He knew he'd gotten his way when Prophet barked the address Tom had seen on Christopher's driver's license into the GPS.

Prophet knew the address by heart, after all these years.

The house was a small, well-kept colonial in the suburbs of a Texas town that was closer to the morgue than where Christopher had been found. Prophet hadn't spoken a word on the fifteen-minute ride, and the tension in the car was palpable. Prophet parked, slammed out of the car, and was halfway up the walk before Tom got out. Figured it was better if he was the one to make first contact anyway.

Prophet was almost to the door when a small, blonde woman opened it, put her hands on her mouth, and then hugged Prophet like he was a long lost son. There was an obvious tension between them, because Prophet hugged her back far less enthusiastically.

Tom waited them out, let them talk to one another in low tones before Prophet turned to acknowledge that he existed. But Prophet must've already talked about him, because the woman said, "Mr. Boudreaux, I'm Carole Morse."

"Please, call me Tom."

"Tommy," Prophet interjected, and Carole Morse rolled her eyes at him and waved them both inside. She'd been crying—her eyes held a watery redness and the skin around them was puffy.

"Have a seat, Tom. You, come help me," Carole told Prophet, and they disappeared into the kitchen. Tom caught a glance of dish after covered dish piled on the kitchen table. Because that's what grieving people did—they cooked and baked because there was nothing else to do. For Carole, grief seemed to be something hidden behind closed doors in the dead of night when no one else was around to see it. To show it, especially around company, would be disrespectful somehow.

She reminded him so much of his momma.

He turned toward the mantel, glanced through the pictures of the family and realized that Prophet had stayed here often. There were many photos of a younger Prophet with his arms around a guy who must've been John. Prophet was guarded in these photos, maybe even more than he was now.

He looked up when he heard raised voices from behind the closed kitchen door—Prophet's and Carole's—but it only lasted for a moment and then it went quiet again.

When they came back out of the kitchen, Tom turned from the mantel and sat on the couch across from Prophet and Carole. She pushed a lemonade across the coffee table for him—homemade, sweet and tart and perfect.

"This is great—thanks."

Her face lightened for a moment as she said, "It's Prophet's favorite."

She turned to fuss at him. It was odd to watch him being mothered, because while he respectfully allowed it, he obviously wasn't happy with it, or with her. It was subtle, and Carole probably didn't notice. But Tom did, and he made a mental note to ask Prophet about it later.

"We're sorry to bother you during this difficult time," Tom told her.

Carole nodded, clasped her hands together. "Christopher's been gone for so long. We've been mourning him for years." She trailed off, as if unable to say anything more. Both men remained quiet until she cleared her throat and said, "I don't know how much I can help you. My husband's not here. He took a job yesterday for a drive into Mexico. Said he can't sit around because he keeps thinking. The service starts tomorrow night."

"That's all right—I'd rather talk to you," Tom said, ignoring Prophet's glare. "Were you in contact with Christopher?"

He expected Prophet to tell him to shut up, but instead, the man asked Carole, "How often did Christopher send you money?"

Carole excused herself after half an hour to take a phone call, probably more condolences. Prophet paced around the room a little, trying to tamp his agitation down. Being in this house again for another not-good reason was clawing at him. He hadn't been here since well before he and John were captured. Maybe it had been a holiday or a random leave, but all of those visits had been few and far between anyway. Crushed in by the memories, his chest ached and his throat tightened. Running out of the damned house would be the smart thing to do.

But somewhere along the line, he'd stopped being smart.

"You knew she was in contact with him from the time we caught this case," Tom said finally. "Which meant you probably knew he was cage fighting. And you let me go on about it."

"Yeah."

"Fine. Did I pass your test?"

Prophet ignored that. "Knowing Carole was in contact with Chris doesn't help shit. We already knew where he'd have been fighting, which is a block from where he was found in the dumpster. I'm betting he made good money. He was a big kid. Strong. John taught him to spar, and the old man was a semi-pro boxer in the Navy. If he'd been doing this for years, he probably made enemies . . ."

He trailed off and shrugged. He walked over toward the stairway, walked a few steps to look at the pictures that went all the way up the wall. Tom joined him, noted the military medals. And more pictures of Prophet.

"You lived here."

Prophet looked around. "Sometimes." *When things were bad.*

Being here . . . he was sixteen again, and a big part of him wanted that. Looking back, sixteen was easy. At least compared to everything that had come after. Sixteen was John, fighting and freedom.

But sixteen led to seventeen. In some ways, seventeen had saved him, and in others . . .

"There are as many pictures here of you as the rest of the family," Tom pointed out.

"I'm photogenic. And they liked me."

"God knows why," was Tommy's response, and it actually made Prophet smile. He was glad his back was to the man so he couldn't see it. "John enlisted with you?"

"Yeah. Mrs. Morse wanted him to try a year of college and he pretended to leave for school, but he enlisted with me instead. Said he always knew blowing shit up would be way more fun." His hand brushed the Purple Heart hanging in the shadowbox.

"Do you have one of those?"

"Natasha told you I served, right? Order five gross of pencils one time . . ."

"She said it was twice."

"Same thing," Prophet dismissed, but Tom shook his head, and Prophet hated that the man already knew how painstakingly accurate he had to be when it counted. "So you're in?"

He could've been referring to the case, to EE, to partnering, but Tom's answer came without hesitation. "I'm in. Have been."

"Bullshit."

"I told you my history; I wanted to make sure I was ready for this. Didn't want to fuck it up for a partner."

"Then don't." He glanced between Tom and a picture of John behind him. "We should go."

"She wants us to stay for dinner."

There was no fucking way he could do that, not at John's table with Tommy, and not for so many other reasons he hadn't known when he'd thought of this place as home. "No."

"You could—I'll grab dinner back at the hotel."

"We have shit to do tonight." He thought about Christopher in the morgue. "We have a lot of shit to do tonight," he repeated for his own benefit, ignoring the way Tom stared at him. Correction: ignoring the way Tom's dark-eyed stare made him feel, trying to tell himself it was nothing, that Tommy Boudreaux couldn't see right through him. And that Prophet didn't actually, in some weird way, like it.

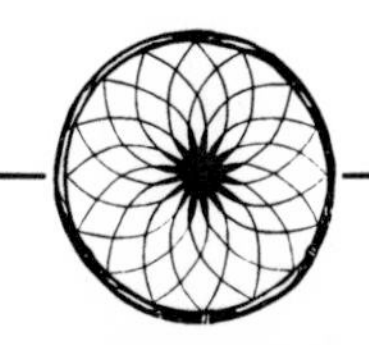

CHAPTER SIX

Tom steered the car in the direction of the highway, surprised that Prophet had thrown him the keys. The man sat next to him, playing with the radio, looking in the glove compartment. Playing with the mirrors.

"You realize I'm driving?" he asked.

"You're not using your mirrors right," Prophet insisted.

Before they'd left Carole Morse, she'd sent Prophet upstairs to put in an air conditioning unit. And she'd pulled Tom aside, told him, "You watch out for that boy. Don't let him get hurt."

He'd wanted to ask how he was supposed to watch out for someone who didn't want anyone to get close to him, but somehow, he figured she knew that it might be an impossible task. Knew, and loved him anyway, which made Tom want to at least try to honor her request. "I will, ma'am."

"Good. Because if you're lying to me, I'll hunt you down. Don't think I can't."

She was the second person in as many days charging him to take care of a man who seemed very well versed in taking care of himself. What the hell did they know that he didn't? "Carole's a nice woman."

"She told you to watch out for me, didn't she?" Prophet asked.

"How'd you know?"

"The A/C unit she sent me to put in was already in the window." Prophet smiled ruefully as he plugged into the GPS the address to a motel in the downtown area. A woman's voice told Tom where he could go, and he immediately turned it off.

"I'm good with directions," he explained.

"Because of all the voodoo?"

"You're going to find a doll that looks a lot like you with a pin in its—"

He glanced down at Prophet's lap before he uttered the word, but Prophet stopped him with his hand up. "Okay, okay, man, don't even joke about that shit." He shifted in his seat. "Now I gotta check to make sure it's all working properly."

Tom just laughed. It felt good to do so, but it sounded rusty as hell. The past years had really done a number on him.

But the longer they drove, the quieter and less fidgety Prophet got. It was odd. Disconcerting, and he couldn't believe he missed the sarcasm.

You don't miss it—it just means something's wrong.

At least he was half-right. Because all through check-in, Prophet let Tom take the lead. He booked two adjoining rooms on the second story, one of which was a suite, because he figured they might need more room.

He wasn't feeling generous enough to give Prophet the suite, though. It was better that way, would force the man into contact with him.

He hesitated, then opened the door on his side of the adjoining rooms and knocked. Prophet opened his side, and Tom stepped back and said, "I figured this was personal. I just didn't get how—"

"Save it. I liked you better when you were being an asshole."

"*I* was the asshole? And you're actually admitting to liking me?"

Prophet snorted a laugh, but no humor reached his eyes. Tom had only dealt with him being loud and insolent, so he didn't know how to handle the quiet, moody man next to him.

Not my job to handle him.

But it was, and maybe not only because Phil had asked him to. Okay, ordered him to. "How about dinner?"

Prophet shook his head.

"Come on—there's a diner right across the street. I'll grab takeout."

"You can do whatever you want. Tom."

"Okay, that's it."

Prophet blinked.

"Freaking me out. Calling me by my right name. That's complete bullshit and you know it."

Prophet just shrugged. "It's all I've got right now."

He went into his room, shutting his door behind him. Tom waited and then picked the lock to Prophet's door and went in after him.

"Get the hell out of my room."

"No," Tom said, feeling a little stupid now that he was actually in here.

"I don't need you worrying all over me like some goddamned mother."

"According to Phil, you do."

"If you're here because Butler wants you to mother me, then definitely get the fuck out."

"That's not the only reason."

"Get. Out."

"Make me."

"Fine. Stay. Do whatever you want. Watch me sleep if that's your kink."

"That's not my kink."

When Prophet began to strip, Tom figured out pretty quickly that the man could be his kink, and despite cursing himself up, down, and sideways, he stayed for the damned show. Backing down had never been his strong suit, and Prophet wasn't really paying attention to him anyway.

Maybe that was the most annoying part—Prophet was throwing his clothes off, heading for the shower buck naked, and he didn't seem to give a shit that Tom was watching.

Yeah, the man had obviously been raised by wolves. What the hell did it mean that Tom was attracted to him?

Means that you're attracted to assholes.

When Prophet was in the shower, Tom went back to his own room, but left the doors between them open.

He grabbed his laptop and sat at the small table, muttering, "If you're not going to work on this shit, I will," and Prophet called "I heard that" from the shower.

"Fucking dog ears."

"Fuck you."

Tom typed *fuck you* so he could get the last word, and then he began to do the research he'd been wanting to do since the morgue.

After half an hour and lots of hot water down the drain—and humming that same damned song—Prophet came out of the bathroom with a cloud of steam trailing behind him and a towel hanging low on his hips. He used another towel to semi-dry his hair and walked around talking to himself while yanking clothes out of his bag.

He caught Tom's gaze through the open door and asked, "What are you doing—posting to your blog?"

Tom resisted the urge to say anything. Besides, giving Prophet the finger was easier, and then he was back to his search through Houston police records for the initial investigation report on Chris's case, knowing Prophet would read over his shoulder anyway.

And he did. The man had no sense of personal space or propriety—he leaned over Tom and dripped all over him and the keyboard.

"Could you not fry my laptop?" Tom asked, pushing it back, but Prophet didn't answer, just scrolled down and read quietly, then moved away and went to find his clothes.

Tom watched out of the corner of his eye, saw Prophet pull on old jeans that looked comfortable as hell—no underwear—and a soft, worn T-shirt from an old AC/DC concert. As he grabbed for his sneakers, he called in, "Great job on the research."

Tom got up and walked into Prophet's room. "Are you going to be able to handle this case?"

"Leave it alone, Tommy." Prophet grabbed his black leather jacket and headed for the door. "Don't wait up."

"You're going out? Why are you fucking with our window of opportunity? That woman we just left cares about you. I figured that might make you not stop working on this case until you got to the bottom of it. If not for you, at least for her." It was a shitty thing for him to say and he knew it.

"I'm not staying here under your insightful gaze, that's for damned sure." With that, Prophet slammed the door on any further conversation, and Tom groused angrily to himself for half an hour as he researched gyms in the area before changing into sweats and a T-shirt. He left his wallet and weapon behind, and headed for the gym he'd pinpointed as the most likely one to gain him an invite to a cage fight.

It was open twenty-four seven, a dirty hole-in-the-wall you had to buy your way into, but it did have all the necessary equipment and rings for training in boxing and hand-to-hand. There were some brutal practice sessions going on.

Why was he even doing this? He didn't owe Prophet shit.

But you owe Phil for giving you this chance.

"Whatever it takes," he told himself as he wrapped his hands in tape and headed into the main part of the gym to get noticed.

"Wanna spar?" one guy asked him right away. He was big and broad, a perfect match for Tom. But he had to play this just right—couldn't make it look too good. He'd get invited to the cage matches because they'd think he'd lose, but not get his ass completely kicked.

He let his drawl deepen as he agreed and answered a few personal questions from the trainer, designed so he couldn't sue if he dropped dead.

Tom had done this many times in his youth, in a much less structured setting, in order to prove himself tough to a community that would never accept him. He'd figured that being accepted didn't matter, as long as they'd stopped fucking with him after he'd proven himself in fight after fight. And, for the most part, they had stopped. Physically, anyway.

Fighting always brought him right back there to that familiar place of violence. Had Phil picked him because he knew how hard Tom had fought growing up? Because his teen years weren't something he put on his resume.

The fight started slow, but escalated when Tom cuffed the other guy hard on the ear. The guy came at him like a charging bull, and hearing his fist hit flesh with a solid slap was more satisfying than it should've been. His temper flared, and he hated that he had a lot of excess anger to work off, because fighting always brought shitty memories with it anyway. His immediate reaction was always to not give up until the other guy wasn't moving, but this time, he forced himself to hold back.

It wasn't easy, because he was pissed at Prophet, and that's who he pictured as he fought. But even though he wanted to wring his partner's neck, he didn't have a lifetime of pent-up anger against him, so he was able to dial himself back just enough.

The guy ended up on top of him, and Tom could've bucked him, tried halfheartedly, but he knew the performance would gain him entrance into the fight club. The blood dripping down his cheek was worth it, especially when one of the gym managers approached him quietly in the back room.

He was rinsing his face, checking to see if he'd need stitches, when he heard, "You fight in one of the Louisiana rings?"

Tom glanced over at the guy, but didn't say anything, so he continued, "S'all right, boy. We've got the same kind of leagues here. You need a manager?"

He pressed a towel on the cut, hard enough to quell the bleeding. "Got one. I've done a few fights up the East Coast, but nothing like you've got here."

The guy nodded. Right move. "Tell him you've got a gig. Pay's good." He handed Tom a blank card and rattled off an address. "Midnight tomorrow night—you're on right before the main attraction."

"Really?" he asked with just the right hint of naïveté.

"Yeah. People love watching a newbie get his ass kicked before they win money."

Bingo. "Well then, I'd hate to disappoint them."

He'd gotten them in the front door. It would be up to Prophet to kick the rest of them down.

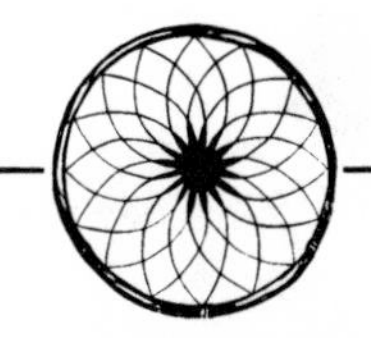

CHAPTER SEVEN

W*hy are you fucking with our window of opportunity?*

First of all, fuck the *our*, and second, because he wanted to be anyfuckingwhere else, but Prophet had made promises. His partner could stick his research—words on paper never thrilled Prophet as much as finding real live evidence.

It was colder than he remembered as he stalked neighborhoods he and John used to roam as teens, but then again, spring in Texas was always unpredictable. When he was younger, the unpredictability, coupled with the seediness of this area, had felt right to him.

Still did. Nothing had really changed. The strip of bars was still there, some with different names. Sex shops. Gambling games. MC and gang hangouts. You had to be careful where you stepped as a young kid alone. Christopher definitely would've made some missteps, no matter how much he'd tried to learn from John and Prophet.

Prophet and John *had* been kids, despite everything—stupid, funny, take-on-the-world kids. Christopher had never really had that chance, not with his big brother gone.

You weren't there for him either.

He told himself to shut the fuck up, slid through a crowded alley, bodies brushing his. *Everything changes and nothing changes.*

He paid his way into the building where the fights were about to get underway. They started at ten and ended well after midnight, and he watched the first one, swaying, cheering bodies pressing against his. He'd brought a bottle of whiskey in with him and drank from it as he watched.

The kids who fought looked younger than he'd remembered. The fighters his age were all angry as hell. It was fucking depressing as anything.

He stared at a program and nudged the guy next to him. "I thought that Christopher was fighting tonight."

"He got killed a few nights ago. It was in the papers and everything."

"No shit?"

"Yeah. Everyone here was really upset. They even did a tribute to him last night before the fights. Did you know him?"

Prophet shook his head. "Just heard the rumors."

"It's a shame. He was a good kid. Respected. To be killed in a random robbery . . ." The guy trailed off and then got caught up in the action inside the ring.

Prophet slipped off toward the back rooms. They were empty, since the fighters waited in the pit with their managers, and he picked the lock to the club manager's office. He checked the computer first, disabled the security cam, erased his image, and gave himself a five-minute window by running the old footage on a loop.

The office was pretty well organized, with a file for each fighter. In Chris's file, he found several receipts for a boarding house, with a room and phone number noted neatly on each one.

He rubbed the ache in his chest at the thought of Chris living in a shitty motel room. But after he didn't find anything else helpful, he left the club and did his penance by going to that motel. Chris's room was still locked, probably just the way he'd left it, because the police hadn't known where he'd been living. According to the report, they'd asked the club manager and several of Christopher's friends and no one had known anything.

So they were covering for him, but the question was why, because there was nothing here of any importance, nothing incriminating, no drugs or alcohol.

No cell phone. And one hadn't been found on Chris's body. Everyone had a goddamned cell phone these days.

He checked under the mattress and found cash stuffed there—mainly twenties and some hundreds that, with a quick count, totaled nearly four grand. He pocketed the money for Carole, along with a receipt for a prepaid cell phone, and what looked like a key to a PO Box. He'd check with the local places in the morning.

And then he pulled up short and stilled when he caught sight of something in his periphery. It was a brief moment, the figure in camouflage a blur as it passed, and Prophet closed his eyes and prayed that when he opened them, he wouldn't see John's ghost.

He opened his eyes and cautiously scanned the room.

Empty.

And now he'd try to convince himself that it had been a trick of light, or the memories that Christopher's death had forced to bubble to the surface.

He left the room without looking back, sure that if he did, he'd see John reclining on the bed in his BDUs, a cigarette dangling from his mouth and his boots dusty. He closed the door behind him and went to the crime scene, which was a few blocks over, and still corded off by yellow police tape.

Nothing, except for some blood on the ground that made Prophet ache again. "I'm sorry, Chris," he whispered into the night, and the helpless feeling that overtook him was too much to bear.

He headed a few blocks over, the opposite direction from the hotel. And from Tom.

Prophet's blood thrummed. He needed to fight or fuck, or maybe fight and fuck at the same time. And he knew he wasn't going to get either in his motel room without fucking something up. He couldn't afford that now. Not until they figured out what had happened to Christopher.

He'd always believed in an eye for an eye. And he would get it, no matter the cost.

The doorway with the eight ball was still there, even fifteen years later, halfway between Chris's motel room and the building where the fighting happened. Prophet went down the alley behind three guys who were obviously regulars. They slipped right past the giant guarding the door, but he held out a hand to stop Prophet.

"Private club, son. Need a membership."

"Son?" Prophet raised a brow, and the giant raised a brow back. "I'll buy in." He showed a roll of cash and got a slight move to the side to let him enter.

"You don't find what you're looking for in there, you come on back and see me." The giant grinned as his gaze raked Prophet from head to toe.

"I'll keep it in mind," Prophet told him, and walked through the narrow hallways that seemed to pound to the beat of the techno music. He bypassed the bar and the dance floor, went toward the maze of hallways at the back of the club that smelled like whiskey, smoke, and sex.

There were poker games back here—high stakes ones—but that's not what he was after. If he could fuck his way through the line of men in the backroom, he'd do it, and hell, they were three and four deep in there. In the half-light, most of them looked damned good too.

He strolled through, finding a spot against the wall. Before he'd turned around, there were three men closing in on him. They didn't ask any questions, didn't say a word—one of them just tugged at his hair, pulled him close at the same time he pushed Prophet back against the wall. Normally, Prophet would've taken off the guy's head. Tonight, he just let himself be taken in.

The first man sucked on his neck while the other two closed around him on either side. One of them put a hand across Prophet's throat, holding him in place. One of them bit him, another scratched. The first guy dropped to his knees and unzipped Prophet's jeans. As he stroked Prophet's cock, the others concentrated on his neck, his chest . . . on telling him what they were going to do to him.

"What the fuck are you waiting for?" he asked roughly. The guy between his legs rolled a condom on him and got to work sucking him off, and he suddenly felt hemmed in instead of turned on by the other two. He pushed them away, not caring how pissed they were, not wanting to deal with anything more than the feel of the hot mouth on his cock.

Tom's face flashed in his mind at that goddamned second, and that wasn't a good sign at all. Especially not when he tried and failed not to come while thinking about his partner. The orgasm blasted through him, nearly taking him out at the knees, Tom's knowing smile dancing in front of his closed eyes. He leaned his head against the wall for a second and tried to goddamned breathe as the guy stripped his condom away for him.

Too fucking complicated. All of it.

And, as the orgasm faded, he felt guilty and left before the guy was off his knees. These days, he was always trying to fuck his past away—maybe his future too—remembering and forgetting all at the same time. And none of it worked. It never did.

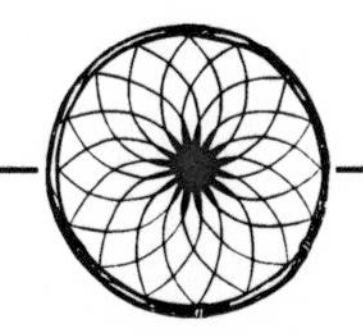

CHAPTER EIGHT

Tom walked through the parking lot of the motel just after one in the morning. His nose throbbed, but it had stopped bleeding, and nothing was broken. He'd iced it for a while, shooting the shit with some of the gym rats, coming up with his cover story for the fight on the fly, including the part about his asshole of a manager. AKA, Prophet's role.

He knew he'd see most of those men at the underground arena.

Halfway to the motel, he'd started to get that hinky, being-followed feeling, and he hadn't been able to shake it. The adrenaline rush from the fighting left him shaky, but had shaven the edge off his anger and left him able to notice shit like being tailed again.

Instead of heading straight up to his room, he stopped at the soda machine. He put the change in, pressed the button and bent to retrieve his soda. Another hand got there first, and he looked up into Prophet's eyes.

The man had been fucking. The smell of smoke and whiskey did nothing to mask the smell of sex, and even if that hadn't been obvious, the look on Prophet's face was. He was smoking a cigarette—a hand-rolled one—and Tom saw scratches on the side of his neck. And a bite a bit farther down, and goddammit all to hell . . .

"Problem, Tommy?" Prophet mimicked his drawl, managing to make it sound good.

"While you were fucking, I was working."

"They don't give little gold stars at EE the way they do in the FBI."

"I'm not in the FBI."

"Maybe they stick them on calendars out on the bayou?" Prophet asked. Tom pushed past him hard enough to throw Prophet off balance, thanks to the whiskey the man had imbibed, and walked up the stairs. Prophet recovered quickly, followed him.

"So yeah, you've read my file. Big fucking deal," Tom threw out over his shoulder.

"No, I didn't. But I could've found out every last goddamned thing about you."

"Why didn't you?"

"No point."

That was definitely a dig, but Tom kept his mouth shut. He wasn't about to be goaded into revealing how a scrungy kid from the bayou had gotten a chance at the FBI. How a shining star had fucked up bad by letting the idea of a curse get in his way.

He's bad luck.

On the walk up to the second floor, Prophet was silent. It was only when Tom opened the door to his room and Prophet followed him inside that he took Tom by the shoulders and studied the cut on his cheek. "You got jumped."

"I was at a gym." When Prophet didn't say anything else, he handed him the blank card.

"You got jumped while you were working out?"

Tom rolled his eyes. "It's our engraved invite in. Tomorrow night. We can't miss this opportunity."

"And you're doing the fighting?" Prophet asked doubtfully, pointing to the cut. "Because apparently, you're not that good at it."

"I did that on purpose."

"That's what they all say when they lose. Dude, I'm sure being sheriff kept you in shape and all—"

"Deputy sheriff. And you could kill someone. You'd have to hold back way more than I will. I've been out of the game a lot longer. Besides, they'd recognize your military training."

"So? I'm sure there's other ex-military there."

"Not many—not anymore. The guys I met tonight at the gym told me they stopped taking a lot of them because they're too unpredictable. They'll see you coming a mile away. Besides, you can't fight with those." He pointed to the current banes of Prophet's existence . . . besides himself, he supposed.

"I can cut them off!"

"You've tried."

"But you haven't." Prophet handed him a knife from his pocket, but Tom shook his head.

"Not happening. You've got broken bones in there."

"One's just a hairline fracture," Prophet scoffed. "I've had plenty before." He left Tom's room, closing the door between them.

Letting Prophet take the casts off and fight would be the smartest thing Tom could do. He wouldn't've minded watching Prophet in the ring. The man moved like a sleek predator, walked quietly. Did everything with an economy of movement that revealed his training, but only if you knew what you were looking at.

Well, it was probably the military training, but maybe he'd been born like this, lethal as hell. Some were.

He chewed on that while he shoved a chair under the main door and then showered, letting the hot water sluice over his tired, soon-to-be-sore body. He wrapped himself in a towel and headed for the bed when a short knock at the outside door made him aim the weapon he'd taken with him into the bathroom at what turned out to be Prophet's chest.

The man didn't even wait for Tom to say *come in.*

You invaded his privacy first.

"Relax, Cajun—I brought you something." Prophet was carrying a big box of donuts and Tom's key card.

"Is that your idea of an apology? And I don't even like donuts."

Prophet scooped the box up, took a donut out, and bit into it. "It's the thought that counts, right?" he asked, his mouth full of sugared jelly donut.

Tom supposed he should be grateful that his feral wolf of a partner thought any kind of apology was necessary at all. Maybe it was even a first. But honestly, he wasn't sure what Prophet would be apologizing for. For leaving earlier? For going out and literally fucking around instead of working? For telling Tom there was no point in reading his file? For alternately making Tom feel like he had a chance with a partner and then slamming him back to reality?

But maybe that was his plan. Because keeping Tom off balance was a good way for Prophet to make sure Tom didn't see how affected *he* was.

Suddenly, Tom felt better. "Yeah, it is, I guess."

Prophet glanced at the chair under the door. "What aren't you telling me?"

"I feel like I was being followed from the gym."

"Like that same feeling you had on the plane?"

"Yeah. You don't?"

"I always feel like someone's following me." He put down the donuts, went into his room and came back with wires and video equipment.

Tom watched him work in silence for fifteen minutes, rigging their doors and windows with cameras. He put down a small monitor on Tom's bedside table. "You can see anyone approaching."

"Thanks."

"What's next?" Prophet asked as he worked through a second donut. That dozen wasn't long for the world.

"I set you up as my manager. They won't care about the former military thing if you're not fighting."

"This isn't a good idea, Tommy. You'll get hurt."

"I'd think you'd like to see me get the shit beat out of me."

"No, I'd like to be the one doing it."

Even though he knew that Prophet more than half meant it, there was something suspiciously like respect in his tone, and it made Tom realize that something had changed between them for the better. And because of that, for just a brief moment, he thought about telling Prophet about his partners, warning him about the bad luck, before they got any farther along. But it would give the man more ammo against him—and he might insist that Tommy be pulled from the case. "I think this is too personal for you."

"We're allowed to work personal cases. Phil handed this case to me."

"And told me to watch you," Tommy reminded him, and Prophet made a *pffft* sound and waved him off. "C'mon, Proph. We both know this is the fastest and most effective way in."

"And the most dangerous."

"Well, yeah. Nothing about this job's safe, partner."

"Then we do this my way."

In EE, there was no tenure or security. People stayed or went on Phil's say-so—that was in the contract. Despite Prophet's personality, he had to be doing something right to have been around for so long. He had to be worth listening to, and Tom would be stupid not to try to learn from him. "Okay, fine. Just tell me, though, is this a typical EE case?"

"No. That first assignment—the Eritrea trip—that's typical. You'd spend time there with me so I could get you up to speed and get you more training. Out of the actual missions we take on, I'd say eighty percent are in-and-out jobs—a day's work, at most two. Some require months of setup and surveillance—Mick handles a lot of these. And then there are the week-plus jobs—they're typically the most dangerous."

"Are those the ones you're mostly assigned to?"

"I guess you'll find out if Phil keeps you around."

He was beginning to hate it when Prophet got the last word.

He'd thought merc work would be in and out, a fast hit, a quick rescue.

EE had their own set of rules and procedures, mainly put in place to ensure the safety of its operatives. Phil was a stickler for check-ins and updates, but those were done with the push of a phone's button or a texted code. Phil also monitored his operatives through their EE phones, which was something the bureau wouldn't do because it would be considered an invasion of privacy.

Phil had told him that he didn't give a shit about Tom's privacy when he'd handed him the phone. And that was a small price to pay, because when push came to shove, EE allowed them a lot more freedom with their methods and from rules in general.

Indeed, they were definitely entrenched in a case where rules seemed to be the last thing on anyone's mind.

"By the way, I went to the ring where Chris fought," Prophet told him. "Got a key to a PO Box and a phone number. If it's his, maybe we can find a phone bill or something and pull those records."

"Wait, you were there, at the fighting ring? Tonight?"

"Is there a fucking echo in here? Yes, the ring. Tonight. Can you use your oh so special skills to help?" Prophet mimicked typing, and Tom shot him the finger.

"Should've known."

"I like being underestimated."

Tom stared at him. "No, you don't, actually. Give me what you've got."

Prophet handed him a printout and the key. Tom began typing, Prophet remained oddly silent, and ten minutes later, Tom told him they had a match to a PO Box in town but the number was for a throwaway phone.

"At least we've got something. We'll go check out the box as soon as they open." Prophet called the cell phone number from the motel phone—got no answer but left a message asking for a call back to his number and promise of a reward, no questions asked. "Worth a shot, right?"

"Right," Tom said, because that's what it seemed like Prophet wanted him to say.

Prophet stared at him for a long second. "I think it's time we both put our cards on the table about what we think happened to Chris."

Tom nodded, wondered if that went both ways. But it didn't stop him from saying what he'd thought from the beginning. "I think he was killed fighting a blood match."

Prophet nodded slowly as if Tom had confirmed his own instinct. "Blood match equals death wish."

Sometimes. But mainly, it was a fight until one of them was down and not getting back up. There was no tapping out. "Sounds like he was messed up after his brother died," Tom offered, and pretended he didn't see Prophet's fists clench. Still, he braced himself for a punch that never came.

Instead, Prophet told him, "He'd been doing this for years. All of a sudden, he agrees to a blood match? Doesn't make sense. Because he didn't have to do that—he was a top fighter. He'd be raking in money—more than I found, but then again, he's been sending it to his mom for years now. He was also a crowd favorite. Blood matches are different."

Tom ran a hand through his hair. "That means I have to get invited to one."

"No. Fucking. Way."

"Got another idea?"

Prophet blew out a frustrated breath. "Let's just get you through the first fight, okay? Because Phil will kill me if I get you killed."

"Fine."

"Can you shoot a goddamned gun?"

"Little bit," he said, his drawl deeply laced with sarcasm.

"And you track."

"How would you know that if you didn't ask about me?"

"Your eyes."

Tom shot him a look. "You know Cajun lore?"

"Not just Cajun."

"So what's your specialty?"

"Natasha didn't tell you that?"

"Rather hear it from you."

"I'm good at a wide variety of things. Best? Building and detonating bombs. I can build them from anything."

So they could track anyone or anything and destroy it. They were a good team, on paper. "Did you like the CIA?"

"I lasted less than a year. What do you think?"

"Maybe they didn't like you."

"Good one. And no, they didn't."

"The FBI doesn't like me now much either." That wasn't entirely true—he'd left on his own steam rather than see the shrink and take the recommended leave, and they hadn't been happy to let his training go to waste. "Why'd you leave the CIA?"

"They wanted me to kill people. I was scared," Prophet deadpanned, but then said, "I don't like doing jobs on faith. I need a reason. I think I'm owed that, considering what I was being asked to do the majority of the time."

It was the most honest Prophet had been with him. "Thanks for telling me."

"Welcome." But his cheeks flushed like he wasn't used to sharing anything or being thanked. He shifted in his chair a little and said, "Sun's almost up."

"Want to grab breakfast here?"

"Let's try the diner. See if we can get a lead on who's following you."

Prophet believed him. He blew out a soft breath of relief, and it was only then that he remembered he wasn't dressed.

Prophet seemed to have locked onto that at the same time, but only said, "Before you fight, take out the piercings."

"Shit." Tom glanced down at the silver bars that went through each nipple. Of course, the piercings in his dick would be more difficult and couldn't be out that long. He motioned to the front of his towel. "Maybe I'll just wear a cup."

"Can't."

"A jock, then. It's not like he's going to fight my dick."

Prophet shrugged. "It's your dick."

"Fuck me." Taking out the Jacob's ladder piercings was a pain in the ass. They'd start to close quickly once he did, and then he'd need to put in smaller gauge piercings after the fight.

Which he didn't have. "Gotta find a piercing place."

"There's one three blocks up," Prophet offered. "We'd better get you there and back in enough time to eat and sleep before tonight. You've got to be there by nine."

"What, now you're my bodyguard?"

"For now, I'm your partner."

Prophet had suspected the tattoos. Now, up close and personal, he'd gotten an eyeful of the tribal-like markings, all in grayscale along Tom's shoulders and back and both biceps, with a few trailing down his forearms. But it wasn't all lines. There were some symbols there, artfully mixed in. You had to look to notice, like a *Where's Waldo* kind of thing. And Tom was pulling on a shirt, stopping Prophet from doing just that.

It seemed like they went down under Tommy's towel too, but Prophet wasn't about to pull it off to check. Although . . .

"Don't even think about it," Tommy warned, yanking on jeans and throwing off the towel at the same time.

"I'm just curious."

"Then get your own."

"You don't seem like the tattoo type, Tommy."

"What type do I seem like?"

"At first, the really annoying kind. But there might be hope for you."

"Gee, thanks."

"Slim hope," Prophet corrected, with emphasis on the word slim. "Let's just go."

He assessed Tom for a long second. The guy was on edge and in some pain. Needed sleep. "You want me to pick stuff up for you?"

"You wouldn't know what to get."

"How do you know?" He gazed down at Tom's crotch and back up. "Can't I just ask someone, 'Hey, his dick's pierced and he needs stuff'?"

Tom rolled his eyes. "Yeah, that'll work. Come on." He glanced over his shoulder. "You gonna get a piercing?"

Prophet furrowed his brow and shook his head.

"Afraid of pain?"

"Don't need anything extra to identify me."

"Are you always looking over your shoulder?"

"I've got a bounty on my head in four countries. And outstanding parking tickets and moving violations in seven states. Including Texas. Coming, Cajun?" were Prophet's last words before he went out the door.

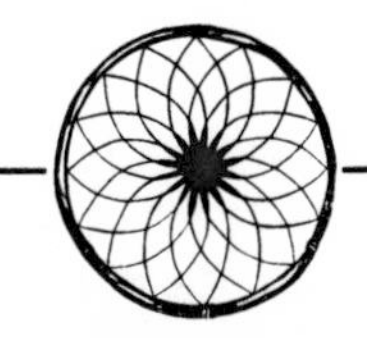

CHAPTER NINE

Prophet woke Tommy and got him to the building that housed the underground fight by 9 p.m. If you showed up later, you were disqualified, and they'd lost enough time as it was. The men at the door clocked them both in, took the invite card, and ushered Tom away for weigh and measure while Prophet lingered, mixing with the light crowd in the hallways.

A few people remembered him from last night, nodded, shook his hand.

Prophet spent some time registering his fighter, using one of his many fake IDs. Payments were all cash, but there were forms to sign, saying that the owners of the ring—which was illegal—couldn't be sued.

He shook his head as he signed. The forms looked exactly the same as when he and John had fought here, but he still didn't recognize anyone at the door or behind the desks from back then. And it was even more crowded tonight. Probably because a newbie was fighting. News like that spread fast around here.

He'd avoided the back rooms last night, but being inside them, hell, it was like stepping back in time. Nothing—everything—had changed, and he was more off balance than he'd thought he'd be. He shifted irritably. His casts were hot and itchy. A few women had stopped by when he was talking to the other managers and had written their numbers on them. A few men, too, although more surreptitiously.

Prophet ran his hands over one of the numbers, a guy named Dale who looked like he was up for anything, and dismissed the idea of calling him. Last night hadn't solved anything. Sex never solved anything.

Since when did you get to be such a killjoy about sex?

After an hour of nosing around more, with zero results, he went to find Tommy. He was in one of the private rooms along the left side of the hallway. The open locker room ran along the right.

Prophet watched him silently from the partially opened door. He wore only shorts, and this time Prophet took advantage of the opportunity to look. He was well built. In shape. There were scars Prophet would've expected to see from a former special agent, and Tommy's head was down, like he was in some kind of trance, as if this was what he needed to do to psych himself up.

He didn't seem like he was having a moment of doubt, but rather, a moment.

He was a man gearing up to hurt someone.

Tommy looked younger than his years. This wasn't necessarily a young man's game though. It was dirty, underhanded, and sometimes older and wiser was better.

The questions Tommy had asked him earlier still rang in his ears. Of course this was too fucking personal. And Tom had every right to ask if it was. But Prophet was still angry he couldn't fight, and even though it wasn't Tommy's fault, in Prophet's heart, he was unwilling and unable to separate the two.

If nothing else, Prophet prided himself on his ability to be irrational. Everyone was always raving about how being cool, calm, and collected was the best way to be. Prophet found the exact opposite worked most of the time.

Tommy raised his head and stared at him, and Prophet wondered how long Tommy'd known he'd been standing there. "I'm up against the challenger to the champion. Suddenly, I'm the main fucking event." His voice was even, but there was an underlying tension.

"Lucky you." Prophet came in, shut the door behind him. "It's because you're a giant."

"Is there a compliment in there somewhere?"

"They say the bigger you are, the harder you'll fall. Everyone loves to watch the big guys fall."

"Great."

"You're fighting a thirty-five-year-old. The champ's thirty-seven, so you're in the right age group."

"I wouldn't have thought that. I guess I don't know as much about this as I thought."

"They have a couple of guidelines they follow for the youngest fighters that generally weeds them out more quickly than the older guys," Prophet explained, glad that the man could admit he needed help. "If they're twenty-three or below, they're classed by weight division, but only fight others within a certain age range. But if someone blows through those guys, they move you up with guys like you. Fast."

"What about rules for the kind of hits? I hear there are none."

"You heard right."

"Then who decides the winner?"

When Tommy had decided to bullhead his way into the fight, he hadn't really cared about the rules or consequences. Now, though, it appeared that was all he could think about, and Prophet figured it was better to be honest and see if his partner backed out. "Three judges determine when it's time to call the fight. Straight pinning won't do it."

"How's that different from a blood match?"

"For a blood match, the loser is the one who's unconscious."

"And people pay to see this?" he asked disgustedly.

"It's not that different from the ultimate fighting people pay to see on cable. The crowd—most of them have never done anything illegal in their lives. This makes them feel like badasses. Brings out everyone's primal side."

"You almost sound like you condone it."

"If people stuck to their own morality code, it wouldn't be a problem."

Tom pressed his lips together for a moment, then said, "I just thought we'd be doing something . . ."

"Bigger?" Prophet asked, and without waiting, said, "Saving lives is always big."

"There's no one to save, Prophet."

It took everything Prophet had not to punch Tom. "There's always someone to save."

And he'd fucked up again. Tom shut his mouth, grabbed the tape and began wrapping his hands until Prophet broke the silence. "You're doing that wrong."

He stepped forward and took the tape from Tom. He undid what Tom had started and rebandaged his knuckles quickly but with care. Tom had taped as if he'd be putting on gloves—Prophet taped him quickly, in a different pattern that Tom probably wouldn't be able to replicate.

Even with the casts, Prophet was surprisingly nimble, holding Tom's hands in place. He was between Tom's thighs and the whole thing was oddly intimate. And even though Prophet was attending to him, Tom could see that the man was clearly someplace else. But he looked up when he finished and said, "All done, Tommy," and just like that, he was back.

"Thanks." And before he could help himself, asked, "Who's Dale?"

"Just some guy I met here."

"And why is he writing his number on your cast?"

Prophet shrugged. "Guess he thinks I'm hot," he said easily, but there was a light flush on his cheeks for a few seconds.

Tom felt an unnatural gnaw of something in his gut. Couldn't be jealousy. Had to be concern. Yeah, concern for his partner. "Just be careful."

"Always am, Tommy." He paused, and Tom wondered if he was going to say something else on the subject. But he didn't.

"Can't knuckle it like a bar fight or you'll break bones in your hand." Prophet held up his cast as an example. "Think dirty moves. Open palm stuff. Nonprofessional. Think about how you fought before anyone actually stepped in and taught you."

"Fighting for your life," he heard himself say quietly.

Prophet met his gaze. "People are betting against you."

He'd heard it before. "What do you think?"

"If you fuck this up, I'll have to hurt you."

Tom balled his hands into fists, the tape stretching surprisingly well. "You'd love that."

"I might." Prophet dug into his pocket and grabbed for Tom's hand again. Before Tom could ask, Prophet had tied a thin leather bracelet around his wrist. Tied it, then hid it under another length of tape.

"What's it for?"

"It's for me," was all Prophet would tell him as he walked out of the room, but Tom hadn't noticed Prophet wearing it. He fingered it through the tape, figured there was a story behind it. Maybe he'd find out someday, but for now he simply left it alone and followed Prophet into the main warm-up area.

It was crowded tonight. The sound traveled up inside the space below the metal rafters, creating an echo that made the room seem stadium-like with its noise level.

He watched the other fighters in the holding pen. Some looked overwhelmed. One wore headphones and drifted off. Tom was pretty sure he was high. But none of them were the man he was set to fight.

He didn't get to see him until he was in the ring being introduced to the crowd. He heard a few jeers at his name but didn't pay attention. Couldn't. Blocked all the shit out and prepped for a fight.

The man named Ivan who stepped into the ring with him was a fucking giant. Bald and smooth, and if he sweated, it would be hard to get a grip on him.

For a nanosecond, Tom wished he'd thought about shaving his body, but then rejected the idea. But he was glad he'd taken out the piercings. This was all like an extremely interesting porno he'd seen, minus the nudity and the winner fucking the loser. At least he hoped that last part wouldn't happen, because he had zero interest in Ivan.

Helluva time to be making jokes, Tommy, he told himself in his best Prophet voice.

He thought about why Prophet had put the band of leather on his wrist, before taking his mind off anything but not getting his ass kicked. His focus narrowed to tunnel vision; the only thing in front of him was the man he had to beat to the judges' satisfaction in order to move to the next round.

Ivan signed up for it and he's not an innocent bystander, he told himself. He couldn't back out now anyway, not when the gates locked with a loud slam that echoed in the sudden, unexpected silence. The whistle blew seconds later. There was no coming together, no clasping hands. It was brutal strength, the grunt of bodies slapping together, the sounds of fists to flesh.

He'd met Ivan in the middle, slammed against him, taking the man down by hitting him in the back of his knees. His advantage probably wouldn't last for long, but he couldn't worry about it. He punched and elbowed and kicked, losing track of everything else, until the screams faded and his world narrowed to just his fists and Ivan's face.

It wasn't long before he smelled the blood. Didn't know if it was his or Ivan's or part of their mingled frenzy. He couldn't care.

He also smelled fear, and it mixed with the scent of the ring tanged with sweat, all sharp in his nose. The sour scent of defeat and desperation, the hunger of the crowd, their animalistic cries, all blended in his ears until everything was just a beat in his head, the rhythm he needed in order to fight.

His feet slid along the mat, his body following by rote. Better that way, to be detached, watching it like an outside observer. The man groped for him—Tom pushed back and then swung, fist connecting with face.

Age doesn't matter in these leagues—what does is how far you're willing to go—how hard you're willing to fight.

He was willing to go all the goddamned way, especially after Ivan boxed his ears. Tom shook his head in an attempt to get rid of the ringing, and it made the big man smile and call him a "goddamned pussy." And that made Tom lose his shit.

Goddamned pussy . . . boy, you'd better toughen up . . .

Bon à rien. Bad loque.

The past called to him, and he didn't remember anything after that. He just kept moving. Slamming. Yelling. It might've been hours or minutes, it didn't matter. Nothing did except fighting.

He saw Ivan's lips moving, saw him attempt to get up. Tom jumped on his shoulders, keeping him down on the mat.

"Back off," someone was barking into his ear, and he was dragged back by several pairs of hands, his wrists yanked into the air, cheering filling his ears.

His anger was still surging, but he needed to see Ivan, to know the extent of the damage. His own body was too numb to know if he was hurt, wouldn't until the adrenaline came crashing down but he didn't care. He asked the man next to him about Ivan, tried to push through, but a wall of people were blocking him. They probably thought he wanted to hurt Ivan further, and he couldn't blame them. He caught sight of a stretcher before he was forced along, shoved into a training room, and almost lost his balance as the door shut and locked behind him. He caught himself and crawled onto the table.

They'd locked the door for his safety, nothing else. They'd told him that at the start of the fight, but it still gave him an overwhelming sense of claustrophobia.

It seemed like hours, but was probably closer to minutes, when he finally heard voices. Loud. When hands touched him, he was up, slamming someone into a wall.

"Tommy. *Tom*."

Prophet. He focused, found he was pressing Prophet tight against the concrete with his body, a hand wrapped around the man's neck.

Prophet's gray eyes were surprisingly non-angry. He supposed Prophet could throw him off, but he hadn't. "Tommy, you okay?"

Was he? Absolutely not. He let go of Prophet, and then Prophet was leading him back to the table. Holding him up, although they both pretended that wasn't the case. The adrenaline left his body suddenly. Painfully.

He was in better shape than when he'd been in the FBI. The parish had kept him busy with constant calls for all different things, from domestic disputes to drug sweeps and grave robbers, but it wasn't the kind of busy he craved. He'd stayed for as long as he could, until Phil had materialized like some kind of guardian angel and rescued him from rotting away in his self-imposed hell.

Work out. Catch bad guys. Drink homemade moonshine. Rinse, repeat, throw your life away.

He couldn't let his daddy win. Not this time.

"Yo, Cajun." Prophet was snapping his fingers at him.

"You snap like that again and I'll break them off," he said irritably, and Prophet actually looked pleased. Whether it was the threat or the fact that he'd pushed Tom into making a threat, Tom couldn't be sure.

It was like coming out of some kind of fugue state, except he remembered.

And you were worried that Prophet *would fuck up your chance for a comeback.*

Prophet was running his hands over Tom's face, checking for broken bones. Tom put his hands on Prophet's casted wrists and held them still for a moment. "How's Ivan?"

Prophet slid his arms out of Tom's grasp. "You won, Tommy. That's all you need to know."

Bon à rien.

Bad loque.

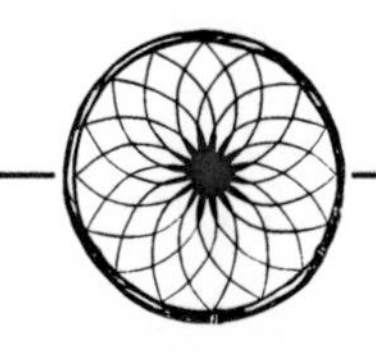

CHAPTER TEN

The fight had been ugly. Brutal. The man in the cage with Tom had been out for blood and money. Tom was taller, the man named Ivan broader, but in the end, it hadn't mattered.

Tom had been like a goddamned tsunami in the ring, a dormant volcano that seemed utterly safe until it blew the fucking roof off the place. Whether or not he did it purposely to get an invite to the blood match—which was where the out-of-control, hard-core types were most suited—wasn't something Prophet wanted to delve into.

It had been fast. Dirty. And Prophet understood what Tom had meant by professional training. It had been a long time since Prophet had really fought in a down-and-dirty brawl without being able to rely on his training to subdue people easily and quickly. He would've stood out like a sore thumb.

Not that Tommy hadn't. And Tommy had won, over the crowd's favorite. Normally, that would've earned him boos and jeers, but it was such a worthy fight that the crowd was still chanting his name.

Cajun. Cajun. Cajun.

Tom raised his head, finally hearing it. "You're a complete and utter ass," he mumbled, and Prophet couldn't deny it. But at least the Tom he sort of knew was nearly back, that vacant look gone from his eyes.

Tom's nose was bruised, not broken. One cheekbone was swollen, his bottom lip bleeding. Prophet would need to check him out further, but it appeared he'd be fine. He reached for some of the supplies they kept in the rooms—butterfly bandages, peroxide, gauze—and attended to Tom's face first.

Tom kept still, the energy finally drained from his body. "Am I in trouble?"

"I think we both might be." Tom's demons had surfaced during that fight. Whether he'd had an inkling that could happen, Prophet had no clue.

"I wouldn't have killed him," Tom said deliberately, like he knew what Prophet had been thinking.

"I know."

"How?"

"Because you could've killed him with your bare hands in one movement." What Tom had done was more primal. Personal.

"You gonna tell Phil?"

"What? That you won a fight?"

Tom rubbed the back of his neck and groaned. "Fuck, Proph," was all he said about that, and then, "We should get out of here."

"I haven't gotten my money yet."

"Seriously?"

"No, Tommy. I guess your joke meter got jostled in the fight. Come on." He moved to help Tom off the table just as two beefy-looking assholes crowded the doorway. Tom stiffened, his fists clenching. He swallowed, and his vacant-eyed look came back. "Stay cool, T. I've got this. Do you understand?"

He waited until Tom met his eyes and nodded before turning to the men. He kept a hand on Tommy's thigh to center him as he said, "My fighter won—got my cash?"

"Boss wants to talk to you."

"Money first." He turned his back on the men to face Tom, mouthing, "They gone?"

After a beat, Tom said, "Yeah."

"Good." He frowned. "You're in pain."

"Some. My ribs mostly."

"You got a decent knock to your head, too." That's what seemed to have started Tom's frenzy. "You've got a pretty good temper on you, Cajun."

Tom didn't answer, because what the hell could he do but agree, so he just sat silently, letting Prophet fix his lip and feel around his ribs to see how badly he winced, and tried not to let the guilt race through him.

And once again, Prophet was there with him physically, but his eyes held that same faraway look they'd had earlier. Prophet had done this before, cared for someone just like this, and probably here, in this club. Maybe, undoubtedly, Prophet had fought as well, but in this role, he was the fierce protector. And Tom had honestly never felt protected like this in his entire life. As uncomfortable as it made him, Prophet was almost hypnotic, rubbing him down, checking for bruises and sprains, icing his hands and ribs, treating the cuts.

Prophet was comfortable here.

"You fought here," he said finally.

"Yep. Long time ago." He took off the tape with a remover that left Tom's skin intact. Tom had been prepared to just rip it off, but literally putting himself in Prophet's capable hands seemed like the better decision. "They're going to come after you."

"Was it always like this?"

"It's big time money now. Fights get recorded, shown on YouTube," Prophet answered without answering, something he was proficient at.

"Did you know I was gonna hurt him?"

"Yeah. I just didn't know if it would be on purpose."

"And?"

Prophet stared up at him. "I still don't, Tommy."

Tom saw the manager in the doorway behind Prophet and tensed when the guy growled, "That asshole fucked up my fighter."

Prophet looked calm, gave him that same *I've got this* look, and Tom forced himself to relax.

"He's got a temper." Prophet shrugged, turning halfway from Tom but still making Tom feel shielded. "PTSD or some shit like that. He kicked your guy's ass, fair and square, and I want my goddamned money."

"Didn't stop for the judge's call."

"Now we've got rules?"

"He can't come back here."

"Plenty of other places to take our money," Prophet said. The man stepped forward, slapped the roll of bills into Prophet's hand, and walked out.

"We're gonna get rolled in the parking lot," Tom said resignedly.

Prophet tucked the bills into the front pocket of his jeans. "I know."

The invite for the blood match would come when they were outside. It was how Prophet remembered it working all those years ago. The boys he'd fought with had spoken about it in hushed tones. The fighters who went to the blood match weren't allowed back into the regular fights, even as audience members. There were all sorts of rumors about what happened to them: paralyzed, run out of town. Killed. Prophet had always surmised it wasn't anything as dramatic as that. Maybe the guys who disappeared had been threatened to stay away or paid enough that they didn't have to fight again. But then again, who the hell knew?

Tommy was dressed now, hood over his head, hands stuck in the front pocket of his old Louisiana U sweatshirt. Prophet guided him out. A few guys had waited for him, called out *Cajun*. But no one came close to him, like they were all a little afraid of him.

Tommy seemed a little afraid of himself.

Before they got halfway to the car, a short guy who looked like his nose had been broken one too many times slunk around from behind a crappy old serial killer van. "Crowd loved your boy, but he might be a little too much for this venue."

"Ya think?" Prophet shoved Tommy forward, and thankfully, he complied.

"Got an offer for you."

"We're not interested in fighting here again."

"Not here." The guy slid him a card. "This is different. Your guy can keep kicking ass and no one will stop him. Money's bigger. Stakes are higher."

Prophet stared at the guy, wondered if he'd been the one to give Chris the same speech, and why Chris would've fallen for it. Had Chris gotten out of control in the end, like Tommy?

"Where and when?"

"Cross Street, tomorrow. Come at ten, fight's at eleven. No one but you and your fighter." The guy shook his hand, and Prophet fought the urge to break out hand sanitizer. Or punch him. Tom could push himself to get in the ring tomorrow, but it wasn't smart. The guy didn't give a shit about the fighters—and the thought that he might've been involved in Chris's death made Prophet's fists clench.

He tried to calm down, counting backward in his mind, but that counting to ten shit never, ever worked. It actually made him madder.

"You in?" The guy asked.

Prophet opened his mouth to say, *No, we're not*, when Tom said, "We're in."

"It's gonna be a good one," the guy said with a grin.

"Fuck off," Prophet told him, but Tom nodded at the guy even as Prophet dragged him away.

They'd almost gotten to the truck when it happened. The men—maybe five of them—came rushing out of the back alley where they'd obviously been lying in wait.

He wanted to tell Tom not to fight, but Tom wouldn't have listened. He was already charging toward them like he was a bowling ball and they were the pins.

Prophet grabbed one of them, slammed him against the hood of the truck. Pinned him, wanted to ask him if he was one of the guy's who'd beaten Chris to death. But the way he went down, the way Tom took the others down, told Prophet that they weren't capable of that kind of violence.

They'd been ordered by the boss to do this, but they were more bouncers than fighters. Prophet recognized a guy who'd been hanging out with Ivan in the back room, as well. He came straight for Tom, but Prophet stopped him by once again slamming his body facedown against the hood of the nearest car.

"Tom, let them go," he ordered. Tom was half sitting on one of them—two others had already run off, and the other was crumpled on the ground.

Tom stared at him—that long, faraway stare, and no, the guy wasn't fully back yet from wherever this fight had taken him.

"At least we got the invite," Tom said finally, letting Prophet peel him up from the ground and giving the guy under him a chance to run. Tom leaned against Prophet, who did a half walk, half carry back to the car.

"I'm not letting you fight again."

"Not letting me? That's rich." Tommy pushed him away. "This is what we were assigned. I'm doing my job."

Prophet stopped arguing, because it was useless. They had twenty-four hours until the fight. There was always the chance that someone else would try to kill Tommy before that.

Who knew that would be the most comforting thought of the day?

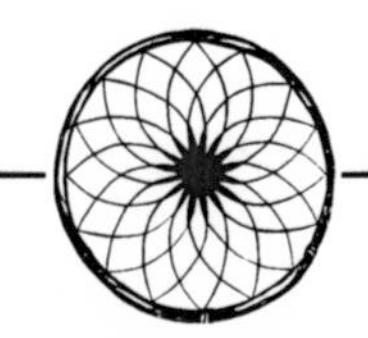

CHAPTER ELEVEN

Tom had known fighting again would change him, make him revert back to the fighter he'd been in his youth. Maybe he'd even wanted to. At least *that* Tom had fought for something.

The pounding rush of blood to his ears still hadn't cleared. If anything, it'd gotten worse on the drive back to the hotel. His ears popped as he walked up the steps, and he pushed past Prophet into his room, stripping as he headed to the shower.

The spray rained down like hot needles along his bruised and scraped skin. He hissed as he forced himself to stay under, scrubbed viciously with the soap. He washed his hair, stayed in as long as he could stand it, until he realized that still being able to smell the ring had nothing to do with how clean he was.

He wrapped himself in towels—one around his waist and another around his shoulders and walked out of the bathroom to find his piercings in the bag on the desk.

Shit. He'd forgotten all about them. He grabbed the bag and opened it.

"You're going to do that now?" Prophet asked. He was sitting at the small table like he'd been waiting for Tom, watching the security camera footage.

"Holes start to close fast." He threaded the bar quickly through his left nipple, hissing at the slight sting of pain, which made him hard.

And Prophet watched the whole thing with complete and utter interest.

"Dude, that had to hurt."

"That's the whole point." His voice was rough, his hands were shaking, and, in tandem, his head was beginning to throb. He refused to tell Prophet any of it.

But Prophet was next to him, taking the remaining piercings from him. "I'll do it."

"No."

"Why?"

Because I'm gonna get hard if you touch me. "Fine."

Prophet capped the piercing Tom had already put in. Then he tugged the other nipple toward him and slid the piercing in, capping it expertly while Tommy watched. He didn't bother to hide his erection through the towel.

He knows you're already hard.

"Okay?" Prophet asked, and Tom could only nod yes. "Towel off."

Tom dropped it. Wanted to say something like, *I have to be hard for the piercings to go in*, but he couldn't. And Prophet didn't seem to care, and he didn't know how insulted he should be about that.

"You're sure?" Tom asked.

"Yeah." Prophet stared at him, and he didn't want to make a bigger deal of the whole thing, so he grabbed his dick, positioned it up against his stomach, and let Prophet slide the piercings in. He tried to ignore the fact that Prophet had dropped to his knees and that his mouth was inches from Tom's dick, but he couldn't help but watch, fascinated, as Prophet threaded the piercings in, waiting for Tom to catch his breath between each one.

When Prophet finished with all five, Tom pulled the towel back around him loosely and went to the bed. He sat back against the pillows, and Prophet watched him silently for a few moments before saying, "You're your very own whipping boy. How's that work?"

"Working great." He didn't protest when Prophet came forward with salve and then pressure bandage. Then ice. Everywhere. Bags of it on his shoulders. Two for his ribs and hands. Another for his cheek and nose.

"Head all right?"

"Can't feel a thing," he lied.

"Figured. That's when you do stupid shit."

There was no judgment in his tone. "Sounds like you've been there."

"My whole life," Prophet concurred pleasantly.

"I liked you better when you were an asshole."

"Most people would agree with you."

His head had started to ache. Fights always triggered his migraines, like his body remembered the emotional and physical responses and repaid him in kind.

He didn't care, welcomed the pain and the hurt inside, embraced it like an old friend as he tried to ignore Prophet. He wanted Prophet out of his room so he could have his privacy, his . . .

Life? Yeah? Which one, T?

He told himself to shut up. Closed his eyes and drifted off.

It felt like seconds later when he woke with the pain slamming against his right temple.

"Should've known," he mumbled.

"Cajun, sit up."

"No."

"Stubborn." Prophet pulled him to sitting, propped on pillows. "Lying down when you have a migraine isn't good."

"How'd you know?"

"My mother had them."

"Calling me a girl?"

"Cajun, I've been calling you that since we met."

"I'll kick your ass," he said weakly.

"Yeah, didn't know you had a temper," Prophet drawled.

"What gave it away?"

Prophet snorted. "Let's take that migraine medicine."

"I can't believe you read my medical files."

Prophet looked offended. "That would be an invasion of privacy. I looked through your bags."

He'd have rolled his eyes, but that would've hurt too damned much. "Don't need anything," he managed instead before he walked unsteadily into the bathroom, knelt, and got sick in the toilet.

He knew how this would go. First the pain, which he could deal with, and then the sickness, which he hated. Doc at EE had insisted that Tom tell him every damned bit of medical history, and thank God he had, because he'd given Tom medicine. Medicine he wasn't using because he couldn't stop getting sick long enough to do so.

After a few minutes, he asked, "Hand me the pills?"

Prophet handed him the suppositories instead.

"Not gonna keep down pain meds without it," Prophet said way too reasonably. And he was right. The migraine had come up too quickly, and he was too far gone. "You sure it's not a concussion?"

"He didn't hit me hard enough."

"Hard enough to piss you off," Prophet told him, and yeah, that's when Tom remembered really losing his shit. The ear boxing.

Goddamned pussy.

"Shut up," he told Prophet. And the voices in his head.

"Not until you let me help you."

The whole *show Prophet no weakness* thing wasn't going well.

He got up, and his head spun. He leaned against Prophet's shoulder without meaning to, but when he went to pull back, the man held him there with a gentle hand on the back of his neck.

"Stay. It's all right."

But it wouldn't be, not in the morning. Not when Tom wasn't drugged and Prophet would make fun of him again, or worse—be a bigger asshole to him.

Not when he had more fights to go before they broke this case.

"I've got it," he mumbled. Pushed back and saw stars. Fucking, fucking migraine.

"You are stubborn, T." Tom swallowed as Prophet traced his bottom lip with his thumb. "Why?"

"Won't rely on anyone."

"Yeah, I get that." Prophet's eyes told him that he did, honestly and truly, and that made it a little easier to sink back against his shoulder. "For tonight, T. I've got you. We're partners."

"You don't want a partner."

"Do you want me to start singing, 'You Can't Always Get What You Want'?"

"No. Please. My head."

"People would pay good money for my singing."

"In Hell, maybe."

"Smart-ass. T, you gotta let me help you."

"No. Got it."

"Fuck. No, you don't. You want me to hold you down and put it in, I will."

"Have you arrested."

"For what? Force of suppository?"

Prophet wasn't going to give up, and fuck, maybe this could be more humiliating. But it couldn't. All he could do was curl up on his side on the bathroom floor and let Prophet help him. Prophet used a glove and some lube, inserted the medication quickly and easily. Professional. No jokes. Nothing but a cloth with water and alcohol for his forehead, sips of ginger ale, and use of pressure points to alleviate the pain, and finally, when the antinausea medication took effect, Prophet helped him back to bed.

"It's okay, T. I've got you," Prophet told him again.

I've got you.

Tom wondered why the hell that suddenly mattered so much.

It took Tommy about fifteen minutes to start nodding off. Prophet got the pills into him before that, and they stayed down. As Prophet watched, Tom's body, which had been curled tighter than a drum in the semi-upright position, began to relax. First, he let his legs down from where they'd been pulled up to his chest. Then his arms relaxed, and finally, he turned onto his side.

The man was handsome in that brooding way. Scruffy now, which he hadn't been a couple of days ago, when he'd arrived all buttoned up and ready for work. He'd looked more like a Fed then, but now he looked . . .

He looked good.

During the fight, he'd been angry. Stunning.

"Who were you fighting tonight, T?" he murmured to the sleeping man, grateful to not get a response. Because he really didn't want to know. Because then he might need to reciprocate.

None of his partners had ever been stupid enough to get personal with him, and by that, he didn't mean naked. Even Mick, a man who seemed to know him as well as anyone did, knew that Prophet and personal questions didn't mix.

Tom might ask them, might push the envelope with things like going to visit Carole and asking about Prophet's CIA career, but the fact that Tom appeared as fucked-up, if not more so, than Prophet was a crowning achievement.

As if he felt Prophet's gaze on him, Tom's eyes opened. After a second of blinking, he said, "You're taking care of me still."

"Told you I would."

"I didn't know you had such maternal instincts."

"Fuck you, Cajun. You know, I could've come up with other worse names for your fight, and don't think I wasn't planning on it. Cajun Heat. Voodoo Daddy . . ."

Tom groaned. "I'm already in pain—isn't that enough to make you happy?"

"Could always be happier," he said. "Shit, I think I saw that on a talk show. I need to go back to war or something."

Tom snorted. Was quiet for a few minutes, and then mumbled, "Not weak."

"No, you're not."

Tommy seemed satisfied with that, closed his eyes, and let Prophet hold the pressure point in the tender web of skin in between his thumb and forefinger. That spot relieved headaches, and Prophet would sit here like this all night if it meant helping Tommy.

He wondered how, in such a short period of time, their roles had been reversed. Wouldn't Phil have a blast with this.

Or maybe this was all part of Phil's plan.

Assholes. Both of them. Prophet didn't need to stop mid-mission to take care of his partner. He could take care of himself—always had, always did—but this taking care of others shit had stopped for him a long time ago.

In small doses, he could do it, like he helped Mick out on missions. But Mick was capable of dealing with his shit, most of the time. And they'd known each other for years.

He'd known Tom two days and already he was calling him Tommy most of the time—and Tommy wasn't correcting him—while mothering the damned man. He didn't want to mother anyone. It was why he'd left home a long damned time ago and stopped taking care of people.

Not John, though.

No, not John. And if John were still around, maybe Prophet would still be taking care of him. And maybe he'd be resenting it by now.

You resented it then. You're just pretending you didn't because—

He clamped down on his thoughts, refused to let them materialize any further.

Tom turned then, mumbled something about *pain* and *Cajun* and *bad luck*, put his hand on Prophet's chest. He said some other stuff in Cajun French, and Prophet cursed and shoved the man's hand off him.

Tom replaced it immediately, grabbed the front of Prophet's shirt in a fist to tug himself closer. This time, Prophet didn't resist, just cursed again under his breath, and watched Tom's even breathing.

How he could look so peaceful after everything that had happened tonight was unbelievable. Prophet wasn't peaceful after violence—never had been, never would be. He was a rolling ball of energy, adrenaline, and anger, and tonight he'd had to tamp it down for all that nurturing shit.

He hated it.

Tom sighed and rubbed his cheek against Prophet's shirt.

Seriously?

Once Tom seemed to settle in—still touching him—Prophet called the diner and paid off one of the waiters to deliver his order so he could fuel up. Extricated himself from Tom's grasp long enough to grab the bag, pay the waiter, and bring it in, but Tom was restless whenever he left the bed, seemed to be searching for him. So Prophet stayed close. Ate through the night, watched movies. Medicated Tommy. Went over strategy. Dozed fitfully, but that at least was par for the course.

Mick texted him—something about Blue scaling down the side of a building for fun. He thought about texting back and asking Mick and Blue to come help him. To take over.

But he didn't.

Instead, he tried to stay awake. One minute, he was watching the awful goodness of *The Expendables*, and the next, he didn't know what the fuck was going on.

He blinked rapidly, but his body remained still. He was trapped in quicksand and he refused to panic. Had to get his bearings.

He listened again. Loud talking. His weapon was pointed toward the sounds.

The room tilted like a funhouse ride, the first sign that this wasn't all real, that he wasn't where he thought he was.

Concentrate. The sounds . . . not artillery fire or the enemy. Still, he didn't lower his weapon. Scanned the darkened room, the flickering light from the TV illuminating the man on the bed . . .

Tommy.

Texas.

Chris is dead. And this wasn't a war zone.

Or was it?

Fuck. He buried his face against his arm, wiped away the sweat, and forced his breathing to regulate. Because he heard screams, the kind you only heard if someone was dying. His first instinct was to cover his ears, but this wasn't real, so it wouldn't help.

Tom mumbled something.

Prophet put the gun back under his pillow and tried to settle back into bed. His body trembled slightly, the way it always did when he came out of these flashbacks, and he focused on Tommy so he wouldn't have to look around the room and catch sight of the ghost in battle fatigues.

He needed to stay next to Tom, because he didn't want his new partner—as fucked-up as he was—to see Prophet equally so.

Great team you've put together here, Phil.

Tom immediately made contact with him again. At first, Prophet thought Tommy might just fall back to sleep with his face on his chest, but then the man moved so they were face to face. He murmured something Prophet didn't catch, before pulling Prophet close and kissing him. Like really kissing him, not caring about his split lip, open-mouthed, tongue-fucking, zero-to-sixty kissing that had Prophet kissing him back.

Tom's erotic growl of surprise spread heat through Prophet's entire body. He gasped in Tom's mouth, a soft huff, and his hands came up to rake through Tom's hair, against his scalp, half gentle, half tugging harder when Tommy responded by arching his pelvis against Prophet's.

A moan rumbled in his chest, and he was fucking gone when Tom stroked his tongue against the roof of his mouth before tongue-fucking him back.

He rolled Tommy onto his back and lay on top of him. Tom's hands grabbed at his hips, Prophet's casts cradling Tom's head.

Fuck, he loved kissing. Fucking was obviously great, but kissing was really how you could figure out how to take someone down in the best way possible.

He was still off-center from the flashback, but this was grounding him. Making him *feel.*

This kiss could ruin him.

"Wanted to kiss you . . . at the airport," Tom told him against his mouth.

"I wanted to see more of your piercings."

"Seen them all, up close and personal." Tom ground up against him, and Prophet kissed him again and again, and Tom's kisses back were a combination of promise and connection.

"Fuck. Sleepy," Tom murmured against his mouth.

Tommy.

Tom, he told himself sternly as he pulled back, like that would make a difference.

Tom, whose hands had moved up Prophet's body to pull his shirt off, stroke his face, then moved to his eyes before he stopped, looked uncertain.

"Prophet, get yourself checked," he said quietly. "Your eyes . . ."

Prophet forced himself not to freeze. "Yeah, m'fine, T. Drugs are fucking with your hoodoo."

"Yeah," Tom echoed, his brow furrowed in concentration, like he was desperately trying to remember what he'd just been talking about. Between the drugs and the sex, Prophet would make sure that didn't happen.

When he brought his mouth back down on Tommy's, a part of him was back at seventeen, kissing a different man, but a bigger part knew exactly who he was kissing. And he didn't bother to stop.

Tom fell asleep under him. Prophet was both grateful and slightly offended. He fought sleep for as long as he could, and when he woke, there were no flashbacks. Just Tom's hand on his cock.

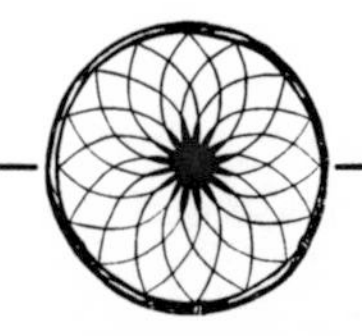

CHAPTER TWELVE

Tom had had an extremely vivid dream that he'd kissed Prophet. That Prophet had kissed him back, rolled him underneath him, held him.

He touched his face and swore it felt like he had beard burn. His lips were swollen, the split one throbbing a little more than it should, and Prophet's chin was red too.

But if Prophet wasn't saying anything, what did that mean? Because if it had really happened, the man had been lying on top of him, not the other way around.

"Better?" Prophet asked gingerly, and yes, Tom was sleepy and drugged and, unsurprisingly, feeling no pain.

"Better." The headache was still there, lurking behind the narcotic haze, but he didn't have the wherewithal to care. He shifted a little, and then realized why Prophet looked so odd.

His hand was between Prophet's legs, just resting there, like it belonged. He pulled it off the soft cotton of the jeans, muttered, "Fuck. Sorry," while also realizing that Prophet had been hard.

"S'okay. You were pretty restless." Prophet reached over and grabbed him another towel with ice for his head, placed it gently where Tom had been holding the other one while he'd slept.

"You're nice when I'm on meds," he told Prophet.

"That is definitely the meds talking."

"Don't."

"What?"

"You're placating me."

"And you're using big words," Prophet grumbled.

Tom snorted, got up, and went to take a piss. He washed up and brushed his teeth too, then asked Prophet if they had any caffeine. He was slightly unsteady, didn't know if it was day or night out, and man, whatever Doc had given him was good stuff.

"Here." Prophet pressed a can of Coke into his hands, and he chugged it. When he finished, he saw Prophet splashing his face with water at the sink, which was situated outside the bathroom. He watched him towel off and then just stare in the mirror, a faraway look in his eyes that Tom wasn't sure he liked at all.

"Anything wrong?" he asked.

Prophet seemed to snap halfway back to reality. "Nothing, man. I'm all good."

"No, you're not."

"No, I'm not. But I'll be fine in the morning."

"It is morning," Tom pointed out. "I think."

Prophet snorted. "Thanks for the update."

"Sorry."

"For what? Correcting me?"

Tom shrugged. "That you had to help someone you didn't even want as your partner in the first place."

He saw the scratches, the fading hickey on the man's neck, and he didn't like it. He was just high enough now from the meds not to overthink things. He was a big ball of want and Prophet was in his sights. He ran a hand down Prophet's bare back before he could stop himself, and the man stilled. Tom didn't care—he'd wanted to touch Prophet for days now. And Prophet wasn't stopping him, just watching him carefully in the mirror.

Tom met his eyes.

"Like what you see?" Prophet asked, his voice a quiet yet dangerous rumble, heavily laced with sarcasm.

Even so, Tom answered him seriously. "Yes."

"That's because you're seeing two of me."

Tom laughed because he couldn't help it. Punch drunk—he could see why they called it that. "Fucking meds . . . make me . . ."

"Tired?"

"Horny," he corrected with a loopy smile. Swallowed hard, but man, the meds were like goddamned truth serum.

"Guess that secret's out of the bag."

"You have secrets too."

"Isn't that supposed to be a secret?"

Tommy wagged a finger at him. "Don't. Not when I'm on drugs."

Prophet smiled, that lazy, sleepy smile that made Tom want to fuck him, and turned around in the small space Tom had left him. And Tom didn't move.

Prophet didn't make any attempt to push him away, either. Instead, he reached down and ran his hand down Tom's arm toward his wrist, the one with the leather bracelet. "You didn't take it off."

"Neither did you."

Prophet played with the bracelet, spacing out a little, and Tom wanted him back in this reality, with him. Put a hand over Prophet's, who said, "You talk in your sleep."

"Did I say anything interesting?"

"You put your hand on my dick."

"And it turned you on?" Tom asked.

"Fighting always makes me hard."

"So my fighting turned you on?"

Prophet gave him a lopsided smirk. "I'm not that easy, Tommy."

Tom stroked a hand between them, going all the way down to the waistband of Prophet's jeans—and they were sitting low enough that all Tom had to do was give a tug and they'd be history—and then brought his hand up to cup the back of Prophet's neck. "Think you might be."

He ghosted his lips against Prophet's shoulder, and the man shivered but didn't move. He wouldn't go down easily, and that was the best part.

Eventually, Tom would worry about the consequences. But there was enough distance between then and now for him to remain as close as he could to Prophet.

Prophet ran his fingers through Tom's hair, then put a hand on his cheek. "This is the worst idea ever," he mumbled, and Tom agreed with a nod. He was still holding Prophet by the back of his neck, and he pulled the man's face toward his, leaning in for a kiss.

Prophet offered no resistance. Let Tom pull him close, crush his mouth against Prophet's in a hot, hard kiss. Tom forced his tongue inside Prophet's mouth, and after what seemed like forever, Prophet's tongue played against his.

Prophet still held Tom's wrist, and it was as if they were both suspended like that, Tom trying to pull Prophet closer and Prophet trying to keep an arm's length between them.

Fuck that. Tom wasn't going to stand for it. He jerked his arm from Prophet's grasp and pushed him back against the sink.

The kiss started out rough and got tender and then rough again as they fought for some kind of foothold, any dominance. It quickly grew to *holy fuck I can't stop this* levels. Hard and soft, and it lit his entire body on fire, and oh holy Mother Mary, he was going down hard.

But he'd make sure Prophet went down harder.

Except he had to make sure he was right about this. That Prophet wasn't just letting him do this because of the drugs . . . or for some other stupid reason, like wanting to tell Phil that Tom had assaulted him.

He pulled back, narrowed his eyes. Needed to know if this was real, or if Prophet was jerking him again, the way he loved to. But based on the flush on Prophet's cheeks, the rapid pulse, the pupils, Tommy knew he wasn't kidding.

Knew for sure when Prophet reached out and put his hands on Tommy's waist and pulled him close so fast it was hard cock to hard cock, match to flame and sparking a totally spectacular meltdown. Epic. Memorable.

This was going to kill him, one way or the other.

Tom's cock ground against his. Prophet was still wearing jeans, Tom shorts, and this was a very bad fucking idea.

Really, literally a bad fucking idea.

But Tom was watching him carefully. Somehow those drugs managed to make him more perceptive instead of less, which wasn't the way it should be working. "Come on—let's go back to bed," he told Tom.

"What do you think will happen then?"

"I'm going to fuck you."

"Suppose I wanted to fuck you?" Prophet asked.

Tom raised his eyebrow, and Prophet cursed softly, remembering. "You insisted on putting it in there," Tom reminded him with a smirk.

"Fuck me."

"Yeah, I'm trying, Proph." Tom's voice was quiet but firm. Like he wasn't taking no for an answer.

Prophet bit back a smart remark, afraid he wouldn't be able to pull it off. Instead, he attempted to stare Tom down. But the man appeared to be impossible to unnerve.

This whole thing was messy and complicated and fraught with a myriad of issues, apart from the fact that Prophet didn't know if he actually liked Tommy, and he was sure Tommy didn't really like him either.

But the drugs were working their magic on Tom, and they were both obviously horny and fueled by the adrenaline rush of the fight.

This could be an effective way to get rid of a partner, Prophet thought. And that made his gut churn a little, but he didn't stop to question why, not when Tom crushed their mouths together and walked them backward at the same time, ending up with his heavy body on top of Prophet's on the bed.

Prophet allowed it. Conceding gave him the feeling that he was in control when really, he wasn't. Not at all.

His casts were getting in the way—or at least that's what Tom said when he pushed Prophet's arms up over his head. And then he reached down to take off Prophet's jeans and his own shorts in a couple of swift movements. He was moving Prophet's thighs, getting him into position . . .

"Tommy, dammit." Prophet heard the frustration in his own voice, even as he allowed Tommy to manhandle him. "Not used to . . ."

"Being in the bitch seat?" Tommy asked with a twisted smile. "You might like it."

He wanted to bite out, "Doubt it," but he couldn't. His breath came out of his nose in a soft huff, body going taut as the blood thrummed into a hot roar that threatened his sanity. He was goddamned falling apart. But hell, if you were going to do so, this was the right way to go.

Tommy's hand skimmed his eyelids and then lingered a second too long there, and the motion would have been imperceptible to almost anyone, but Prophet wasn't anyone, and he needed to tell

Tommy to never, ever mention what his goddamned Cajun voodoo ass had just seen. Again.

But maybe he wouldn't have to. Tommy seemed to shake it off, maybe remembering Prophet's earlier words. He was still loopy.

Because having Tommy know would be the worst fucking thing Prophet could think of.

Tom had pounced on Prophet because he'd been feeling no pain. And he took complete advantage of the fact that Prophet's hands were clumsier than they ever would be otherwise because of the casts. Granted, he was surprised that Prophet lay there, on his back, arms above his head—now he was just watching, a little warily, but he was so damned still.

Coiled to strike? Could be, but Tom didn't think so. He bent down, kissed the man again, and Prophet offered no objection, kissing him back with fervor.

"You can move, Proph," Tom murmured against his ear after he tore his mouth away.

In response, Prophet turned his head so Tom could nuzzle his cheek. Which he did.

It wouldn't stay like this—Tom knew that. But as long as Prophet was pliant—and naked—Tom had no problem taking advantage of him.

He'd take any advantage he could get.

He pushed back off Prophet a little to run his hands along the man's chest, his fingers straying along the scarred skin—he catalogued a bullet hole, two knife slices, small scars he couldn't place—and then he squeezed a nipple between his finger and thumb and Prophet jumped.

Tom wanted to see that again and again. He fingered the nipple and bit the other one at the same time, ground his thigh lightly against Prophet's cock, and yes, the man raised his hips off the bed in response.

Fuck, the guy would look good with piercings. Tom bent, sucked and bit his nipple again, murmured, "If you were mine, I'd make you pierce it, just because," low enough that Prophet couldn't hear, bit and sucked again, and Prophet's body jolted.

When he glanced up, the nipple still in his mouth, Prophet asked, "That all you got?" He'd tried to sound bored, but his cheeks were flushed, eyes glittering with arousal.

"Is that a challenge?"

"You're the one who started this."

That wasn't entirely true, but Tom didn't want to argue. He wanted to fuck. Hard, fast, and maybe this was the drugs, but he was beyond caring.

He wanted to see Prophet lose his shit even more.

He dragged his tongue down Prophet's hot skin, flicking, biting, licking as he took the most direct path to get him between Prophet's legs.

He traced the lean, tautly muscled line of Prophet's hip with his tongue. Prophet tasted sweet, as if the donuts and candy he ate ran through his blood.

Prophet remained oddly submissive, watching Tom with a gaze that made Tom quake, might've felled him if he were sober. But now, he was king of the goddamned world and Prophet was all his, stretched out like a sacrifice.

"You do this with your other partners?" Prophet asked suddenly.

Tom rubbed the scruff on his cheek against Prophet's inner thigh, and the man jumped a little. "Never. You?"

Prophet shook his head, stared up at the ceiling. Oh no, Tom wasn't having that at all. He pressed a finger along Prophet's perineum, replaced it with his tongue. Prophet groaned, hips lifting, and there, attention was in its proper place.

He wanted to remember all of this, the scent of Prophet's skin, the weight of his cock in his hand. More than that, he wanted Prophet to remember this, wanted to embed it into his brain and onto his body.

Prophet's cock was long and thick and begging for Tom's mouth. Prophet hissed when Tommy sucked on him before taking him halfway.

"Tommy." That was it. That one word, but the tone of voice nearly had Tom coming on the bed.

He took Prophet's cock deep into his throat, and Prophet arched up into him, fucking his mouth with several strong thrusts of his hips. Tom let him for a few moments and then stopped him with a firm grasp on both his hips, pinning him.

"More," Prophet bit out as Tom sucked him, handled his balls. Tom ran his tongue directly up the vein on the underside of his cock, pressing firmly for good measure.

His eyes never left Prophet's face, not even when the man closed his eyes.

Tom was going to hunt Prophet—track down everything about him for good measure.

"Fuck, if you keep doing that . . ." Prophet cut off mid-sentence and groaned as Tom worked his tongue around the head of his cock, probing, pressing, driving him crazy. He wanted Prophet to come as many times as he could tonight. Relished in the control he had, because he hadn't had any earlier, and Prophet had known it.

Now that the roles were reversed, he wasn't going to lose his advantage.

"Sadist," Prophet bit out as Tom moved himself back up.

"You say that like it's a bad thing." Tom pulled his body back up Prophet's so they were chest to chest. His fingers dug into Prophet's hip as he rocked his pelvis against Prophet's.

"Fucker. Gonna come," Prophet warned.

"No, you're not." The loopiness was wearing off, leaving him slightly unbalanced and desperate to hang onto the control. "Not yet, Proph. Gonna make it good for you."

He flexed his hips again, a slow, torturous grind of cock against cock. Prophet's arms remained over his head, fingers curled into fists as much as they could be.

Would Prophet touch him if they weren't there, or were the casts just a convenient excuse to remain somewhat submissive?

"How good?" Prophet asked. His breath came in quick pants. He looked, somehow, like a goddamned angel.

Tom slid a knee between Prophet's legs, splitting them apart, forcing them wide with his body.

He's afraid of hurting me. Because Prophet was reacting—all the signals were there, beyond the hard dick. The flush, fast breaths, fingers tightening into fists around the ends of the casts.

All this time, Tom was worried about exactly the opposite. But he had an unbreakable man under him. He growled at the thought of Prophet trying to protect him, leaned in and kissed him again. The kisses turned hot, wet, their bodies arching against one another, sliding together in a hot, sticky, sweaty mess of pleasure. Prophet began to rut against him.

He wanted Prophet begging.

He kept his mouth on Prophet's, their kisses frantic as he pushed up onto one elbow and grabbed for the lube. Prophet's thighs opened for him easily and he eased one finger slowly inside of him.

"You don't have to flirt, T. I'm not a chick."

"That mean I don't have to buy you dinner afterward?"

"No, I definitely want dinner." Prophet paused. "Maybe I am a chick."

"I really hope I remember that when this is all over."

Prophet snorted, then groaned when Tom added a second finger and twisted. "Yeah, that's it. Fuck."

Prophet tried to grab onto something and when he realized he couldn't—not really—Tom reached up and placed one hand, then the other, so Prophet could grab at the bottom of the headboard.

"Don't let go," Tom told him. Prophet looked at him, his eyes slightly dazed, since Tom hadn't let up on the finger fucking, purposefully leaving Prophet on edge.

Tom pulled back, reluctantly removing his hand to open the condom so he could roll it on carefully over the . . .

"Piercings," Prophet said, his brow furrowed.

"You're the one who put them back in. Don't worry—you'll enjoy the hell out of them." He rasped a tongue over Prophet's nipple, then bit the nub again.

"Fuck."

"Thought so."

"Fuck you," Prophet managed as his cock drilled Tom's stomach. Tom pulled back to finish with the condom, and Prophet ignored Tom's request not to let go of the headboard, shifted his weight and flipped onto his stomach.

Tom had expected that, although he was disappointed. He could've insisted Prophet stay on his back, better yet, could've flipped the man back over himself, but he allowed Prophet to settle in on his elbows and knees, casts hitting together with a dull thud.

He made a mental note to scratch the man's number off those later, replace it with his while Prophet slept. If he slept.

Yeah, that was the goal—to fuck Prophet so hard and well that he slept like a baby.

He moved so he was chest to back, thigh to thigh, the contact like a wrestling pose. He bit down on Prophet's neck where it met his shoulder, enough to leave a mark as he entered him.

Prophet hissed at the intrusion, but Tom didn't stop. A slow, smooth push through the pain would make Prophet's body yield to him.

"Relax, Proph," he said, more of a demand than a request, and the tension in Prophet's shoulders dissipated as Tom held his hips, rocked against him.

"Fuck. Fuck," was all Prophet said when Tom didn't give him time to recover. He didn't need it, not the way Tom had opened him, was pressing him, holding him impaled with his cock. "Tommy . . ."

That's the way the man should always sound when he says Tommy.

Prophet pushed back against him hard, once, twice, which allowed Tom to sink inside him faster. They both cursed at the same time—Tom in Cajun French—stilled like their lives depended on it.

And then Prophet rocked up, snapping his hips and forcing Tom to move to his rhythm.

"Fuck, Proph," he ground out. Prophet laughed, but it was a good laugh. He sounded free. Happy.

"You're right—piercings are good."

Prophet was the one who was high now. Tom managed to wrest back control by bucking at an angle that made Prophet stiffen and give a near whimper.

"Yeah, Tommy, like that."

One of his hands was on Prophet's shoulder as he rocked his hips back and forth, the other on Prophet's leaking cock. Prophet was matching him stroke for stroke, his head against the headboard, which in turn slammed the wall, the bed threatening to break apart. Tom's entire body was reduced to a heartbeat.

"Tommy!"

He didn't know why he hadn't wanted Prophet to call him that. Now, he didn't want Prophet to call him anything else. Tom sped up, his breath coming in halting gasps. "Come on."

"You first," Prophet said. "I have . . . more . . . self . . . control."

Tom pulled back. Slowed down. Prophet arched, trying to make it happen faster, but to no avail. Tom angled, hit his prostate fast, three times in a row, then backed off with shorter strokes that made Prophet moan louder and drop down, his shoulders hitting the mattress, arms sprawled in front of him as he started to lose control.

Prophet had expected the bleed-off of aggression from the fight to the sex, the leftover adrenaline. But, although Tom wasn't gentle, which was something Prophet never tolerated, it was like Tom was able to separate aspects of himself. He'd fought, he'd won—now it was time for the hedonist in him to play.

Or maybe he can just turn the fighting off.

But Prophet had been around men with bad tempers long enough to know better. Tom hadn't just been fighting Ivan in that ring. Maybe he hadn't been fighting Ivan at all.

The past was crowding in on this case from all directions. Prophet could fight, which was what he did best, or he could let himself drown in it. He closed his eyes and let himself drift away, back into the past, to a different bed, to a boy teetering on the edge of manhood. He could pretend so fucking easily.

Tom's hand moved from his cock to his nipple, squeezing it hard, bringing him back.

If you were mine, I'd make you pierce it. Just because.

He shuddered, and Tom said, "Stop leaving."

Dammit. Did Cajun Voodoo Man know goddamned everything?

He shivered under the big hands that manipulated him. They were doing more than just looking for a quick fuck—the touches were lingering, like burning hot ribbons along his skin.

His cock ached as Tom touched him, fingers digging into his skin, like Tom wanted Prophet to remember him, remember this.

And fuck, he would. Knew that already, because his body wanted more.

He didn't know why he needed this so badly. Tommy thrust against him, the piercings rolling inside him in just the right places, his hand on Prophet's cock.

Prophet's climax was like a gathering storm, swirling furiously, thunderously fast and uncontrolled, part wrath, part beauty, mixed with a little pain, and oh fuck, *yes*. Tom kept up a steady stream of dirty talk. Maybe it was the drugs, but Prophet didn't think so. It was a mix of English and Cajun French and Prophet's orgasm was long and drawn out, left him wrecked, weakened, unable to stop shuddering.

Tom yelled as he came seconds later, pumped inside of him, still hard and Prophet swore he could feel him come through the condom. It was dirty and messy. Raunchy. And when Tom's hand caught in his hair, forcing him to turn his head and look into Tom's face, Prophet complied. Couldn't pretend he didn't have the strength to look away.

Tom was forcing him to watch, to acknowledge. To not sink into the past, for comfort or self-flagellation.

Tommy seemed intent on taking care of him as well as taking charge. Prophet couldn't get too comfortable with this, couldn't enjoy it, because then . . .

Because then.

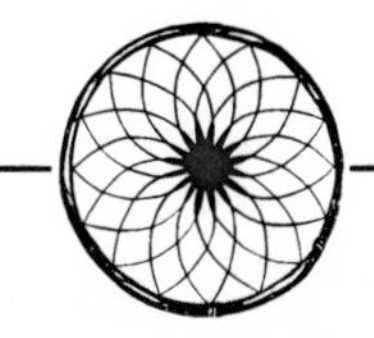

CHAPTER THIRTEEN

"What're you doing?" Prophet asked, his voice roughened by lack of sleep rather than sleep itself. For the past half an hour, he'd appeared to be resting with his eyes slightly open, while Tom tried to come down from the sex high that had rolled into the post-migraine drug high.

Tom wondered what the hell Prophet was scared of when he closed his eyes. Knew better than to ask. But he hadn't been able to resist grabbing a marker to draw on Prophet's casts. The man hadn't noticed until Tom was well into covering up the other phone numbers on the casts. Prophet stared between the casts and Tom, gave a small smirk, but didn't complain.

"Go back to sleep," he told Prophet, although he was still hazy too, in that place between dreaming and waking, where his body felt good and he wasn't sure any of this was real. Where he was still high enough not to really give a shit that he was doing something he'd never do if he wasn't.

But Prophet leaned in to watch him drawing the nautical star that mirrored the one Tom had tattooed over his heart. He'd gotten far enough that you couldn't see Dale's phone number any longer. "Nice star."

"Figured you'd appreciate that."

"I know you covered the number."

"Good."

"Good that I know or good that you covered it?" Prophet asked.

"Yeah."

"You're fucked in the head, Tommy."

Tom grunted, kept drawing. He was stringing together what was left of the numbers now, mesmerized by the way he was able to connect everything. That's what he liked most about the work he did—there were patterns in everything, in crimes, in good and evil, in life in general. Sometimes he felt like he could follow those paths forever.

Sometimes he feared they'd lead him down to hell and back.

Haven't they already?

"You draw your own tats too?" Prophet's voice grabbed him out of his reverie.

"Some of them." Tom sketched around the names, using some tribal symbols, a sugar skull, and anything else that struck him. Art tended to mesmerize him and he liked being able to follow his mind's lead without having to think on it.

"Where'd you get them done?"

"Got a friend in the business."

"An ex?"

Tom frowned. "Kind of." The man who'd inked him was truly the last person he wanted to think about, talk about, especially right now. "Don't you have any exes?"

Prophet laughed. "If I did, you know they'd all be after me. With shotguns."

"Only the men, or the women too?"

"Take your pick. I'll fuck anyone for the job, T. Don't tell me you wouldn't. But for my personal life, men suit me. Always have."

"No questions? No angst?"

"Not about that."

He answered that so easily. But just because it seemed like Prophet had let him in didn't mean the man had *actually* let him in. Tom hadn't been so high that he didn't know the actual difference.

Prophet reached out to trace the dreamcatcher on Tom's shoulder and biceps. Tom fought the urge to shudder at the touch, but stopped what he was doing. He could let Prophet trace his tattoos all day long. "You have bad dreams, Tommy?"

Tom didn't answer, because it didn't really seem to be a question. Instead, he asked, "Do you want me to draw you one?"

Prophet glanced at him and, after a second's hesitation, shrugged like it didn't matter. But it did.

Tom sketched on the inside of Prophet's right cast, since he'd covered the left with tribal markings and the skull. He started with the circle, a difficult proposition on the surface and the angle, but he managed, filled it in with a similar look to his. And then he drew the feathers carefully, so they curled around like Prophet's arm like an embrace.

It might've taken minutes or hours, but Tom was bleary-eyed when he finished. He looked up and saw Prophet studying it.

"Does it work?" Prophet asked.

"You never know how much worse things could be," Tom told him.

"Are you always this wise, or is it the meds?"

Tom laughed. "Definitely not always. How long do they have to stay on?"

"Who the fuck knows. I think Doc just does it to torture me. He told me that the next time I take my casts off myself, he'd put them on with pink wrapping. Like that would stop me. Like I'm afraid of pink." He paused. "Okay, I'm a little afraid of pink. But I'd just wear long gloves or something."

There was silence—comfortably so—as Tom finished. He closed the pen, flexed his hand that had gotten stiff from the drawing. He'd also gotten close to Prophet, moving next to him to get the right angle on the cast, his hip brushing Prophet's cock. And now his own had a more pressing need than covering up phone numbers.

The light dappled across Prophet's face. He looked more relaxed, less on guard than he'd ever been. But somehow still lethal.

Always lethal.

Prophet turned onto his back, arms over his head again, casts sprawled on the pillow. Tom's erection nudged Prophet's thigh as he thought about Prophet tied up, and Prophet shook his head.

"Did you take Viagra instead of migraine meds?"

"Maybe," Tom murmured, wrapped a hand around Prophet's cock, which was hard again too. "Would you mind?"

Prophet's answer was between a grunt and a laugh. Tom ran his thumb over the head, circling lightly, unable to resist leaning down to suck the tip into his mouth.

Prophet inhaled sharply, threaded his fingers into Tom's hair. He closed his eyes and groaned when Tom stroked in earnest, lifting his hips off the bed in a big cat-like stretch, letting Tom take control of him again. "Think I didn't get enough?"

"Think you need sleep."

Prophet's eyes opened as he studied Tom's face. "You're going to put me to sleep this way."

"Gonna try," Tom told him, his hand pumping Prophet's cock slowly, then faster when the man refused to tear his gaze away. He couldn't read the man's expression, not until his mouth dropped and his eyes glazed.

"Yeah, like that." Prophet's voice was hoarse, body tense. His casted hand reached out to hold on to Tom's biceps, the one with the dreamcatcher.

Tom caught him staring at it when he came.

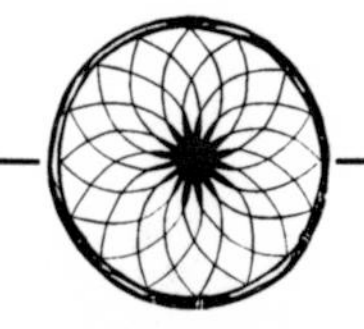

CHAPTER FOURTEEN

Prophet slept on and off, better than he had earlier, but he chalked that up to orgasms, not the dreamcatcher. Still, he couldn't stop staring at it, both the one on Tom's arm and the one on his cast.

It was just after five in the morning. Old habits of waking at oh dark hundred were hard to break and far too ingrained for him to even bother trying.

Tom wasn't restless now. His face was smushed into the pillow he was holding, cradling almost, all curled up.

Get out while you can. Because Prophet couldn't remember the last time he'd actually woken up next to someone when it wasn't in a foxhole or a safe house. And that wasn't half as dangerous as this shit.

He rolled out of bed, his brain already trying to formulate a plan, both for dealing with what had happened and with what lay ahead, especially in regards to the blood match. He opened his computer and found two things—an email from some guys he'd met in the audience who'd known Chris, wanting to meet with him today, and an IM from Cillian telling Prophet that he was alive and not to try anything with his couch.

No promises, he typed as he sat on the bed next to a passed-out Tommy, and in a minute got a response back of, *How's the partner?*

Great in bed, Prophet thought. Typed, *Same. PITA.*

You paused.

So?

When you pause, means you're thinking of a lie.

"Got to be kidding me," he muttered. *Go spook someone else. Maybe I'm a slow typer.*

Where is he right now?

Prophet turned his head toward Tom's prone form. *Sleeping.*

Next to you?

No.

Now you typed too fast. Also a tell.

Fuck off, Cill.

Getting involved with a partner . . .

We aren't involved.

You're fucking.

Prophet typed, *No.*

Too fast. Is he good?

Yes, on the job.

Ha. For the record, I'm excellent at both.

You're also never home.

Give me a reason to be, Cillian typed, then signed off immediately, allowing that last thought to linger in Prophet's head.

Guess I'll suck on that for a while, Prophet thought to himself, then wondered why the hell he felt guilty about flirting with a man he'd never met, and then cursed because the reason was lying in the bed next to him.

Then he showered, dressed, alarmed the place to alert Tom to intruders if he woke before Prophet got back with food. He had to get out of there, get some air, some space, and he headed across the street to the diner.

Once there, he sat at the counter with a coffee as he waited for the take-out order and wondered what the fuck he was doing fucking his partner.

He blamed it on the case. On the fact that he'd started seeing John's ghost. He used to dream about John. John would be lecturing Prophet, and he'd wake, and it would feel like it had been so damned real.

Now, the man was lecturing him in person.

"Just because you're seeing a ghost doesn't make me dead."

John, leaning on the other side of the counter, wearing his old-school desert BDUs, dirt on his cheek, and the same pissed-off-at-the-world expression he'd always worn in public.

In private, Prophet had been able to wipe it off his face. Most of the time. Now, he told John, "Fuck you and your ghost riddle logic."

The waitress who was delivering his food looked at him but didn't seem bothered, simply shook her head. "This place, everyone talks to themselves."

He looked back up to see John smirking.

Can't go there again, buddy. I almost fucking lost myself. Lost everything.

"Try harder," John suggested in the immortal words of their CO before he disappeared.

Tom woke alone and sore in more places than he'd thought possible. His head had the lingering throb of a migraine hangover. He shifted cautiously, since his body still ached all over from his various fight club injuries. Thankfully, the shades were all drawn, so the room was bathed in darkness, despite the early afternoon hour indicated by the clock.

Nowhere to go but here. Nothing to do but get the kinks out before tonight's fight.

The door opened and closed, and he heard Prophet saying, "Don't shoot. I've got breakfast."

Tom hadn't noticed he'd pulled his weapon, an old, ingrained FBI habit that was resurfacing with this case. He stared at Prophet and then slowly lowered the gun and put it on the table next to him. Prophet nodded, moved forward, and unpacked the big bags of greasy diner food that Tom wouldn't touch on a normal day.

Post-migraine, he couldn't get enough. "How'd you know about the breakfast food?"

"You mumbled about it in your sleep."

He wondered what else he'd said, decided maybe he didn't want to know.

Prophet didn't offer anything more, just dug through the bag and brought some of the food over to Tom, who settled back against the pillows and ate the breakfast biscuits and hash browns and gulped the coffee when it cooled. He was getting to half-human again. Sleep and time would take care of the rest, but the irritability that always followed his migraines was growing.

Prophet treating him like a stranger, refusing to acknowledge what had happened last night, made things worse.

What'd you expect him to do? Cuddle?

Prophet still wasn't saying much. He ate standing, staring down at the computer screen like it contained the secrets of the universe. Tom prodded at his sore lip—made worse by the kissing, but it was a damned good ache. Still, ice wouldn't be a bad idea. He dug a hand into the ice bucket next to the bed, wrapped a couple of cubes into a napkin and held it to his lip. At least the Steri-Strip had stayed on.

If Prophet noticed him doing this, he didn't indicate it. Tom heard a *ding* and then Prophet started typing with one hand.

"Who's that? Natasha?"

Prophet's face held the ghost of a half-grin as he shook his head. "Just some asshole spook."

"Met him on one of your missions?"

"Actually, he lives in the place below mine."

"Cozy. So you two make popcorn and watch movies together?"

"Funny. But I've never met him."

The look on Prophet's face wasn't for a guy he'd never met. "Didn't take you for the sexting type."

Prophet snorted, shook his head, and just kept typing. He looked younger. Happy. Which annoyed the ever-living fuck out of Tom almost as much as Prophet trying to pretend last night hadn't happened.

Fuck, he hated the migraine hangover even more than the goddamned migraine.

Finally, Prophet closed the lid and said, "I got a call from someone who says they knew Chris. I'm going to meet him and his friends a few blocks over."

"You're not going alone."

"Have to."

"I'm your fighter—wouldn't it make sense that I'm there, showing that I'm not hurt? Pretending that I'm not? If word gets around that I'm up and about, that's better for the blood match."

Prophet seemed to consider that as he ate another breakfast sandwich. But Tom's natural patience had worn thin, had already been stretched to its breaking point. Coupled with recalling how badly he'd lost control in the fight, he began to suspect that Prophet thought of him as a liability.

Well, fuck that. He shoved himself out of bed and went to the shower. It would be like Prophet to leave without telling him, but he didn't. He waited for Tom to get dressed. Watched that part, even, as Tom's cheeks flushed and he turned toward Prophet. "Are things going to be weird because of last night?"

"Surprised you remember."

"I remember everything."

"You fucked me because of the drugs, Tom. You would've fucked anyone last night."

Tom slammed Prophet against the wall before he could stop himself. "Go fuck yourself if you believe that," he rasped as his body pleaded for mercy.

He backed off, grabbed his gun and wallet and shoes, and walked out the door.

The meeting was fucking worthless. Prophet sat in the diner next to Tom, who looked like he wanted to rip everyone's face off, as three young guys told them what a cool dude Chris had been. Had no enemies. Fought cleanly. Even management liked him, and they didn't like anyone.

"What about blood matches?" Prophet asked finally.

"No way," the guy named Rally said. "No fucking way. He didn't need to do that shit."

The other two guys were concurring, jumping in with, "He was getting famous . . . he didn't have a death wish . . . was a good guy."

"He was fucked-up over the death of his brother," Rally added. "Said he was doing this to honor his memory."

Prophet's throat tightened at the mention of John. He looked over the other men's shoulders because he couldn't meet their eyes, half expected to see John's lanky body leaning against the diner wall, sarcastic grin on his face.

He wasn't sure if he was disappointed or relieved when the image didn't appear.

Maybe you're going goddamned crazy.

Or maybe he'd always been there. "You'll call me if you find out anything else?"

"Yeah, we will. Fucking scary, man. We just want to fight," Rally said. He hesitated, like he wanted to say something else, but he stopped himself.

Tom put a hand on Rally's forearm. "Spill it."

Way to be subtle, Tommy.

"It's just that . . . in the last week or so, he seemed really . . ." Rally shook his head. "I don't know—fucked-up. He was forgetting practices and he was always on his phone, checking his voice mails. And Chris hated the phone. Half the time, he left it in his room."

"I checked his room at the motel, didn't find his phone," Prophet said.

"He liked to pay cash for everything—it's not exactly a tax paying business we're in. He used a throwaway," Rally explained, which wasn't anything Prophet didn't know.

"Did he have an email account?"

The three men all laughed a little, and Rally said, "He hated all that shit. He said that if someone wanted to get in touch with him that badly, they'd come find him face-to-face."

As if realizing what he'd said, Rally cursed softly under his breath, and Prophet swore he saw John's reflection in the glass window next to him.

"We've got to get a list of the guys Chris fought. And their family members. Hospital records too. This has to be about revenge," Prophet was saying as he took the rental car around a corner on two wheels and Tom held on for dear fucking life.

"Want to let me drive?" he asked as he slammed into the window for the third time in just as many minutes.

Prophet ignored him in favor of yelling, "Someone wanted him out of the game—they probably beat him to make it look like a blood match," because the window was open and they were going so goddamned fast it was like a wind tunnel in the car. And Prophet was motioning with his hands. Both hands. That were not on the wheel.

"Guess that's a no. Watch out for the . . ." Tom looked behind him. "Red light."

"Don't you think that's what happened?" Prophet demanded.

"Those guys said Chris was well liked."

"No one's that well liked," Prophet said, and Tom had to agree on that. "Gotta stop and check the PO Box."

He jerked the car into a space in front of the mailbox place, and Tom grabbed the key from him. "I'll do it."

"I'm coming." Prophet was out of the car, storming toward the shop, and people moved out of his way instinctively. Tom opened the box.

Empty.

Prophet stared at it, and Tom said, "Proph, let me ask—" but it was too late. Prophet was already at the counter, scaring the young guy who worked there to fucking death.

"Sir, I can't tell you any of that. These are protected by—"

"Fuck the law," Prophet said calmly. Too calmly. "You can give me the information or I'm going to take it, but either way—"

"I don't know. The one guy paid for the box every coupla months. Cash. He never gets a lot of stuff here. Last month, some guy came in and asked me to put something in the box—"

"What?"

"Just a letter!"

"And you remember that?" Tom asked dubiously.

The guy looked sheepish. "He paid me a hundred bucks, because we're not supposed to do that."

Prophet threw his hands into the air. "That, he does."

Tom remained focused. "Do you have the security footage?" He pointed to the camera.

"We only have three days' worth of tape and then it erases over itself."

Tom wrote his number down, gave it to the kid and thanked him. "If anyone comes around asking about that box in particular, give me a shout, okay?"

He gave the kid a fifty so he'd be remembered too. Prophet nodded his approval but he was still muttering under his breath about *fucking archaic postal laws* and *stupid, stupid security tapes that didn't help for shit*.

And then Prophet got behind the wheel again, before Tom could stop him, and there was another round of driving like Mr. Toad's Wild Ride.

He sighed with relief as Prophet pulled into the motel's parking lot and stopped on a dime in the spot, although for a second it looked like he might go right through the door in front of them. "But what about the checking of the phone and stuff? That's out of character."

"Threats," Prophet said as they got out of the car. Tom was closer to the stairs but Prophet was on his heels. He opened the door of the room and let Prophet in first before the man ran him over. He was intense and intent on figuring this all out immediately.

It was hard to stay angry at the man when the case was so obviously causing him pain, so Tom let any resentments about Prophet's earlier comments about fucking anyone when he was drugged go for now, closed the door behind him, and said, "We'll break it, Prophet. I'll look into those records now, and then maybe we'll find out more at the blood match."

"You're not fighting tonight."

And *ding*, the anger was back, with a vengeance. "The hell I'm not. It's the only way to get inside—that's your best chance to meet the men behind the blood matches and find out more."

"It's over."

"It's so far from that, and you goddamned know it. Just because you can't handle being fucked—"

And, so much for letting shit go.

"I can handle anything you have. It's not about that." Prophet's voice was low and dangerous, running right up Tom's spine. "You should've told me you weren't sure you'd be able to keep control."

"Would you have?"

"No."

"Well, there you go. You don't get the only say in this, Prophet. You're not my boss—you're my partner, in case you forgot."

Prophet's voice dripped with Prophet-like sarcasm as he said, "No, I didn't forget your sacrifice for the cause."

"I got you your main lead and now you're acting like I screwed everything up," Tom said, unable to keep the fury out of his voice. He wasn't talking only to Prophet now, but to a voice from the past and all of this was fucking with his head.

You fucked this up, boy.

The case was going fine until you got involved, Tom.

No one's going to vote for bad luck.

Prophet had the nerve to shrug and turn his back. Tom charged him, silently, but Prophet must've been waiting for it to happen. Tom hadn't exactly been subtle about his anger.

His body hit Prophet's hard, without restraint, plowing the man into the wall. Prophet let himself hit it with a grace that shouldn't be allowed, got his bearings, and before Tom knew what hit him, Prophet had him pinned.

It shouldn't have been that easy. But Tom had let his anger both blind him to the dangers of pissing his partner off and stop him from assessing the situation more carefully.

As Prophet held him, his cast across Tom's neck, his body pinning Tom's to the ground, Tom finally realized what Prophet was capable of. There was a carefully restrained violence coiled inside of him that would be far worse than anything Tom could unleash—and what Tom was capable of when pushed was fucking scary.

Now, to be on the end of his strike . . . maybe he should be afraid. Run like hell when the man shoved away from him with a muffled curse.

Instead, Tom stood and shoved back against him. Fuck giving up. No one pulled shit on him.

"Stand down, partner. I don't want to hurt you," Prophet said calmly.

"I'm not in your military."

Prophet bared his teeth unconsciously, and Tom took another swing. This time, fist met target. Pain jolted through his arm like he'd hit a steel plate instead of the guy's cheekbone, but just like in the ring, he wouldn't give his opponent the satisfaction of showing it.

Prophet slammed him across the chest, and then, before Tom could protect himself from what he knew was coming, caught him twice in the diaphragm, effectively stopping him from breathing or standing up straight. He put his hand on the back of Tom's neck as Tom saw stars swimming in front of his eyes. None of this had taken any effort from Prophet.

"Anger makes you weak, Tommy," Prophet told him in a tone that let him know that today was his lucky one.

"I won my fight with Ivan."

"At what cost?"

"You tell me."

"Better you don't know," Prophet told him.

"Fuck you."

He stopped fighting, though, which made Prophet loosen his grip. That allowed Tom to shift and get away. It was a move he'd learned early in life, and it continued to serve him well. He got in a few hits before Prophet subdued him again, and what the fuck was wrong with him? The man had double casts, for Christ's sakes.

Could anger really fuck him up that badly?

"You're not going back into that ring," Prophet said, in a voice that left zero room for argument. "I'm not going to be responsible for you again."

At those words, he sagged, and Prophet let him go. He caught himself before he hit the floor, grabbed ahold of the table to steady himself. Tried to breathe.

As much as he didn't want to admit it—or talk about it—he was a liability to his partner like this. Exactly the opposite of what he'd been trying to prove.

Maybe he had to stop trying to prove shit to everyone. But it couldn't be that simple.

He heard Prophet's phone ring. A text message alert.

Prophet simply said, "Fight's been canceled," and threw Tom his phone.

Tom caught it with one hand, read the messages on the screen still doubled over. Demanded, "Did you have something to do with that?"

"And if I did?"

"I thought you wanted to find out who killed Christopher?"

"Not at your expense."

"I didn't think you gave a shit."

"I don't. I just don't need another goddamned thing on my conscience."

"Neither do I." He felt like punching a wall, and at that moment, he realized how right Prophet was about how fucked-up Tom was. Utterly defeated by that, he sank into the nearest chair. "I'll fix it, somehow. Okay? I can control it. By the time it's rescheduled, I'll be ready, and then I can help."

"Tom. Tommy," Prophet started, his voice gentler than before. "Not your fault."

"Then whose is it?"

"Whoever made you have to fight like that to start with."

Not going there. "If Chris died from a blood match," he said, bringing it back to the mission where it should be, "he can't be the only one who has. Word would get out. Someone would've pieced beating deaths together."

"Those kids are too new to the scene, too young to know."

Tom disagreed. "They're exactly the ones who'd be most plugged in."

"How about a search for beating deaths in the last year and see what matches we get?" Prophet asked. "I'm guessing you can get into the relevant databases."

"I thought we were supposed to let Natasha do all of that?"

"You always follow rules, Cajun?"

"Lately, I've been trying."

"How's that working for you?"

"Fuck. You." Tom grabbed for his laptop and tried not to groan in pain.

"That's the spirit."

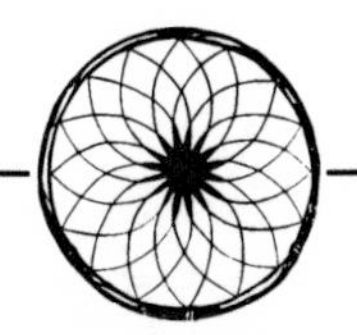

CHAPTER FIFTEEN

"There's nothing that matches," Tom said after four hours of searching for beating deaths in conjunction with the location of the blood match—or at least the general area. But the building was abandoned, owned by the city, which meant anyone could break in, hold a fight, and leave with no consequences. Another dead end.

While he'd been staring at the computer, Prophet had alternated between looking over his shoulder, randomly pacing, and handing him ice wrapped in towels for his ribs. "How the hell did you ever do recon?

Prophet glanced at him. "I can be still when I need to be. But right now, I don't need to be."

Tom sighed, rubbed the back of his neck. Prophet moved his hands away and used the tips of his fingers to massage the bunched muscles.

He let himself sink forward to give Prophet better access, and he was sure the man would snort and stop.

But he didn't, making Tom ask, "Why?"

"Why what?" Prophet's fingers were like magic, digging into the sore muscles and tender spots on his neck, working out the kinks.

"Why are you being nice?"

"Gotta keep you on your toes."

"Or throw me completely off balance."

"Only for your own good."

Maybe that was true. Prophet hadn't threatened him with Phil once. But that didn't mean all was forgiven, at least where Tom was concerned.

After several more minutes of massage, Tom was convinced that Prophet was literally pulling all the fight out of him and turning him into a girl, because he heard himself ask, "Do you really believe I would've fucked anyone last night?"

He winced after he said it.

"I don't know you all that well, Tommy."

No, he didn't. But Tom couldn't shake the taunt from his mind.

Does it bother you that he might be right?

Prophet still didn't stop the massage, going over his temples, down his shoulders. "I'm better without the casts."

"I don't know if I'd survive that."

Prophet chuffed a laugh, his breath warm on the back of Tom's neck. He was tracing the tattoo Tom had there, but that's not what he commented on. His fingers trailed down to the exposed feathers from the dreamcatcher on his right biceps. "You have bad dreams, Tommy."

Tom didn't answer, because it hadn't seemed to be a question. Not really, because Prophet was yanking Tom's shirt over his head. "You're good at calming people down."

"I'm good at a lot of things." Prophet's casted hands slid down his chest, fingers flicking his piercings. "Can't do a lot with my hands. Gonna have to use my tongue instead."

Oh, yeah. Prophet's submissiveness was long gone. The man behind him was a stalking panther, and he wasn't going to stop until he had his way.

"If we fuck now, then you'll know it was me fucking you and not the drugs," Tom said, pushing himself up and turning to face Prophet.

"We are going to fuck now. And you can try to prove to me whatever the hell you want," Prophet growled before putting his mouth on Tommy's. Because enough talking. It was time for the goddamned kissing, hard and fast and smooth and slow and any and every way in between, until Tommy was humping his thigh.

He allowed it, wondering if he should just keep kissing Tommy and let him get off like this, because fuck, that would be hot. But he was too far gone for that. Instead, he pulled back and turned Tom around, pushed him down, chest first, against the table. Kicked Tom's thighs apart and sank to his knees because he hadn't been kidding about using his tongue. Breached Tom, who nearly shot off the table, but then stilled. Tom's entire body shuddered, and Prophet buried his tongue deep, speared it in and out, opening the man so he could ride him hard. Tom began to hump the table, but Prophet held him steady so he couldn't.

Tom was cursing. Begging.

Prophet quickly fished the condom out of his pocket, tore his jeans down, and suited up while Tommy turned to look at him. Prophet fisted a hand in his hair, holding the man's cheek down to the table while he entered him, hard and fast. He didn't stop, rocked his pelvis back and forth, watching his cock slide in and out of Tommy. Tommy, who'd raised his hands over his head to clutch the underside of the table. Tommy, whose muscles and ink formed the perfect, masculine lines along his back, his skin shining with sweat.

"Harder, Proph."

Yeah, he could do that. This had been the warm-up.

Tom grabbed around for him. When he couldn't reach, he accepted his fate and brought his hands back to the table, holding on for dear life while Prophet took him, harder, faster. The table shook, Tom's body shook, and he yelled, a cross between a curse and Prophet's name, biting it out fiercely. Especially when Prophet stopped moving just when he knew Tommy was about to come.

"Fucker." Tom struggled to get up, to rock his hips, to get Prophet moving again. But Prophet was still grabbing his hair, holding him in place. "Fuck me now."

Prophet couldn't hold back at the plea in the man's voice, pounded into him, listening to Tommy groan like Prophet was hitting every single sweet spot at once. Bucked against him, fucking himself on Prophet's cock even though he wasn't in the right position to do so.

Prophet let him do all the work, liked watching him completely lose control.

He trusts you.

Most men did. Why, Prophet didn't understand, since he barely trusted himself most of the time.

"Proph." It was a plea. He took his hand away from Tommy's hair, touched his cheek as he slammed the man's prostate without stopping, giving him exactly what he needed. Tom's ass clenched around him as he bared his teeth and came with a roar.

Tom's body locked in climax as Prophet rode roughshod over him. He was goddamned helpless and he loved it.

Hated that he loved it, that Prophet could unlock him and his secrets so easily.

Was Prophet that good, or had Tom given them up without realizing it?

His muscles gradually relaxed, his eyes focused, and *he* realized that Prophet hadn't come yet. The man remained hovering over him with the semi-patience of a predator, still hard inside of him.

"Fuck."

"Yeah," Prophet agreed, his voice husky. Tom's only comfort was that Prophet was half out of control himself. Hanging on by a thread.

Using the little strength he had left, he pushed his ass back, drawing Prophet's cock deeper into his body. He was already overstimulated and that made the pain/pleasure line finer, which made him thrust back over and over again until Prophet hissed and pushed fingers through Tom's hair again.

"You like that, Proph?"

"Yeah. Make me come, Tommy. Make me."

He took that challenge, worked as hard as he could, despite his position, to fuck himself on Prophet. Soon, he felt like he was going to come again before Prophet, although the man was close, so close. Three hard bucks back against him and Prophet lost it, nearly howled as he came in a pumping rush, tightening his grip painfully on Tom's hair, which made Tom come again, a small orgasm but still one so close to the first that he felt like he could die happy.

He didn't know how long he lay there, Prophet partially leaning on him, the table creaking. Finally, Prophet dragged him to the bed. When Tommy climbed in, Prophet was right behind him, shoving them both under the covers with a satisfied groan.

Tom turned into him, not caring if Prophet didn't want that. He pushed himself up with a grunt. Wrapped himself around Prophet, needing that contact. Prophet conceded by slinging his arm across Tom's back, his fingers tracing the inked skin. Feeling the raised scars they covered.

Tom stiffened. First instinct was to pull away.

"I know they're there, T. No need to run."

"I'm not."

"Good. Did I fuck the fight out of you?"

"Never. That doesn't mean you should stop trying," he murmured sleepily.

"You're in so much goddamned trouble, Tommy."

"Tell me something I don't know."

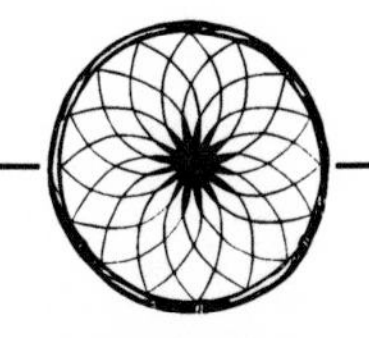

CHAPTER SIXTEEN

Tom woke alone in the bed. He shifted to see the bathroom door open and Prophet standing naked outside the running shower, struggling to get plastic bags over his casts.

He was cursing, low enough for Tom not to be able to make out distinct phrases, but he knew the look on the man's face well enough at this point. He could only imagine how frustrated he was with the whole cast thing.

Tom watched him for a second, guessing that if the man could take him out without breaking a sweat, he could shower with the awkward things on his hands. He propped up on his elbows, trying not to laugh as the rubber band Prophet was trying to put around his wrist broke, snapping his finger.

Sometimes, it's the easy things that end up being the hardest.

Finally, after what seemed like hours, Prophet got everything rigged and stepped into the shower.

It was then that something propelled Tom out of the bed and into the bathroom. He pulled back the curtain, ignored Prophet's surprised look and mutterings of "Fucking privacy is a God-given right," and instead squeezed some shampoo onto his palms, stepped halfway into the shower, and threaded his hands through Prophet's wet hair.

For a long moment, the man stood in shocked silence as Tom massaged his way through the blond locks. And then Prophet dipped his head back a little, putting it into Tom's hands. It was a subtle move, but it kept Tom's hands in his hair.

"Feel good?" he murmured.

Prophet gave a soft groan that sounded like a yes. Tom continued rubbing and kneading, then moved him under the shower, rinsing the soap out of his hair.

"Need help washing other places?"

"Yeah. I'm really dirty."

"I can't believe you said that with a straight face."

"I can't believe you'll do it anyway."

"I feel sorry for you."

"Yeah, right." Prophet smirked, one eye opening lazily. "You gonna join me in here? Or don't you want to get wet?"

"Right now, it's all about you."

"Just how I like it." Prophet's breath hitched when Tom ran a soapy hand over his cock. Groaned out another couple of curses as Tom pulled him toward an orgasm he probably hadn't planned on having. At least not that quickly.

He hadn't really been able to brace himself, was probably counting on Tom to hold him up, but Tom was amazed that the man could remain as steady as he was through his climax. He watched the close-eyed smile spread over Prophet's face as he cleaned him off again.

The man was still hard, but relaxed. It gave him a chance to study Prophet's body again, because he couldn't seem to get enough of that. Like he was trying to commit the man to memory. His skin was tawny, like it had recently seen some sun. No ink. Many scars, old and newer, and Tom wondered if there'd come a day when he'd know the story behind all of them. Or any of them.

"Want to talk about it?" Prophet asked.

"About what? The orgasm I just gave you?"

"Who you were fighting?" Prophet's voice held no judgment. He sounded relaxed as hell, and that, in turn, allowed Tom to remain calm.

"Figured my defenses are down?"

"Mine aren't?" Prophet asked wryly. Tom smiled even though the man's eyes were still closed. Knew he'd stand here letting Prophet lean against him as long as Prophet would let him.

And he hoped Prophet would stand there a long goddamned time. "So I'm violent. Deal with it."

"I am," Prophet said through gritted teeth. "You want to own it? Anytime now."

"Calm, cool Prophet."

"Not a chance. I just hide it better than you." He paused, opened his eyes. "Is this what got you kicked out? Or was it because you held this back?"

"None of the above."

"I'm trying to help, T. Talk to me."

He thought about telling Prophet to fuck off, that he couldn't push Tom out and expect all the answers.

But he didn't. "It was the premonition thing. My partners kept getting killed." He waited to see something on Prophet's face, but there was no disgust or anger.

Why do you want to push him to anger so badly?

"How's that your fuckup?"

"I was supposed to be there with them."

"Where were you?"

"For the last one, not following a directive. I had a gut instinct. Thought I could follow it. Thought I should be allowed to."

Prophet watched him carefully. "Was your gut wrong?"

"No."

"Do you think you could've saved your partner if you'd been there?"

"I would've been killed too."

Prophet frowned. "Did you tell your partner not to go there?"

"I did. But he didn't want to get in trouble. We were always getting in trouble because of me, and he was a more by-the-book kind of guy."

At least Prophet understood. The man had the same instincts, the same issues with following orders over common sense and gut feelings.

Together, they could be dangerous. Dangerous, but good, in more ways than one. They understood one another, and Tom wondered if Phil had known all of this before partnering them.

He doubted anything Phil did was by dumb luck.

"Tell me something. If your partners had followed your gut instead of the rules, would they be alive?"

"Yes."

"Did you tell them to?"

"Yes."

"So how were they really partners? Sounds like you've had pissing contests, not partners."

"I should've tried harder."

"Died with them, right, Tommy?"

Tom couldn't even pretend he hadn't gone there himself. "On the plane, you believed me."

"Yes." Prophet paused. "Phil knows all this."

"I didn't tell him."

"It wasn't a question. Phil knows all this. He gets all of our background info. All of it. He's the one person in all our lives who knows every goddamned thing we've ever done. So if he knows it and hired you, why are you so fucking jumpy?"

"Are you not hearing me? Three partners, dead." Plus, his mentor had been killed after he'd made full agent, but even though Tom wore all his guilt, he couldn't take credit for that one.

"I heard. And I'm still alive."

"Because you listened to me," Tom said decisively as he shut off the water.

Prophet's lip quirked. He was holding back a laugh. "So if I want to stay alive, all I need to do is listen to you. Check."

"You fucker." He shoved him, but Prophet caught his wrists, even with his hands wrapped in plastic.

"What are you looking for? My attention? Because you've got it. You had it when you walked into EE."

Tom narrowed his eyes, couldn't believe Prophet was admitting it. "Same."

"Okay then."

"It'd be okay if you told me about John."

Prophet didn't say no, but he shuddered. Tom wanted to assume that was because of the sudden loss of warm water, but he wasn't entirely convinced. He patted the man dry, rubbed his hair. His cheeks held a rough stubble.

"Need me to shave you?" Tom asked.

"Depends."

"On what?"

"If you like the rough?"

Jesus. He blushed. Fucking blushed, and Prophet nodded. "No shave today. And by the way, it's okay that you like to fight."

"I don't like it. Not more than anyone else."

Prophet snorted. "Most people don't like to fight at all. Correction—most normal people."

"Guess that excludes you."

"Yes, it does."

"I don't like to fight. I'm just good at it. There's a big difference, don't you think?"

"No."

"I don't know what you want me to say, but you're acting like a shrink."

"I've had a lot of practice with them. They're fun to fuck with."

"Just like me?"

"Truthfully? You're not all that fun in general." But he was smiling as he said it.

After Prophet dressed and Tom showered himself, he figured the man would find a way not to talk about John. But to his surprise, Prophet sat back against the pillows on the bed that was still made and said, "What do you want to know?"

Tom sprawled on his stomach facing Prophet, not bothering with clothes, and the words "John Senior" came out of his mouth, surprising even him.

"What about him?"

"You tell me."

"I can do that." He paused. "You think he's a lead."

"Not sure."

"Cajun voodoo?" Prophet asked, with zero sarcasm.

"Trying every possible avenue." Because they weren't any closer to finding out who had killed Chris. There were lots of leads and false starts and red herrings. They'd pieced together how Chris had lived, that his death had been a malicious ending for a kid who was well liked, that he'd played by the rules in a profession where there were few or none, that he'd helped his mother.

Prophet was staring down at his casts. He looked up at Tom and admitted, "Got a phone call that the fight's been rescheduled for tomorrow night."

"And?"

"And I hope we get another fucking lead before that."

Tom didn't question whether or not that meant Prophet was going to let him fight. Instead, he asked, "Suppose I see something when we're talking that I don't think you want to talk about?"

Prophet glanced up at him, his gray eyes sharp. "Then don't mention it."

"Okay."

"But the case stuff . . ."

"I'll tell you. And you'll listen."

"I will, T. I just don't buy the blood match thing. Not because I don't want you to fight, which I don't. It's just . . . why would Chris agree to do this? To kill someone with his bare hands for money? Because the Chris I knew . . ."

"I know you don't want to believe it, but John's death changed him. You said so yourself. So did Chris's friends."

"They weren't his friends. They didn't know him back then. And no one changes that much."

"Maybe he wanted to die."

"No. He wouldn't do that. He was helping his mom. He wouldn't have abandoned her."

"Then maybe someone—something—forced him into that cage. Gave him no choice. And then they didn't give him a fair fight." Tom paused. "You're hiding something."

"I don't have to tell you shit that doesn't have to do with the case."

"And tell me what part of the secret you're carrying doesn't, Proph?"

Prophet's fists clenched, and Tom braced for the punch that would likely break something on his face. Since it had all been broken before, he didn't worry much. It would all go back together in some semblance of just fine.

But Prophet took a deep breath and clenched his jaw hard. Tom said nothing more, because there was a devil behind the man's eyes that was dangerously close to the surface. Tom had hit a nerve and cursed himself for it, for causing Prophet pain, even though that hadn't been his intention.

Then what was?

To see what's behind the mask.

Prophet exhaled, looked up at the ceiling, because he couldn't look at Tom while he talked about this. Could barely get it out anyway, so he just went fast, thought of it like pulling off a Band-Aid. "John and I traveled around for the entire summer starting when we were fifteen. Mrs. Morse thought we were working odd jobs landscaping. Fuck, it was dangerous and scary and every other day we were pretty convinced we were going to die. There were no rules. Not that there are many now, but back then the fights were held in abandoned buildings where you couldn't bring in any ID."

"You guys were good then."

"John got beat up pretty bad the first few, but he caught on quickly."

"And you?" Tom prompted.

"I was born with violence inside of me. It's only a matter of where or when I let it out." He'd resigned himself to it—and come to terms with it—a long time ago.

"You could never be an abusive man, Prophet."

"You don't know shit."

"Maybe, but I know *that.*"

"More Cajun bullshit," Prophet said, but he couldn't stop himself from smiling a little. "It was mainly John who fought anyway." He finally glanced over at Tom, who was looking at him like he'd revealed something extremely important. Made him overexplain, which he rarely did. "John needed to fight more than I did."

"Why's that?"

"It was just something inside of him. At the time, that's what I thought. And then, when I found out what—who—he was fighting, it made sense. Then again, maybe it was inside of him all the time anyway. Maybe even if his father hadn't hurt him, he would've been like that."

"Abuse?"

"Yeah, physical." Prophet stopped, because he couldn't bring himself to say more. He pictured John in the hotel room after they'd graduated boot camp. They'd gone out, partied all night, stumbled home drunk, and maybe it was the stress of boot camp—because their drill sergeant had been a complete asshole—coupled with the alcohol, but John had started talking about his father, like he hadn't been able to help himself. He told Prophet about the abuse, about the fact that John Senior had regularly come into his room since he'd been a preteen and fucking raped him, telling Prophet like it hadn't mattered to him, like it had all rolled off his back. Like he was trying to prove he was too tough to let that bother him. Just like they'd both done their entire fucking lives.

Prophet hadn't bothered trying to get through to him about it. Even as John had talked about it, it was apparent that it was just that—talk, like John was telling *a* story, not *his* story. After, John had closed it off, bricked a wall, and Prophet had been lucky to be on the inside of it, for the most part.

And John had loved him. John *could* love, so Prophet had figured that was most important.

"So much for the perfect family, right?" Prophet added. He had told Tom that about the Morses earlier because he had so badly wanted it to be that, and because if he threw Tom off the track, then he wouldn't have to face Carole Morse. "I was the one with the fucked-up mom. I thought John's was perfect. Wanted them to be."

"Except they weren't." Tom paused. "Is that what you and Carole were fighting about?"

"It's hard for me to go back there, knowing what I do. I told her at John's memorial service. I had to tell her, just in case. And after I did, she threatened John Senior with a knife. A fucking kitchen knife."

"She really didn't know?"

"I have to believe she didn't. Otherwise . . . fuck . . ." He shook his head. "John was a master at hiding things. But that's why John Senior rarely comes home anymore—after all that, she didn't leave him. Maybe she was afraid of how it would look or maybe she needed him to support her and so she hung this over his head. And maybe that's why Chris was sending her money. I'm sure the abuse didn't begin and end with John."

"So you think Carole was abused too?"

Prophet shrugged. "Seems more than likely. I didn't put two and two together at the time, but yeah, there were signs. Mystery bruises. Maybe I just stuck my head in the sand back then. And once I found out about John, I realized I'd have had more sympathy if she hadn't dragged her kids through that shit too. Whether John Senior touched his sons or not didn't matter. They'd have already seen the abuse with Carole and that would've fucked them up too."

Prophet shifted, hating the swirl of emotions the topic brought back for him. At least Tom wasn't looking at him with anything like pity on his face, because he would've lost it. No, Tom was just listening, taking it all in, and so Prophet continued. "The only reason I told Carole anything was to ensure John Senior couldn't get away with that shit with Christopher. I knew John had threatened the shit out of him when he left for the Navy. Last time John spoke to Christopher, Chris told him that his father barely looked at him, never touched him or Carole again."

"You threatened him, too," Tom said quietly.

"Damned straight. I wanted his father to know that nothing had changed even with John being gone, told him that I'd kill him if he touched Chris. He wasn't entirely pleased about that, so he and I had *words*. He went to his son's service with a black eye. He's lucky that's all he got." Prophet glanced at him. "I was so pissed John hadn't told me sooner. It made so much sense, made his anger fall into place."

"So he was an angry guy."

"Let's just say I understand angry guys."

"Because of him?"

"Because of me."

Fuck, Prophet's sudden honesty always disarmed Tom with its unexpected simplicity. Maybe Prophet was tired of being the secret keeper. Tom knew he was.

"Losing John really fucked Chris up, but he never knew about what happened to John when he was younger. I'm sure he saw his father hit John, but that's not as bad as it could've been."

"Sounds like he was actually pretty well-adjusted once he got out of that house."

"He should've done more with his life. John would've pushed him to do more."

"Why didn't you?"

"Trying to make me bleed, Tommy?" Prophet asked, but continued before Tom could say anything more. "Carole told me she'd take care of Chris. She knew she hadn't been there for John, and she promised she wouldn't let it happen again. And I went around for two years, looking for John, so I could bring him back for his family. When I couldn't . . . they were healing. I was a reminder of bad shit. Get that?"

"Better than you know," Tom said quietly.

"You're a good partner, T."

"Just not for you."

"I'm no one's ideal partner. Got to trust me on that." There was no self-pity behind those statements, just a simple declaration of fact Prophet believed with his whole heart and soul.

Tom wasn't sure how to answer that. He wasn't anyone's ideal partner either, but he figured that might be why they worked so well together. "So the last time you saw John Senior was at John's memorial service?"

"Yeah. I didn't know him well before that. I kept thinking, *were there signs I missed?* But I always kept my distance from him when he was around. The guy's just mean. He's a long-distance trucker, so he was never home much."

"Do you think . . . if he'd met up with Chris . . ."

Prophet sighed like it pained him to consider it. Like he had already. "Chris was six foot two. Had a hell of a lot of youth and strength on his side."

"But anger can drive anyone." When Prophet didn't make any kind of snide *you should know* comments, he continued, "If he got in a shot to the head and brought Chris down . . ."

"He could've beaten him to death, and Christopher couldn't have done a thing about it," Prophet finished dully.

"Maybe that's why he wasn't at the house? Maybe the guilt is too much for him?" Tom asked.

"I don't know if the man's capable of guilt or remorse. Can we pull his trucking invoices? Gas and toll receipts?"

"Even better—I can look at some of the cameras." He didn't move though. Not yet. "Why didn't you want a partner?"

Prophet waited a beat before saying cryptically, "I stopped after one."

And then he looked Tom dead in the eye. "By the way, you should've told me about your partners right away. Because I don't scare that easily."

"Do you scare at all?"

"I wouldn't be alive today if I didn't."

"Prophet, what's going on here?"

"With what?"

"With us."

"We'll work on this case. And we'll fuck, if you still want to. And one can't interfere with the other."

"Right. Because nothing is personal." Tom paused. Took a breath.

"Way I figure it, if I'm forced to have a partner, might as well have one with benefits. If you're annoying me, fucking you will be more satisfying than punching you." Prophet grinned, then added slyly, "And I could always punch you afterward."

Tom mentally called him an asshole and then asked, "Did you win your cage fights?"

"Of course." Prophet managed to look offended at the question.

"All of them?"

"You don't think I can fight, Cajun?"

"So this whole time, me fighting, you taking care of me, it's what you did for John."

Something indiscernible passed over Prophet's face. "A role I'm good at."

"Then who takes care of you?"

Prophet opened his mouth to give what looked like it wanted to be a smart-ass answer, but nothing came out. His eyes darkened, a dangerous look. Finally, he said, "When I need a shrink, I'll see one. We've been through this before, and it didn't end well."

"It ended up with you going out and fucking random strangers," Tom reminded him. It didn't matter that Prophet hadn't answered his question. Tom had the answer.

No one took care of Prophet. Prophet took care of Prophet. It must be exhausting to be expected to take care of partners who didn't recognize he needed the same. Just because he didn't seem like he would didn't mean anything.

And you've done a great job of that yourself.

But he was here now. He could make up for it. He'd start with checking on John Senior's whereabouts the night Christopher was killed.

For ten minutes, Tom's typing was the only sound in the room, and Prophet wasn't sure what the hell to hope for.

Finally, Tom said, "I've got his pictures on traffic lights from here to Oklahoma in the twelve hours before Chris was killed. Same with the way back home. Even if time of death's off by hours, there's no way he could've done it."

"So he's out."

"Are you sorry?"

Prophet shrugged. Didn't know what to feel. He'd failed John, failed Chris, failed Mrs. Morse. This was why he wanted to work alone. He couldn't handle letting anyone else down.

"What now?" Tom asked.

"Fuck if I know."

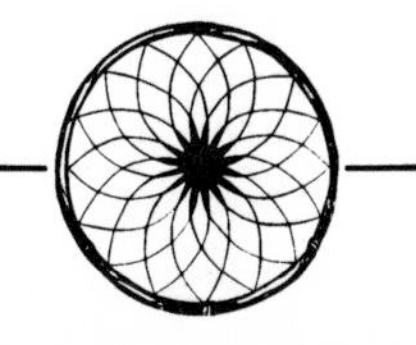

CHAPTER SEVENTEEN

Hours later, when the sun went down and the room got cold, Prophet was still on the opposite side of the room from Tom when he began to hum the now familiar tune.

Tom looked up from his computer, didn't stop himself from asking, "What's that song?" even though he knew he'd just walked down a path he shouldn't have.

Prophet confirmed that by stopping cold, as if he'd been caught. Maybe he hadn't even realized he was humming it. Or maybe it was just that no one had ever asked him about it. "It's from a Celtic group. Flogging Molly," was all he said.

Tom went onto iTunes and found the song easily enough: "If I Ever Leave This World Alive." As the opening bars began, a chill went through him, but he couldn't bring himself to press stop.

Prophet did. It wasn't hard to see that it took all of his restraint not to smash the computer's lid down or throw it across the room as he simply closed it with a firm click.

Tom had asked one too many questions.

"What the fuck are you doing?" Prophet asked in measured tones.

Tom could've said, "Listening to a song," or some other smart-ass remark that Prophet would've tried. But he didn't. Instead, he opened up the computer again and went into his email. Found the one he'd hidden and pressed play on the video file.

As Prophet saw the opening screen, Tom watched him revert to the man in the video. His eyes changed—hardened the way they had when the man tore the tags off him—and he bared his teeth and fisted his hands, his entire body taut as a bow. He looked feral. Primal. Willing to do anything it took to survive.

"How long have you had this?" His voice was calm, which only made him scarier. This had to be a huge invasion of privacy for him, and a betrayal on Tom's part as well.

He forced himself to keep his tone neutral. "You'd be pissed no matter when I told you."

"I'd have a hell of a lot more respect for you if you'd told me the second you goddamned met me."

"Would you? Or would you have used that as an excuse to be suspicious of me?"

"Do I have a reason to be? How the hell did you get this?" Prophet asked, his voice still controlled.

"I don't know. I've been trying to figure that out so I could give you that answer."

"How many times have you watched it?"

"More than once."

"Since you met me?"

"More than once," he repeated as he stood. Prophet punched him then, a slam to the solar plexus that sent Tom down, gasping for air.

"Did you get off on it, Tommy? Or was it the fact that you had a secret of mine that did it for you?"

"Not . . . like . . . that." Tom charged. Had to defend himself against the onslaught. But this was different than the ring. Prophet would never go down.

Because Prophet couldn't make him lose control. Because Prophet wouldn't let himself lose control.

He should admit defeat now. Maybe Prophet would leave him alone. But it was too late. Prophet was pushing against him, winding an arm behind his back. Slamming him to the ground.

"I didn't learn anything on that video that I wouldn't have after a couple of days working with you."

Prophet moved away, then shoved him. He stumbled. Hit the wall. And with the grief on his face, everything clicked.

"Prophet, what happened to John?"

"Shut the fuck up, Tom." The façade had cracked, just for that moment, and then his scary calmness was back, and Tom decided he hated that the most, especially since his expression didn't match his tone when he said, "Just . . . no more."

Tom held up his hands. "Sorry." Grabbed his sweatshirt and left the motel room without a look back.

Prophet shuddered out a few breaths. He slammed his casts against the table, nearly knocking the computer to the floor.

He caught it. Stared at the frozen frame that had captured him hours after he'd killed Azar. That goddamned bastard. He could still smell him.

He'd never seen this video, ever. Why the hell would he need to, since he lived it?

He'd known there was a tape hanging around somewhere. It had become part of the investigation after he'd been rescued. But whoever had sent this to Tom had done so before Tom had even known who he'd be partnered with.

It wasn't Phil—he didn't work like that. And even Phil didn't know half the shit that had happened during that time.

His fingers itched to press play, even though a voice inside his head warned him not to go there. What new intel could he find out? And who would want to hurt him by using this?

Plenty of people.

He leaned in, ready to make peace with it. His hand shook a little as he hit the button and heard the man's accented voice. And he was right back to being inside that room. Alone.

He'd gone from captured to rescued to caged again, by his own kind.

He muted the volume and watched the younger version of himself on screen. Younger, but no more innocent then.

As he watched, he unconsciously rubbed his casted wrists. During his torture, his wrists had been hurt, yes, but that move with the table had cost him, had weakened his wrists. They fractured easily now. The damage would haunt him forever. And if he'd known that then, he still wouldn't have changed a thing.

When the video cut out, Prophet watched himself frozen on the table, heard the conversation loud and clear, then heard the one that had happened before the camera had started rolling.

"Where's Azar?" Agent Lansing had asked.

"I killed him with my bare fucking hands."

"There's no body."

"I ate it."

"Where's your specialist?"

"He's not here."

"Did you kill him?"

"I did my job," Prophet had said.

"There's no sign of Hal Jones, dead or alive. If we have no body, we have reason to believe you're complicit in allowing his escape into the wrong hands."

He'd stared at Agent Lansing. "I didn't beat myself, you asshole."

And that's when things had gotten rough. Prophet dealt with it until the asshole ripped his tags off, and then he trapped the guy. All it would've taken was a simple rock of the table and Agent Lansing wouldn't have asked any more questions. As it was, Prophet had eventually let him up. He'd been questioned for another week straight until they'd released him.

And then the CIA had hired him. Because apparently, their motto was, *If you can't kill it, hire it.*

He rewound and watched it twice more before closing the laptop and going to look for Tom.

He found him on the ground floor, standing near the vending machines, hands in his pockets, looking up at the sky. A cigarette dangled from his mouth—smelled like one of those hand-rolled jobs. Smelled like Tom's apartment and his skin.

Shouldn't have been turning Prophet on. Not now when he was coming out here to . . .

What? Punch the guy for knowing shit that wasn't his fault?

His anger faded. He opened his mouth to say something like, "Come on, Cajun, let's go get dinner," or something equally stupid, which was pretty much as close to an apology as Prophet would ever get.

But before he could get anything out, the back of his neck prickled. Next, he heard the screech of tires as a car careened around the corner, a gun pointed out the window at Tom.

"Down!" he yelled as he dove for Tom, knocking him to the ground as bullets rained down around them. That was as instinctive as his cursing when he realized he'd been hit.

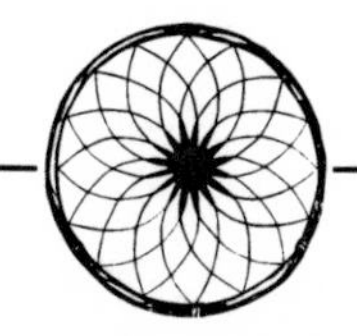

CHAPTER EIGHTEEN

Tom was half buried under the weight of Prophet's body as the car zoomed away and the firing ceased. He shifted enough to see the blood on the ground, but Prophet was up and moving. Barking orders as he took his T-shirt off and pressed it to the bullet wound in his side.

"I'm going to the car. Get our stuff. New hotel." He was texting while he spoke, not looking at the screen but rather at Tom.

Tom ran upstairs, left the motel room door open to keep an eye on Prophet—he could see that Proph had gotten into the passenger's side of the rental holding his arm over his wound and, Tom was sure, his weapon.

In the distance he heard a siren. He was also aware that, in the darkness, people were tentatively starting to peek out of their rooms. In under two minutes, he'd packed both their shit, thrown it into the back of the car, and had them on the open road.

Since they'd checked in under assumed names, anonymity shouldn't be a problem, but Prophet still insisted he pull over and switch the plates on the car. Prophet just happened to have several available. And then he'd pointed to the GPS that was directing Tom to a hotel twenty minutes away. If Tom drove like Prophet.

"Hospital," Tom said firmly.

"No," Prophet ground out as he pressed the motel towels Tom had taken against his side. "Trust me. Go there. Get me inside without anyone seeing me."

"Yes, that'll be easy."

"Thought you believed in magic, Cajun?" Prophet's words slurred a little.

"Fuck you," he said to the man who'd saved his life.

Prophet snorted. "Already . . . happened." And then he closed his eyes.

"Wake up, dammit. You don't get to save me and then die."

"Not dying. Sleeping."

"Open your eyes."

But Prophet shook his head. Tom noticed Prophet's phone buzzing and answered it as he followed the GPS bitch's directions.

"It's Doc. How's he doing?"

"Passed out."

"Sleeping," Prophet insisted.

"Someone's meeting you at the hotel. He'll keep Prophet stable until I can get there."

Before Tom could say anything else, Doc hung up. He cursed, kept driving. He listened to the GPS in between trying to wake Prophet up.

"I'm not sleepin'," Prophet said, in an extremely sleepy voice.

Tom glanced over and saw the blood seeping through the white of the towels. His hands tightened on the wheel, and he refused to let panic wash over him. He turned the radio up—loudly—to country music.

"What. The. Fuck," Prophet managed to yell over the music.

Tom turned it down a bit. "Stay. Awake."

"Turn that . . . shit off . . . first. Christ."

"I knew it'd get you up."

"Torturing someone . . . who's been shot. That's low, T." Prophet's eyes closed again, his breath fast, no doubt from pain and maybe even a little shock.

Tom reached over and squeezed his thigh. Looked over again, and Prophet was looking back at him. "You'll . . . get me there. S'why I can close my eyes."

Because he trusts me.

Fuck.

Tom drove like a complete maniac the rest of the way, fueled by Prophet's words alone. When he finally pulled up in front of the hotel, in record time, there was a guy waiting out front who looked like he belonged in a biker gang, all black leather and tattoos and shitkickers. His hair was dark and short and he looked like he wanted to take a piss on the world. Or at least fuck someone up.

Tom waved from the truck, and the guy shot him the finger and motioned for them to follow him, flicking his cigarette to the side as he walked toward them.

"Guess he's our contact," Tom said. His voice must've held enough doubt to make Prophet crack his lids and say, "Name's Mal. Kind of… an asshole. You'll like him."

"Ah, fuck you, Proph."

"That's the spirit."

Tom wondered why the bleeding man was the one talking him down from the wall, but whatever. It was working. Between him and Mal, they slid Prophet halfway into a jacket to cover the blood, then did a push/pull to get him onto his feet.

"Guys, I got… this," he said, then almost fell forward on his face.

Mal ended up catching him and snorting what seemed to be a silent laugh. Tom glared at Mal and hooked his arm under Prophet's. Mal walked slightly in front of them, blocking the bleeding side because it was becoming harder to hide, and Prophet hung onto Tom and stumbled along, head down, looking very much like a drunk man.

Once in the safety of the hotel room Mal had rented, it was apparent the man had medic training. He had IVs and blood running and was covering the wound, giving antibiotics and fluids. Making Prophet comfortable. Monitoring his vitals.

He did it all silently while Tom watched.

"Is he okay?"

Mal glanced at him and back at Prophet. Tom repeated himself twice more, got no answer and finally grabbed Mal's shoulder.

"You going to answer me?" he demanded, then caught sight of the thick, ribbed scar running across Mal's throat.

Mal signed something that looked like it ended with a curse and then pointed to his ears.

"Can't speak. Hears fine," Prophet mumbled.

"Could've told me earlier," Tom said through clenched teeth.

"No fun that way."

"I guess you're fine."

"Told you," Prophet said, his voice barely audible.

Mal rolled his eyes and looked at them like they were both fucking idiots. At this point, Tom agreed with Mal's assessment. Minutes later,

Mal pointed to the door, and Tom stared at him, because no one had knocked.

Seconds later, someone did knock, and Mal looked like, *told you fucking so*. Tom checked the peephole and found Doc on the other side. He'd met the man on his first tour through EE, and he'd gotten the distinct feeling Doc neither liked nor trusted new recruits.

"Tom," Doc said with a nod. "Mal, you're out."

Mal did as he was told without a backward glance at any of them. Tom did see him hold up his middle finger as he left. He guessed it was kind of like his gang sign. Or his message to the entire world.

"Boudreaux, you going to stand there or help?" Doc asked.

He wondered what would happen if he said, "Just stand here," but decided not to press his luck further. Prophet was groaning a little and definitely past the sleeping and into the passing-out stage.

Doc hurried that along with a shot injected into the IV. Two minutes later, Prophet's head turned to the side, his breathing easier, but his face still alarmingly pale.

"No way I want him awake while we're doing this," Doc said.

"What about the mess?"

"We've got a clean-up crew," Doc assured him. "It's not our first rodeo. Let's do this."

Doc had Tom wiping away the blood as he inspected the wound. Prophet had been hit close to his ribs, with another flesh wound close to his diaphragm, either of which would make breathing painful.

"I don't like where that bullet's sitting," Doc muttered and Tom wondered how he knew where the bullet was without X-rays, but the man had no doubt performed enough battlefield medicine to know. "Too close to the lungs. I'd rather not risk anything happening while we're mid-flight back to EE."

Instead of taking the bullet out, he debrided the wound, then handed Tom a bandage and had him hold it while he taped it.

Through all of it, Prophet's breathing remained steady. Tom traced the other, older scars on Prophet's body with his eyes and, in response, Doc ran a hand over a few of them.

"I always try not to leave too much of a scar," Doc said. "He wouldn't care, but I do. He'll be modeling my handiwork for the rest of his life." He glanced at Tom's hands. "You can go wash up. I'm just about done. Take the shirt off too."

Tom stripped the T-shirt off and threw it into the pile of bloody things, then went into the bathroom and closed the door behind him. He scrubbed the blood off his arms and hands, from under his nails. When he glanced in the mirror, he saw there was some on his chin and neck too.

"Fuck it." He stripped down and jumped into a hot shower for about five minutes. He came out and toweled off quickly, put his jeans back on. When he went back into the bedroom area, he'd really expected to see Prophet up and laughing, making fun of Tom for being so worried.

But the guy was still passed out, a big bandage on his side. So quiet. He looked innocent, which was odd.

"Shit. Proph." He ran his hands through his damp hair as he moved toward the bed.

"Asshole's going to be fine," Doc told him with a frown. "Watch him for me while I wash up and make a few calls."

He nodded, moved a chair closer to the bed, not sure what he was supposed to be watching for. Beyond Prophet's breathing, which was still easy. But the man's fingers were curled into fists—as much as the casts would let him, and they hadn't been like that minutes earlier.

Guess his metabolism burned through pain meds fast. That would make sense, given Prophet's constant need for movement.

He wanted to hold Prophet's hand but resisted. "I almost got you fucking killed, dammit."

He'd been in this position before, but not like this. Not so intimately. His last partner had been shot and killed by a drug dealer, died on the concrete while passersby tried to help. Tom had been three blocks away, stopping the dealer's posse from blowing up an apartment building. Saving multiple lives. Losing one.

Not a bad ratio when you weren't the one involved.

Third time's the charm, he'd told himself before getting out.

"Not your fault," he'd heard time and time again, but he'd never believe it. When three partners die on your watch, you tend to take it fucking personally.

Fucking bad luck.

It's what they said about him behind his back when he'd returned from the bureau and taken the deputy job. He knew the sheriff kept his distance, because, as the man said, "I only got two years before retirement. Seems foolish to die now."

He'd made it. And Tom went up for election, knowing he'd lose. But hell, self-flagellation had become his thing.

"You said John died in combat. You never said . . . fuck, Proph." He didn't know what else to say. Based on Prophet's reaction, Tom had little doubt that John's death was connected to the video somehow. Which would mean John had been killed on the mission Prophet was being interrogated about. He took the man's hand in his and was pretty sure Prophet squeezed it back.

Why *had* Prophet come outside? To yell at him some more? To leave?

His throat tightened.

Hold your shit together.

"If you're gonna fall apart, now's the time to do it," Doc observed. "He's not going to deal well with that shit when he's awake. But I'm guessing you know that already."

Tom hadn't heard him come out of the bathroom, or make any phone calls. "He jumped in front of a bullet for me."

"Sounds like him. And he'll hold it over you forever." Doc fiddled with the IV. "You know who took the shots?"

"I didn't see any faces, but it has to be the guys from the fighting ring."

"Phil doesn't want you to go back in on your own. It's too dangerous now."

Too dangerous for a case that was personal. "Prophet's not going to let this go."

"Probably not. But he's not going anywhere for a little while. And Phil wants you in the office."

Of course he did—to fire him.

Doc continued, "You're going on another mission, if you pass my physical."

"But this one's not done."

"It's done for now. Phil doesn't think this one's worth it right now—taken it as far as it can go."

"It's important to Prophet."

"Yes. And that's why sometimes you need someone to pull you away."

According to the new orders that Doc handed him, he was being reassigned immediately to Eritrea. And it made sense, because no one was in imminent danger with the fighting ring. It wasn't something urgent.

Only to Prophet.

He knew better than to try to question Phil on this. It was where he was needed, and he supposed Phil reassigned partners in the short term when something like this happened.

He went onto the balcony and burned the papers, like he was supposed to. He was flying on an EE plane, so he didn't need anything else but the time. When he came back inside, Doc was getting out a small saw, which Tom didn't understand until he went to the side of the bed where Tom wasn't and said, "Hold his arm while I do this."

He wanted to protest, and Doc must've seen the look on his face before he could school his expression. He immediately went to the previous night, when he'd drawn the dreamcatcher. Had it protected Prophet?

And who, what, would protect him now?

He won't need protection if you're not around.

Doc had stopped, like he was waiting for Tom to say something. But what could he say? They were plaster, not permanent. Maybe he'd fooled himself into thinking any of it could be.

"He's pissed at me."

"Do you deserve it?"

He watched his drawings get sliced in half. "Yeah."

There was blood on the casts anyway. They'd been ruined before Doc cut them off. Ruined from the moment Tom had stopped listening to his gut and forgotten his promise to Prophet.

Bad loque.

Just then, Prophet moved. He was fighting the drugs, his body moving restlessly, like he was pissed off they'd put him out and was doing everything he could to wake himself up.

"He's always like this," Doc commented. "Hates going under."

I know the feeling. "So why do it?"

"He bitches too much otherwise." Doc smiled, but when Tom didn't, he said, "You know he'll be all right, don't you?"

Just then, Prophet clawed his way out of unconsciousness—it was the only way Tom could describe it. It was frantic, like he was dragging himself out of deep water, fighting anyone and anything in his way.

"Step back," Doc told Tom as Prophet flailed. Before Doc could hold him still enough, Proph ripped the IV out. Doc spoke to Prophet in a low voice, full of concern. It was obvious to Tom that Doc and Prophet were close. Then Doc put hands on both Prophet's shoulders as Prophet opened his eyes. He grabbed Doc's wrists, hard, but Doc remained where he was, undeterred. "Proph, it's all right. You're fine. I'm here."

And then Prophet finally blinked. Focused. Looked around, and after a long moment, settled his focus on Doc. "You fucking bastard."

"No choice, Proph."

Prophet looked at everything like he was seeing it for the first time. Like he was reassuring himself, but of what, Tom had no clue. All he knew was that he wanted to go over and sit next to him. Just be there.

Tom smiled, said, "Hey," and Prophet stared at him as if memorizing him. "You okay?"

"Hurts," he admitted, and kept staring at Tom.

"You better not have ripped your side open more," Doc told him, and then Prophet broke their gaze and looked at Doc.

"Then you shouldn't have knocked me out, asshole."

And then he was Prophet again.

Drifting in and out of consciousness, Prophet had been aware of Tommy talking to him. Confessing things. Now, Tom looked like someone had shot his dog, and fuck it all, the guy couldn't be thinking this was his fault.

Yeah, of course he was.

And then, more fucking pain as Doc checked the bandage, which made him grit his teeth and curse like a sailor, just because he could.

"Whatever gets you through the night," Doc said, completely unfazed by the barrage of new and, if Prophet did say so himself, inventive combinations of words strung together like a long, run-on sentence.

It even made Tom crack a small smile, but the guy still looked like hell.

"We're out of here in ten," Doc told Prophet. "Tom'll ride with us, but he's getting a different flight."

Prophet glanced over at Tom.

"Phil's putting the case on hold. Sending me to Eritrea," he said in a tone that sounded like Prophet should magically make that not happen.

Fuck, he was in no shape to go against Phil. And if Tom was needed, Tom was needed. What else was he going to do, play Prophet's nursemaid?

"Go where you're needed," he rasped.

"Obviously, that's not with you," Tom said quietly—angrily—before he turned away to gather his shit.

Prophet turned away too and pretended Doc wasn't watching the entire goddamned exchange. Because something about this case was really fucked, and it went beyond Tom as a partner.

Tom helped get Prophet into the car, drove them to the airport, and helped get him onto the plane with Doc. Before Prophet could say anything else, Tom said good-bye to both him and Doc, a general one that sounded more like a curse, before he stormed off the plane.

Prophet stared after him for a long moment, then turned back to Doc, who was watching him.

"No judgment," Doc said.

"Just put me to fucking sleep," he told Doc, who whistled low under his breath and then complied. When Prophet woke again, he was in EE's infirmary, hooked up to tubes and monitors, and he wanted to turn over and sleep for days.

But Phil was storming in then, checking on him, talking about him like he wasn't there to Doc, as Prophet listened to the prognosis and the long rehab Doc wanted. And finally, Doc left and Phil pulled a chair up to his bedside.

"Who shot you?"

"Ivan's friends. I recognized them—they came after us the night Tom fought. Ivan's one of the main draw fighters."

"What did you do to piss them off?"

Prophet shrugged. "What don't I do?"

"You're going to need to give me more than that."

"I pushed too hard to get intel."

Phil stared him down, and Prophet gave his best half-indignant look. "I don't have any leads. But based on Ivan trying to kill us . . . maybe Chris was too popular. Fuck, I don't know, Phil."

"Can't blame yourself." He paused. "Is going back there a dead end?"

"I'd like to find out what happened," he said.

Phil stared at him. "I don't think that's the best idea, but we'll revisit it when you're healed."

Phil didn't know much about that mission ten years back. Simply that Prophet had lost John and gone off the rails.

Prophet knew that Phil didn't want to dig into deeply classified shit on his operatives, because that would fuck them all over. He knew his limits, but he also expected his operatives to share when—but not necessarily what—they thought something might be coming back to bite them.

Now, Phil patted Prophet's shoulder before he left. Prophet stared at the ceiling, muttering to himself. "I don't think this is connected to John."

"Bullshit," John told him from his perch by the window.

Prophet threw his hands up. "Fucking drugs."

"You got too close, Proph. Pull back. Look at the big picture," John advised.

"I think it's a coincidence." A horrible one. He'd gotten Gary's all-good text with the correct code on the private phone just that morning, assuring him things were fine on that front.

"No such thing."

He refused to look anywhere but at the ceiling, afraid he'd see John smirking at him again. But he still needed to get in the last word. "Sometimes a coincidence's just that."

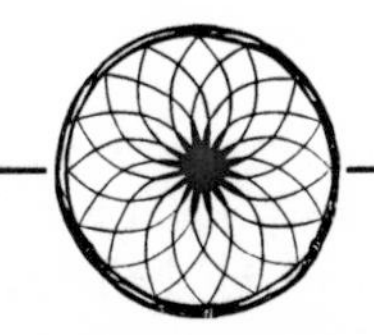

CHAPTER NINETEEN

Tom would go straight from Texas to Eritrea without stopping. At least the flight was on EE's plane, which meant he didn't have to deal with another strip search. On the tarmac, he watched the pilots and crew doing last-minute checks as they waited for Tom's newest partner, Jason Copeland, aka Cope, to show. Tom had met him briefly when he'd been training for EE—Cope had been easygoing and helpful. Natasha had explained on the phone that Cope was coming in from California, so it was easier to meet here on the private airstrip Phil had access to, rather than go back to EE.

"Phil wants to know if you're okay with jumping right back in," Natasha had also said.

He had no choice but to be okay. Prophet wanted that. Phil wanted that. And Tom needed that, so he'd told Natasha that he was fine when all he really wanted to do was ask about Prophet.

Now, he paced the tarmac, hoping he'd just go numb.

By this time, Prophet would be back at EE, but he hadn't heard from him. He thought about calling, but what the hell was there to say? He didn't know if he'd been permanently reassigned or not, but this all felt like one big test. Again.

He thought about the shooting again, rolling it over and over in his brain, and he still couldn't come up with any explanation for why he hadn't known the danger was approaching. As much as he sometimes hated the knowing, he'd come to expect it, to rely on it.

Maybe that's your problem right there.

"I was unprepared. Standing there like an idiot," he said. He'd been wrapped up in that damned video, the look on Prophet's face, the hollowness of his voice when he'd asked about it.

He hadn't been thinking about safety, his own or his partner's. So he had his first failure under his belt at EE, Ltd.

He had so much to prove. He had a second chance with Cope, when what he really wanted was one with Prophet. He had to content himself with the fact that Prophet was alive and recovering. Because while he was really goddamned grateful that Prophet seemed to have broken his partner curse by surviving their time together, how long would that last if they stayed partners?

With that, he caught himself rubbing his arm where the dreamcatcher was tattooed.

You have bad dreams, Tommy.

"All the goddamned time," he said, his temper rising when he thought about the reasons for those bad dreams. In turn, he slung his bag viciously over his shoulder as Cope walked across the tarmac.

Cope was a little shorter than he was, his hair shaved nearly to the scalp in a dark buzz. His eyes were dark too. Tom couldn't see the guy's pupils.

"Good to see you again, Tom." Cope gave him a hearty clap on the shoulder.

"You too, Cope."

"I've got some extra gear. You haven't been to Eritrea yet, right?"

"No."

"And you haven't done anything like this before, if I'm remembering correctly? Your background was domestic—FBI, right?"

"Yes." He'd been offered a few joint task force jobs in the FBI, but he'd turned them down, the way he did to anything team related.

"I'll get you through it. It should be quiet. During the downtime, we'll go over some shit. Weapons. Demo. You know, the good stuff."

"Thanks."

Cope paused, then said, "I heard you had a rough time today."

"Little bit."

"We've all been there. Phil wouldn't sent you to Eritrea if he wasn't going to keep you around." They started walking to the plane as Cope continued, "I worked with Prophet around the time Phil started getting serious about partnering everyone up. We had some good missions. He told Phil we were incompatible." Cope shrugged it off. It didn't look like it was keeping him up at night at all. "What happened with you?"

I got too close. "I got him shot."

"That'll do it."

Tom snorted, and Cope told him, "Look, Prophet's backed me up on several missions since I partnered with him—no hard feelings. He's hit every current operative in EE several times, as well as some who aren't here anymore."

"Because of him?"

Cope shrugged enigmatically. "Variety of reasons. Phil shouldn't bother trying to partner that guy permanently. He's not built that way."

"Not a team player?"

"See, that's the thing . . . he is. Just not forever. Or anything close to it. Hey, he's a good guy. I'd trust him with my life. I like that he'll take over EE when Phil retires." Cope disappeared onto the plane, and Tom followed, his thoughts reeling.

Tom absorbed that, but couldn't reconcile Prophet being groomed to take over EE and Phil forcing a partner on him. But Tom knew from his own experience that everyone had secrets. Forcing Prophet to tell them would mean Prophet would want to know Tom's too. And no fucking way, because the curse might not actually be broken. And he wasn't putting Prophet at risk.

But, even with that, he realized leaving Prophet behind wasn't going to be easy, mainly because, as much as he didn't want to leave him as a partner, he really didn't want to leave the *man*.

Cope clicked his seat belt closed as the plane reared forward faster than any commercial flight ever could. "Ready to move out?"

Tom didn't bother to tell him that he had no choice.

Prophet hated recovery time. It made him more twitchy than usual, and he was twitchy on a good day. Doc had discharged him to home several days after he'd had surgery to remove the bullet but was insisting on that "complete bed rest" crap. He'd left Prophet with just tight wraps on his wrists and the promise that the casts would go back on next week. That would be his big goddamned day let out of his pen. Until then, he was a caged lion.

And he couldn't even use this time to steal anything from Cillian. Well, maybe something light. He checked out Cillian's place, scanning everything, his eyes resting on the couch.

Probably too heavy, but with the right leverage . . .

With his hands on the computer keys, he contemplated IMing the guy. The last time they'd IM'd, he'd bitched about his new partner.

His new partner who was now Cope's new partner. Dammit. He typed, *All your shit's just the way you left it*, not expecting to get an answer.

But the ding of a message came through seconds later. *Home?*

Yeah—recovering. R&R. Forced.

Bullet wound?

Just a small one.

Enough to keep you from stealing my couch?

How the hell did Cillian know Prophet wanted the couch? *For the moment.*

How's the new partner?

Prophet went to type something and realized he had no idea how to answer that. The pause was only for a second, but it was enough to make Cillian write, *Interesting.*

I didn't say anything.

I didn't think anyone could render you speechless.

"Definitely stealing your couch," Prophet said out loud, then typed. *He's fine. He didn't get shot.*

You took a bullet for him. How romantic.

"I'm going to kill this guy." *It wasn't like that. He's okay.*

Where is he now?

With another partner on a different mission.

Heard from him?

Didn't expect to.

Not what I asked. Sounds like neither of you fought to stay together. Must not have been a great partnership.

Prophet considered that. But he couldn't agree. *I'm not a partner type of guy. Nothing he did.*

Right. Guys like us are meant to be alone.

Prophet wondered which one of them Cillian was trying to convince more.

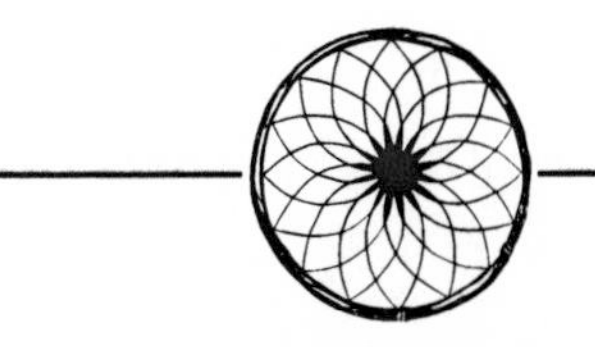

CHAPTER TWENTY

A week into his time in Eritrea, Tom found himself hunkered down in one of the many safe houses along the route out of Mogadishu instead. He could safely say he'd never had much desire to go to Somalia, and certainly not like this, with Cope and American Foreign Service Generalist Shawn Breen, who they'd rescued from kidnappers demanding ransom and the release of political prisoners. They'd also rescued Breen's eighteen-year-old daughter, Amy, who was visiting.

Visiting.

Tom didn't understand that, but apparently she'd come to visit before heading to college, and, like her father, wanted to live a life of service.

She was a tough kid, but definitely more at risk. Cope had dressed her in his jacket and a hat to disguise her as much as possible. She was shaking but holding up better than expected. Since the official US stance in a case like this was "we don't negotiate with terrorists," this was exactly the type of thing EE was built to handle.

Because EE didn't negotiate, either. They used shock and awe on the kidnappers and took back their own. And the CIA had called Phil, and Phil had activated Tom and Cope.

Cope was former Delta, a good shot. He'd given Tom several impromptu refresher courses during their downtime, taught him that Feds trained differently than soldiers. And Tom was definitely in need of soldiering now.

As the bullets flew, Tom realized that he might be out of his league.

"Doing fine, Tommy. Trial by fire." Prophet's voice in his ear. He'd been called in by Natasha, patched in from his home in order to help guide them once Cope realized how trapped they'd be. "Just stick with Cope and try not to shoot him."

"Funny."

Prophet ticked off latitude and longitude of the LZ on the roof of a building four doors down, and Tom pictured him, lying in bed, barking orders. He barked orders naturally, and now wasn't the time to think about Prophet and bed and orders.

Prophet had been leading him and Cope through the streets between the safe houses—because it wasn't safe at all to stay in one for more than a couple of hours at a time—since he had satellite and could actually see what sides danger was coming from. Although it seemed like they were goddamned surrounded. They were being hunted, and getting out of town had never been so important.

"Come on," Cope said, and the four of them were up and running down alleys, Prophet silent in their ears for the moment. But a minute before they were about to reach their destination, Prophet cursed and told them to go back through the alley and head out of the city limits.

It was an incredibly risky proposition, but Tom saw why Prophet was telling them to do so immediately. RPGs were flying through the air like the Fourth of July on testosterone, and the helo was leaving. The only good thing about that was that it took all the attention of the men who'd have otherwise been firing at them. And they'd stayed back just far enough to not be spotted. He and Cope dragged Breen and Amy back through the streets, dodging locals and rebel soldiers, because they couldn't afford a firefight that would draw attention to them. They kept going until they were out of the city and into the desert scrub, their ultimate goal the coast.

Except now they were in the middle of nowhere in the middle of the dark and they'd just have to keep walking the uneven terrain.

That's what Prophet told them. A twelve mile walk to the next extraction point that could be accomplished more safely than inside the city limits.

More safely. Which meant, not really safe at all.

After five miles—or eight klicks, as Prophet and Cope called them—they took a break for several reasons, the first two being Breen and Amy. Cope was helping them out, giving them the pep talk, hydrating them. But the other reason was because, in less than a mile, they'd be walking through an area dotted with rebel soldiers. Hidden rebel soldiers. It meant stealth and complete quiet would be necessary to get them through the last leg of this mission.

But for now, Tom was talking to Prophet. The man was only in his ear, not Cope's now. Cope had Natasha in his, and the two different perspectives were meant to give them double support.

Tom knew the only way he was still going was because of Prophet's voice.

"The best thing about missions is the disconnect," Prophet was telling him now. "You can almost pinpoint when it happens. You're up in the chopper and one minute, your mind's on all the bullshit on the ground—bills, lovers, whatever. And then suddenly, all the noise from the chopper shakes the shit out of your brains and you're all about what's right in front of you and nothing else. All that matters is life and death."

Tom understood. His missions had usually been smaller scale, with less outright bloodshed. "For me, with the FBI, it was about the hunt."

"Well, yeah," Prophet said, like that had always been obvious. "You're a born tracker."

Tom was. Growing up in the bayous, everything was a matter of hunting, tracking, and stalking.

"What kind of cases did you work?"

"Mainly shooters. Some serials."

"You were on the Steele Street case."

Tom's gut clenched. Prophet had read his file, and he'd known that was bound to happen. He waited for Prophet to elaborate, but the man dropped it, saying instead, "Getting on a helo in the middle of the jungle's a little different than what you're used to. Just don't hesitate to fire. They'll come at you from all angles and you've got a huge ratio of enemies to friends."

"Phil had me train with Bob."

"Shit, he's tough."

"Tell me about it." Tom had never been as mentally or physically exhausted in his entire life. It had been worth it—the lack of military training could've been held against him. FBI training was intense, but the focus was different. "This was supposed to be recon. Surveillance.

Boring shit." He heard the uncertainty in his voice and was sure Prophet would call him something unflattering.

Instead, Prophet, who was thousands of miles away and yet so intimate in his ear, told him, "You can do this, Tommy. Fuck your scars. Fuck your past. It all just makes you stronger."

Tommy. Jesus. He swallowed back his fear. "You really believe scars make you stronger?"

"You tell me." He swore he could feel Prophet running a hand over his bare back, like he had in the motel room. The tattoos concealed the scars from the naked eye, and a casual touch wouldn't reveal them either. But there was nothing casual about Prophet—not his bearing, his touches, his gaze—they were all deliberate, no matter how hard Tom tried to pretend otherwise.

"Still standing," he told Prophet now.

"That's all that matters. Use those instincts, Tom. I told you I'd listen, but you need to listen to you too."

"Fat lot of good it did you."

"Well, what the hell happened that day? How'd you lose focus?"

You. "Not sure."

"Okay, you have to go dark now."

"I know."

"I'll keep talking. Cope's ahead of you. Keep an eye on him. I've got your back."

He was about to say *thanks* when Prophet said, "Shut up."

Tom mentally gave him the finger, and yeah, back to normal.

The terrain was unforgiving. As Prophet guided them, he could easily picture the man here. Prophet had obviously walked this path before, and his directions were better than the NVs Tom wore.

But suddenly, Tom stopped moving.

"What's up, T?" Prophet asked, then added, "Go with your fucking gut, man."

Tom did. He moved a few fast steps to grab for Cope, who turned and looked at him.

"Go in the direction you need to. I'm with you," Prophet said. Cope didn't argue when Tom led them west along a narrow footpath.

Prophet guided him along the new path. "Six point four klicks, T," which Tom quickly calculated as four miles, and it was exactly that long until he saw the helo in the distance, the giant steel bird coming toward them like a beacon.

Prophet chose then to tell him, "I checked into the path you avoided while you were walking. Intel now confirms there were rebels waiting half a mile down from where you turned. You were right. You did it, T."

Tom nodded as though Prophet could see him, and then let Cope cover him, Breen, and Amy as they ran to board the hovering helo that would take them out of Hell.

It was like a horror show, the ghosts of the past sitting around him. Staring at him.

John was there. Hal too. And now Chris, staring at him almost sadly.

Prophet blinked, and the room tilted again. Chris was gone and they were back in the desert. Hal was there, sitting next to him in the tent, drinking a warm beer, watching as John prepped the Land Rover they'd drive across the neverfuckingending deserts of the Sudan.

"Five minutes before we move out," John called.

Prophet was sweating and looking between the two men, and even though he knew this wasn't real, because Cillian's fucking couch wasn't in the middle of the goddamned desert, it was as real as it got. And no one—nothing—could pull him out of this.

"You are fucking pathetic." John smirked at him.

He turned to see Hal, watching him with that all-knowing look as he told Prophet, "I'm ready."

"I'm not," Prophet said brokenly, and he didn't want to be broken.

You were born a Drews. Born to shatter and break into a million fucking pieces, and who was going to pick them up?

Who'd want to?

He'd met Hal four days ago. Had spent that time working up a plan with his team to get Hal safely across the desert. Also spent that time with Hal talking his goddamned ear off. Wanting Prophet to *know* him.

"Don't do it, Proph," John told him, and Prophet didn't know if that was John in the flashback or sardonic ghost John, but it didn't matter—his message was always the same warning. "Don't."

"Don't," Prophet repeated now, the word echoing through an empty room and not a tent. He blinked and stared as the desert cleared, as Hal faded away, still alive, and then he was on the bedroom floor, clutching his knees to his chest and rocking.

Yeah, you're really ready to get back in the game.

"You did your job," he told himself, repeated it out loud, over and over while still rocking, because even though he knew it was the truth, that didn't stop it from being one of the hardest things he'd ever done. He hadn't known it would be that soul-wrenchingly difficult.

In truth, he'd never thought he and John and the rest of the SEAL team were invincible, but thinking and knowing were two entirely different things. And even though he'd done several jobs escorting specialists before, the mission with Hal had been different.

Hal had made Prophet sit down with him ahead of time. Had made Prophet listen to him. And he'd made Prophet promise him several things.

He'd regretted making those promises ever fucking since.

Finally, when his rocking stilled, he dragged himself off the floor and to the phone, to make sure Tom hadn't called again. His hands were still trembling, had been from when he'd put the phone down from guiding Tommy through Somalia's underbelly. He'd put the phone down and his head on the desk and he'd woken up in the middle of the desert again.

"Fuck." He shook his head. The shakes and light-headedness had to be from his injury, right? Right. Because if you couldn't lie to yourself, who the hell could you lie to?

He was an amazing goddamned liar.

He pulled the interrogation video up, studied it again for the thousandth time, stared at the phone he'd just spoken with Tom on. Two separate things but somehow, they'd become entwined. Impossibly so.

And Prophet didn't believe in coincidences.

It had been almost a relief to discover that Tom was with Cope. Almost, and that tiny part that wouldn't let it be a relief had pissed Prophet off as much as being paired with a partner in the first place.

Or maybe it was because Phil hadn't even pushed the issue of his staying partnered with Tom. Maybe Phil was making the break for him, assuming that he'd bitch about getting shot in order to get out of it anyway?

Have you always been such a giant, high-maintenance pain in the ass?

Speaking of, Prophet dialed the number by heart for the bi-monthly call there was no getting out of.

Her voice was groggy when she said hello.

"Shit, sorry I woke you."

"That's okay, baby."

Baby? *Jesus.* He gripped the phone tighter. "Everything okay?"

"Same old shit."

"Making friends?"

"You mean, besides the ones in my head?"

"You said it, not me."

"The people here are okay. Better than the last place, I guess. How's your work?"

She was lying. So would he. It was the story of their lives. "Great."

"I still can't believe you're working construction. There's so much more you could be doing."

"Times are tough out there."

"Shouldn't be for you."

He'd been hearing that his entire life, so he didn't answer, let her continue. "I got a call from some guy. He was looking for you."

"What did you tell him?"

"That you won't give me your number." Choking cough. "I need more pills."

"They're regulated."

"Fuck you."

"Yeah, I know. Those were my first words, Mom." He said it without a trace of irony. "You're okay. The doctors say you're doing great."

"And how are you doing?"

"Fine. Just fine."

"That guy who called sounded mad."

"I'll bet he did," Prophet said as un-ironically as he could. "If he calls back, hang up on him."

"Yeah, yeah." She paused and then asked, "Are you coming to visit soon?"

Never. "Yeah."

"You always say that."

"I know." He didn't know what else to say because there was nothing left to say, so he hung up instead.

Calling Phil was out of the question. Prophet was all alone, and although he normally liked it that way, the urge to dial Tommy back was almost overwhelming.

He messaged Cillian instead. Because that fictional relationship was so much more healthy.

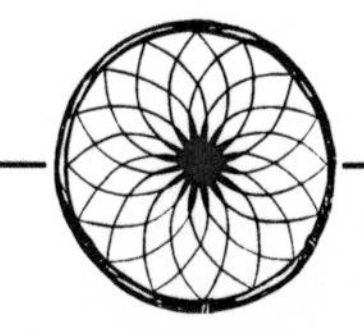

CHAPTER TWENTY-ONE

Tom slammed his fist against the heavy industrial steel door, stood back, and waited. He didn't hear footsteps but he knew when Prophet saw him through the peephole. He could feel it.

He heard bolts moving and then the door slid open quickly, Prophet showing no signs of being in any kind of pain as he pushed.

"How the hell did you get past the security at the front door?" Prophet demanded. "And fuck that, I don't remember giving you my address."

"Nice to see you too, Proph." So much for the warm and fuzzy feelings they'd shared weeks ago over an earpiece during the Eritrea slash foray into Somalia experience. "I used a tracking device. You might be familiar with those."

"You planted a bug on me?"

"Yes."

"And you don't think that was wrong?"

"I don't care."

Prophet blinked. "Fuck. That's something I'd say. You've been hanging around me too long. But that still doesn't explain what you're doing here. Don't you have a home anymore?"

"You pointed out that my place isn't one."

Prophet shrugged as he lounged against the heavy metal door. "You said it works for you."

"Not anymore. Are you going to leave me standing here or invite me in?"

"You were never not invited."

"God, I want to hit you." Tom pushed past Prophet, not touching him as he did so.

"Phil told me I should tattoo *Get in line* across my forehead to save myself the trouble of constantly saying it."

Tom heard the door close and lock, continued surveying the place. It was all open space. Industrial. Modern. Clean, with some cool pieces of sculpture and furniture and pictures, all probably obtained during Prophet's travels.

Prophet walked in his general direction, but left a wide arc of space—and a table that showcased several pieces of stone sculpture—between them. "Why'd you come here?"

"To finish the mission."

"There is no mission. I'm sure Phil told you."

"He did."

Prophet stared at him. "Let me guess, you got a premonition."

"Something like that." It was better than saying *I'm worried about you.* "About what happened . . ."

"Forget it," Prophet said, then stopped. "Which what happened? The shot or the other thing?"

"The shot."

"Like I said, forget it."

Tom took a couple of steps toward the table, and Prophet, asking, "And the other thing? Do you want to forget that?" *Because I tried it. Can't.*

Prophet ran a finger over one of the statues between them. "No."

Want it to happen again? he wanted to ask, but didn't. Instead, he said, "Me neither."

"Are you back because you want to fuck or because you want to help?"

"Both."

"Not a bad answer."

Tom began to walk around the table that separated them. "I have some questions first."

"Then you're shit out of luck, because I've got no answers." Prophet walked away before Tom's slow deliberate strides could catch up with him.

But he walked backward, actually, his eyes never leaving Tom's face. Tom almost smiled at that, but he didn't, simply continued his relentless prowl forward, unable—unwilling—to stop himself. "I didn't come here for more of your 'escape and evade' shit."

Prophet gave a mirthless laugh and stopped in his tracks. "You've been with EE for three months and you're already breaking rules. So much for staying out of trouble and keeping your nose clean."

"Yeah, fuck that." Tom was in front of him now, and the distance would easily diminish if either one of them reached out to touch the other.

Neither did.

"I appreciate the sentiment, but we can't go back out because I can't protect you," Prophet said.

"Really? Because I think you did a really good job when you took the bullet meant for me."

"You're pissed I saved you?" Prophet asked, apparently incredulous.

"I'm pissed you don't think I can take care of myself," Tom corrected. "I'm pissed that you haven't given me a chance to take care of you."

Prophet shook his head. "You've taken care of—"

"Sex doesn't count!" Tom yelled.

"Sex always counts," Prophet informed him, poked his chest with a pointed finger. "And you must have a death wish."

"What I have is a desire to stay with EE. And to finish this job, keeping you out of trouble like I was charged with doing."

"I was the one keeping you out of trouble."

"I know. That won't happen again."

Prophet sighed, stared up at the ceiling as though all of this was killing him. "Whatever. You've already found me. I invited you in. What more do you want?"

"Why do you push everyone away?"

"Because I'm a highly damaged individual with psychotic tendencies?" Prophet's tone was a hopeful question, and Tom couldn't stop his mouth from quirking up in a smile.

He didn't believe that Prophet believed what he'd said. He'd wanted a reaction. Maybe an assurance.

Or maybe he'd just wanted to push you away like he does everyone else. "You're not an easy man."

Prophet laughed a little, the low sound going right to Tom's cock. "You're just figuring that out?"

"First time I'm saying it out loud."

"You've mumbled it a couple of times."

"I don't remember that."

"You talk in your sleep, T."

"Only since I started working with you, dammit." Tom swore that although neither man had moved a step, they were standing closer together. "What else do I say?"

"I plead the Fifth."

"It's my sleeptalking, and you won't even tell me what I said?"

"You said I'm the hottest guy who's ever fucked you. With the biggest cock, too."

"Hrmph," Tom said, stuck a hand into his pocket and fought the urge to rub his cock. "Fucked being past tense."

"Aw, don't be like that, Tommy."

"Tom. And it's hot in here, right? Can you open a window or something?"

Prophet's smile was easy. Lazy. "You don't mind when I call you Tommy when I'm fucking you. Why's that?"

"Because I don't give a shit about anything when you're fucking me."

"You say it like there's something wrong with that." Prophet rubbed his fingers along his own jawline.

He liked to be kissed there, Tom knew. Kissed and licked and sucked and marked . . .

As if Prophet knew what Tom was thinking, he moved his hand to run it through Tom's hair, and for the first time, Tom saw that his arms were cast free. "Doc said you were healed?"

"No."

"Ah, Proph—" he started, but Prophet gently put a finger on his mouth, then ran his thumb across Tom's bottom lip as he said, "I'm all right, Can't show weakness, Tommy. I expect you understand that."

He did, and decided it was as good a time as any to broach the subject he'd been dreading, the thing that had gotten them in trouble in the first place. "Did you watch the video?"

He regretted it instantly, though, when Prophet took his hand away from Tom's lip and simply said, "Yes."

"Learn anything from it?"

"Why don't you tell me what you learned?" Prophet asked.

"Like I said before, things I would've figured out anyway after knowing you five minutes."

"I guess that's supposed to be comforting."

"Interpret it as you will." Tom resisted the urge to comb his fingers through Prophet's hair, the way Prophet had done himself earlier. And then he rethought his decision and wound his fingers into the blond strands. Brought their faces close. "Fuck me, Prophet."

Prophet blinked. Jaw tightened, nostrils flared, all for a brief second in time during which Tom willed himself taut, ready for a rejection that never came.

From the second he'd opened the door, Prophet had known this would happen. He fisted the front of Tommy's shirt and yanked him hard toward him. He let go of the fabric at the last second as their chests slammed together, and he caught the back of Tom's neck in his hand while he crushed Tom's mouth against his.

It was a messy kiss, a mash of tongues, and Tom's moan against him gave Prophet a rush of power and heat that made his dick harder.

Tom's hands scrabbled between them. He was unzipping Prophet's jeans, rubbing his cock, even as Prophet's hands pulled up Tommy's shirt and played with the man's nipple rings. Tugging, teasing, making him jump.

Tom pulled down Prophet's jeans carefully, since Prophet wasn't wearing underwear. In turn, Prophet yanked Tom's shirt over his head.

Naked was the only word thrumming in his mind. Obviously, in Tommy's too.

"Bedroom?" Tom asked against Prophet's mouth.

"Top floor."

"Unless you're not up to it," Tom said, a hand brushing Prophet's side where the bullet had hit.

"Do I look not up to it?" He'd have to be dead before he gave up an offer of sex with Tommy, especially now that the man had gotten him so goddamned worked up.

"I don't want to hurt you," Tom told him.

"Then don't," was all Prophet said before stopping any more concerns with his tongue stuffed in Tom's mouth. He'd put his dick in there too if it'd stop the guy from thinking and make him feel.

Besides, the fucking kissing . . . yeah, it was good with Tommy. Tommy's voice against his ear, his breath warm and sweet, his hands—his hands—touching Prophet's shoulders, trailing down his back, splaying there, under his shirt.

Skin to skin, like the fights.

They stumbled up the stairs together. The sun had gone down and the fourth floor was bathed in near darkness, with barely a sliver of light from the lampposts shining through the windows. Didn't matter. He didn't need lights to see Tommy.

He melted against Tommy, and Tommy goddamned knew it. And for once, Prophet didn't care, let Tom drag his clothes off until finally Tom whispered, "Want your hands on me."

He could do that. Hadn't touched Tommy with his uncasted hands. So he reached out to lay his palms along Tom's tattooed skin, knew he would spend the rest of the night, against all his better judgment, tracing it with his fingertips and tongue.

Whether he wanted to or not. A siren's song.

Prophet read his body like he was reading braille. In the dark, Tom could see the flash of Prophet's blond hair, felt Prophet's tongue on his skin as the man conquered every inch of him and planted his flag.

It would never be like this with anyone else. It never had been before. Tonight, Prophet was ruining him for anyone else, and Tom wondered if Prophet knew it too.

Prophet was between his knees, playing his tongue along Tom's piercings. Tom pushed on his elbows to watch, a sharp gasp escaping when Prophet reached up and flicked a nipple ring hard.

And then Prophet kept him from coming back down to earth. His entire body was a complete slave to sensation, and he was mainly incoherent, save for a few choice words like *fuck* and *me* and Prophet's name, which he said more like a curse, which made the man actually chuckle.

"Do it again," he begged.

"This?"

"That . . . and the laugh."

Prophet did both and then slid Tom's dick inside his mouth to the goddamned root. And Tom's come splashed down his throat with something akin to a howl.

He panted. Clutched the sheets as Prophet held his hips firmly to the bed, draining the last of him.

"You'll come again."

"No fucking way. Not for days."

"Wanna bet?"

"Against you? Don't think so, *cher*."

"I like it when you call me pet names."

"Yeah, I'll call you something," Tom threatened, but Prophet's fingers were back, doing unspeakable things to him.

He dropped his knees to the side as Prophet said to him, "I'm a fucking slut for you."

"I'm a slut for you too," he mumbled, and Prophet heard him.

Nodded, like he knew, and said, "Nothing wrong with that."

No, it didn't feel wrong at all. And that could be a problem, but it wasn't when Prophet's tongue danced over his nipple then bit it, a growl thrumming up from the back of his throat as he did so.

There wasn't anger in Prophet, rather an inherent wildness that Tom had no desire to tame. No, he wanted to ride it, imbibe it, fuck it senseless, and watch it grow wilder. This Prophet was in control, but barely. White-knuckling it, like Tom had been.

But then Prophet pulled back, the way he always did. It was so subtle Tom almost always missed it, probably because he wanted to. And then Prophet flipped him over to fuck him and there was no mistaking why.

So he doesn't have to see your face. So he doesn't have to be fully here.

Whether it was guilt or not, Tom didn't know, didn't care. He'd make sure to keep the man on him as grounded as he could, because it wasn't the time to push Prophet on this. Tom would work with it, rather than against it.

Prophet's cockhead breached Tom's ass, making him draw a hissing breath through his teeth. He thrust back against Prophet's girth, not wanting to wait. "Don't care if it hurts."

Prophet flicked his nipple ring. "No, guessed you wouldn't," he murmured.

And then he tugged, and the delicious fucking pleasurepain flooded Tom's body. He took it—everything. Got on his hands and knees and let Prophet ride him hard, didn't care how the hell wet he was put away.

He came twice before Prophet did.

Prophet's orgasm slammed him against Tom, pushed him down flat to the mattress. He felt Prophet throb inside of him and swore that he could come again. If he weren't so completely boneless and content.

Prophet pulled out, and he bit Tom's shoulder as he rolled slightly to throw the condom into the pail by the bed before moving back to drape himself partially over Tom.

Tom turned his head to see Prophet, his cheek on the pillow, his shoulder on Tom's, his arm thrown across Tom's back. One of his legs splayed across the back of Tom's thighs. "You have patience."

"I came when I was blowing you," Prophet admitted. And that made Tom grunt weakly, and he shifted to where he could reach back to take the man's hand in his before he realized what he was doing.

To his surprise, Prophet tightened his fingers to match Tom's grip and fell asleep against his shoulder, lips touching skin.

Tom didn't want to sleep, if only so he could stare at Prophet's face more, and marvel at how goddamned innocent the man looked when the peace of sleep overtook him. He wanted to stroke a cheekbone, a scar, to kiss him more. But he didn't want to break any of this moment, either, so he settled for trying to memorize it while figuring out where the hell they'd go from here.

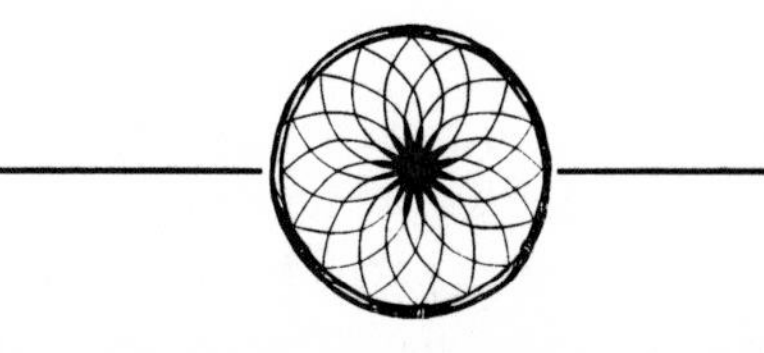

CHAPTER TWENTY-TWO

Prophet got them beers and chips. Ordered take-out Chinese, which they ate in bed as the TV flickered in the background. It was a comfortable silence, until Tom brought up the subject he'd come here about.

Well, the second subject. The first was already more than accomplished, and he had the sore ass to prove it.

"I know you're not dropping this case. Just tell me, is it about closure or revenge?"

"Can't it be about both?"

"You're never going to hear what you need to. It's never going to absolve you. But then again, I don't think there's anything you need to be absolved of."

"Real sweet of you, Tommy."

"There's nothing sweet about me. You, on the other hand . . ." He trailed off as Prophet snorted. But Tom swore he caught the slight flush of red on his cheeks before he turned away.

"I have to do this alone."

"No."

Prophet sighed, stared up at the ceiling. "I already almost got you killed."

"I think that was more my fault."

"That I got shot?"

"Yeah." Tom paused, letting his thoughts knit together, the way he did when he finally stopped to breathe and let his intuition take over. He was—finally—figuring shit out. "This isn't the case we started."

"No, it's not," Prophet agreed, then seemed content to let the conversation stop there.

"So this is the part where you explain things to me," Tom prompted in a slow and steady voice, like he'd use for a child. "Maybe Phil needs to have a handbook for partner to partner communication."

"In or out of bed?" Prophet shot back.

"Sweetheart, I understand you just fine in bed."

"I am not your sweetheart," Prophet muttered. Was he? Or was Tom being sarcastic. Jesus H. Christ. *Sweetheart.* And just when he was recovering from that, Tom shot out, "Are you really going to take over EE when Phil retires?"

"Why? You think fucking the future boss will ensure you a job?"

"Just when I think you weren't raised by wolves . . ."

"But I was."

"Forget I asked."

"You have zero sense of humor, huh?"

Tom shot him the finger.

"Okay, fine. Yes, it's true."

"Wouldn't that take you out of the field?"

Prophet closed his eyes, rested his palms over them. So easy to explain why, but there was no way. And if Tom was still around EE when it happened—which he doubted—then he'd know.

Everyone would know.

"I'll cross that bridge when I come to it. What's this really all about? Did the mission with Cope fuck you up? Because you did just fine."

Tom rubbed the back of his neck, his body language tightening. "It was intense."

"Supposed to be."

"It's different there. No rules."

"Makes it interesting."

Tom barked a laugh, then said, "Cope said he'd worked with you."

"Yep."

"Who else did he work with?"

Prophet wondered why Tom hadn't just asked Cope, but then figured maybe he had and this was some kind of test. Tom was learning too much from him, and it was his own damned fault. "Cope worked a lot with Mick. Still does and still will, but Mick's got a permanent partner." A partner in every sense of the word. Mick and Blue together was such a thing of fucking beauty. It made so much sense that a guy like Mick would end up loving a thief. Sometimes life just got it right. "You got what you wanted—proved yourself to Phil. Maybe even to yourself."

"Who's psychic now?" Tom asked, but he didn't deny that's where his thoughts had been leading him. "Did Phil assign you to me in Somalia because he wanted you to check on me?"

"Paranoid much? I think the job's been rough on you. Think you're dealing with a lot of old shit you should've dug up and thrown away years ago."

Tom snorted. "Like you have?"

"Do as I say, not as I do. Look, I haven't said anything to Phil about you losing it during the fight and I won't. He's impressed with you."

"Thanks, boss."

Prophet cut him a glance. "I'm not trying to make you worry that you're not cutting it by talking about where things went wrong. But I get that what happened in Somalia was a big deal." *And you should've been with him.*

"Okay. And yeah, I'm . . . fuck."

"Just take a breath. You were good. You got the job done with Cope."

"Because I let you get me there."

"Because you worked with a partner. Because you utilized all your resources, including your instincts. But you know that, so what's this really all about, T?"

Tom didn't bother denying what was bothering him. "Phil said that I'm probably going to have to make a choice . . . about my partner. A permanent choice."

"So make it."

"I'm here, aren't I?"

"There's no case, T."

Tom stared at him. "If we're partners at EE, we'd be together for more than one case. But yeah, there's still a case. Don't bullshit me."

"Your Cajun voodoo-ometer working overtime?"

"Yes," Tom said seriously.

Fuck. The last thing Prophet wanted was Tom digging into this further. "Did you come here for me, or the case?

"Does it matter? They're one and the same."

Prophet laughed tightly. "No, they're not. At all."

So make it. Like it was that easy.

Tom didn't want to point out that Prophet wasn't pushing for Tom to fucking pick him. So instead of asking anything else, he stared at the ceiling, noticing the dreamcatcher hanging from the overhead light for the first time. He was about to comment on it when Prophet's phone beeped. Prophet glanced at it and punched in something. "Give me a sec here."

"Is that Phil?"

"No. The ongoing, never-ending conversation with the spook. That's his couch." Prophet waved toward it, the gray sleek lines looking perfect in here. Like it had been made for him.

"He gave you his couch?"

"Gave is such a broad term."

Tom snorted a laugh and stared up at the dreamcatcher again. Between the sex and the comfortable mattress, he could drift off easily.

But he'd come here to figure out his choice. Wanted Prophet's input.

You knew he wouldn't help you decide. "How long have you had that?"

Prophet sat on the edge of the bed, facing away from him, and didn't look up from his phone. "Couple of years."

"You have bad dreams, Proph?"

"Why? You want to be the one to change that?"

"I might."

"A thankless job."

Prophet sleeps with whoever he needs to in order to get the job done, Cope had told him one night when they were shooting the shit, drinking warm Tusker lager and discussing the finer points of sleeping with the targets for the job. He hadn't been trying to get a rise out of Tom, hadn't known there was anything between Tom and Prophet. Instead, he'd simply been explaining Prophet's full and varied sex life and his admiration for how well the guy did his job. That job now included Tom as a notch on Prophet's bedpost.

Prophet put the phone down and turned back to him. "You're thinking too hard."

"You sure giving that guy information is a good idea?"

"He doesn't know where I work."

"You know he's a spook. He's got to know what you do."

"Probably."

"That doesn't worry you?"

"Never has."

"Because he flirts with you?"

"I'm not attached, T."

"Guess not." Tom shrugged. "Lot of men in your life, Proph. It's getting crowded." Prophet frowned, shook his head, and Tom continued. "John. The spook. Doc . . ."

"Doc?"

It was Tom's turn to shake his head. "You're more intimate with them—"

"What the hell, T? I'm not sleeping with them."

That made things worse, except Tom wasn't sure what bothered him more: the fact that Prophet wasn't intimate with those men and could still reveal more to them than he'd ever revealed to Tom, or that Prophet might be fucking him only to keep him at arm's length.

Or the fact that he can read you so easily.

Or the fact that he knew a lot about Prophet, but also knew he'd barely scratched the surface of a very complicated man.

He'd never wanted someone all to himself like this. It was the oddest goddamned feeling.

Prophet sighed. "Look, I've known Doc longer. And the only contact I have with Cillian is through cyberspace. Although you'd be surprised how much you can learn about someone through IM and texts."

Tom grabbed him, pulled him back to the bed. "If you're trying to make me jealous, it's working. I'm going to fuck you on his couch. On your back. On your knees. Bent over the back of the damned thing. And I hope to God he gets it all on tape."

"You really are a kinky fuck, T."

"You bring it out in me. And what about Mal? What's his deal?"

Prophet flickered a glance over him. "Why? *You* want to fuck him?"

"*I* don't want to fuck every guy I ask about."

"Good to know." Prophet paused. "Mal's deal is Mal's deal. If he decides to let you in on it one day, you'll know."

"Did his throat get cut on a mission for EE?"

"Worried about your neck, T?"

"I worry about a lot of things."

"I know." Prophet traced a finger across Tom's Adam's apple. "And no, it wasn't on an EE mission."

Tom supposed everyone who worked at EE had a past, something that set their path in motion toward mercenary for hire. "Sure it's okay that I came here?"

"You mean, is it okay you bugged my phone?"

"Yeah."

Prophet stared at him steadily. "Would've been just as easy not to answer the door."

There was silence again, this time brimming with tension.

"Tom, we talked about this. We partnered for a case and we agreed not to let sex get in the way. It's just fucking."

Tom pulled away from him and sat up then, because he couldn't touch Prophet while the man was trying to separate from him. "You're kidding yourself if you think it hasn't. And if you think that's all it is."

"That's all it can be."

"You still didn't answer what I asked. And I didn't want this either. I was scared of killing another partner. And I'd never slept with any of my other partners, so I'd never had to balance work and sleeping together, so I'm even more freaked out about what's happening here."

"Maybe, for you, all of this is less about sleeping with me and more about you wanting me to help you."

He stared at Prophet in disbelief, but Prophet wasn't joking. And judging by the guarded look in Prophet's eyes, he'd been thinking that for longer than tonight. "Is that what you thought about John and his temper?"

"Sometimes, yeah."

From the way Prophet said it, though, Tom knew it was more than just sometimes.

Bon courage, Tom, you're really up against too many ghost here.

Finally, Prophet asked, "Have you got any of those fortune-teller feelings?"

He was about to tell the man to fuck off when he noticed Prophet was serious, and no doubt talking about the case and not what was happening between them. Which made him want to tell him to fuck off even more. But there was that look in Prophet's eyes that wouldn't let him. Maybe because he wanted to help Prophet . . . and maybe because he knew Prophet was right about Tom needing—wanting—Prophet's help. "Nothing more than knowing this case is far from over."

Prophet frowned, and Tom continued, "It never made sense why I was sent that video."

"When *was* it sent?"

"Weeks before I knew I'd be partnered with you. Before Phil knew, maybe."

"Maybe they were just trying to warn you that partnering with me was a bad idea." Prophet gave a wry smile, then shrugged. "The shooting's not connected to the video, T."

"Right. You told Phil it was Ivan's friends."

"They were trying to teach you a lesson. You went too far with Ivan."

You lost control. Prophet's unspoken words.

Tom blew out a harsh breath. His chest ached. They were back to his temper, again. And he knew he didn't want to be anything like John, because every time Prophet talked about John, there was pain in his eyes. And goddammit, Tom didn't want to bring the man any more pain. He wanted to be the one who could erase it.

Even so, an irrational burst of jealousy bloomed. "How close were you and John?"

"Close."

"Like brothers close?"

Prophet eyed him warily. "Where are you going with this?"

"Did you fuck him?"

"Sometimes. And sometimes, he fucked me," Prophet said easily. "That pique your curiosity?"

Tom had to turn away. It was as he'd expected. He wasn't sure why it was like taking a goddamned bullet. Prophet was using him as a substitute to make himself feel better, and he'd happily gone along for the ride.

"Tommy, what the fuck do you want from me? A rundown of everyone I've fucked?"

"No. You don't owe me anything."

"And here I thought I was the difficult one of the partnership," Prophet mused.

"You are."

"Well good, didn't want to lose my status. If it makes you feel any better, you run a close second, T."

Tom touched the thin leather bracelet Prophet had put on him before the fight. He hadn't been able to bring himself to take it off. And then he saw his own anger flash white in front of him, before it settled into something eerily calm and wholly new to him. "But you'll *help* me with that, right, Prophet?"

Prophet frowned a little at his words, then shrugged and said, "Whatever turns you on, T."

The casual barb of the words were the catalyst, but it was that fucking shrug that pushed Tom over the edge, hard, with both hands. And he was damn well taking Prophet with him this time.

"Yeah, you'll help me," Tom said, his voice low and deceptively calm, his body uncoiling to move closer in a way that sparked Prophet's danger meter. It was like Tom had just processed everything they'd talked about, and Prophet knew his blow-off had been the tipping point. He'd seen plenty of people reach it before in his presence—most of the time, *because* of him—but none had reacted like this.

"Christ, Tommy, have a drink or something."

"Why, so you can take care of me some more?"

"Ah, do what you want." Prophet attempted to brush the topic off, but Tom wasn't letting this go.

"That's what you're doing—you're taking care of me, the way you used to take care of John. You're fucking me the way you used to fuck him too."

"Technically, you've been fucking me too," Prophet pointed out, and Tom smiled, a ruthlessly wicked smile that made Prophet simultaneously break out in a sweat and get hard, like his body wasn't sure which reaction was appropriate.

Before he could roll away, Tom put his full weight on him. Grabbed his arms and yanked them over his head. Held them there. Stared at him until Prophet wanted to look away, but fuck it all, he didn't. Not even when Tommy told him, "Tonight, there's only room for two of us in this bed—and you're going to know who's fucking you."

It was a threat, a promise, all rolled together, enough to make him ache at the realness of it.

Tom had hit his breaking point. They all did, for different reasons. It only served to show Prophet, over and over, what he already knew. That he was meant to be alone, that he tended to drive people away for no real reason he could ever figure out, although now—*now*—he had a reason.

He thought about telling Tom that he wasn't competing against anyone, not really, but that wasn't entirely true. He did sink into the past when Tom fucked him, because it was easier than feeling. Tom—the intuitive bastard that he was—had noticed it several times, had always managed to pull him back for a little while.

Now, Tom wasn't going to let this go.

"Is fucking me going to help you make your decision about which partner to choose?" Prophet asked him, since he'd already pushed his luck and lost.

"Whose bed am I in?" Tom growled in response.

"Mine. For now."

"Keep pushing, Proph."

"What I do best, Tommy." He tried to gain the leverage to turn over, but Tom smiled, shook his head, and Prophet's stomach did a flip-flop. This was going to happen. Never thought he'd be in this position again, literally or otherwise, but he was tired of fighting.

Keep trying to convince yourself that this has nothing to do with Tommy. Pretend it's all about the past.

Tom was intent on stripping him, seemed a little surprised by his submission.

Join the club.

His side still ached. And Tom had weight on him. Prophet could get out from under him if his life depended on it, but it would take substantial effort. And pain, on both their parts.

Did his life depend on it? Something did . . . but he was mesmerized as Tom gently slid his hand under Prophet's wrist and straightened his arm. Took one hand, then the other, and made sure Prophet gripped one of the cold metal bars of the headboard with his fists.

"Don't let go," Tom ordered. "I'll use handcuffs if you don't think you can keep them there."

His entire body shuddered, and Tommy saw it and smiled again.

"Fuck," Prophet huffed, but he didn't move his hands. If anything, he grabbed on more tightly, like somehow that could help him as Tom reached out for the lube and condoms. "You like giving commands, T? Guess you could've made it in the military after all."

"Guess you get off on taking them," Tom countered. He lifted his body enough to stroke Prophet's cock, but kept his knees planted firmly on either side of him, holding him in place. Then he dipped his head to bite one of Prophet's nipples, and Prophet bit back a groan, but who the hell was he fooling?

He closed his eyes, but Tom bit again and again until he opened them and stared into the man's face. "Eyes open, Proph. Entire goddamned time. Got it?"

He swallowed. Hard. Like he had a brick in his throat. "Yeah, I'll play your game."

"This isn't a game. Sooner you figure that out, the better."

He wasn't giving Prophet the chance to get away. This time would be so different, the first time they'd been face-to-face, the first time Prophet realized who was on him, where he was . . . what exactly he was doing in this bed and why.

Tom covered him with his body, but if Prophet really wanted out, he could break away. Tom knew they weren't all that evenly matched for a fight, even though he was bigger, had training.

Prophet had been trained to kill in many different ways by several different organizations. For some reason, knowing he was at Prophet's mercy even though he was on top made Tom harder. He ground his pelvis to Prophet's, covered the man's mouth with his and kissed him until they could both barely breathe. His fingers pressed Prophet's hips hard. He wanted to bruise him, mark him. Make it so Prophet couldn't just *not* forget him, but would also *know* who he was really in goddamned bed with.

Prophet ripped his mouth away, and Tom bit him on the shoulder. Hard.

"Making memories?"

"I'm not just a memory," Tom told him, his voice far more steady than he felt. "You're going to get that tonight."

He eased off enough to grab both their cocks together in his hand. He did a slow catch and drag, pulling and stroking. "This scares the shit out of you."

Prophet didn't answer him.

"You're not going to stop me, are you, baby?" he murmured.

Prophet's eyes remained angry, but they were heavy-lidded too. There was no denying his arousal. He wasn't able to stop the moans from escaping his throat, no matter how hard he seemed to try. He bit his bottom lip like he was forcing himself to hold in an answer, and his hands were clutching the metal rungs so hard they looked like they hurt.

Tom didn't care—not now. He edged off Prophet's body, a forearm braced against the man's chest so he could ease Prophet's thigh up, leaving him access to his ass. He snapped the cap on the lube with one hand, squeezed some out, and pressed into Prophet with two fingers.

He twisted them slightly as he pushed, and Prophet ground out something about "Jesus Christ, Tommy," and Tom didn't wait before adding a third.

Tension bowed Prophet's entire body. He was sweating. But still staring at Tom, although his eyes were getting glassy now.

"You like that, Proph?" He slid his fingers in and out in a relentlessly erratic pattern that didn't give Prophet a chance at relief or control.

The jokes had stopped. Prophet's breaths came in harsh pants, unable to do anything but react as his body responded unmistakably beneath Tom's. Prophet's resistance had faded, but that wasn't the issue. Tom needed to make sure that Prophet stayed *with* him. "Say my name, dammit."

"Tom."

"Say my goddamned name."

Prophet moved his head from side to side. Then, brokenly, he ground out, "Please . . . Tommy . . . don't stop. Okay?"

"You're with me?"

"Yes."

"I like you obedient."

"Don't get used to it."

For a long moment, the two men stared at one another. He was pretty sure Prophet would buck him off, break the hold. But he didn't. Instead, he moved one hand off the metal rail and put it down near Tom's. Tom put his palm against Prophet's, and they wound their fingers together.

"I'm going to fuck you hard. Fast. Messy."

"Just how I like it," Prophet managed.

Tom positioned his cock against him, and with Prophet pushing, Tom ground into him, sheathing himself inside the tight, hot hole.

Prophet took his other hand off the metal rails, reached up and pressed it against Tom's throat. "Fuck me now."

"You want to fight me, Proph?" he asked breathlessly.

"Isn't that what we're doing already?"

Maybe. But it was so goddamned right. His free hand grabbed Prophet's hair in a fist and held him in place, while Prophet continued to hold Tom's throat, his Adam's apple pressing into the hollow of Prophet's palm as Tom pounded into him. Prophet bit out a howl, hooked his ankles behind Tom's back and dug his heels against the man's ass, forcing him deeper inside. Their groans rose above the sound of thighs slapping as Tom leaned against Prophet's hold, Prophet's palm taking the weight of his upper body.

Prophet's neck corded with tension, and he never took his eyes from Tom's face, not even when he broke apart and came so hard it was like he was shattering.

"Tommy . . ." A breath, a whisper even, as Tom came on the heels of Prophet's climax like a scream in the night, hot and fast like an electric jolt that stunned him senseless. Prophet's hand broke its hold, curled around Tom's neck, pulling him down so their faces were close, his body shuddering as Tom's hips jerked erratically.

His last thought was that their hands were still clasped tight together.

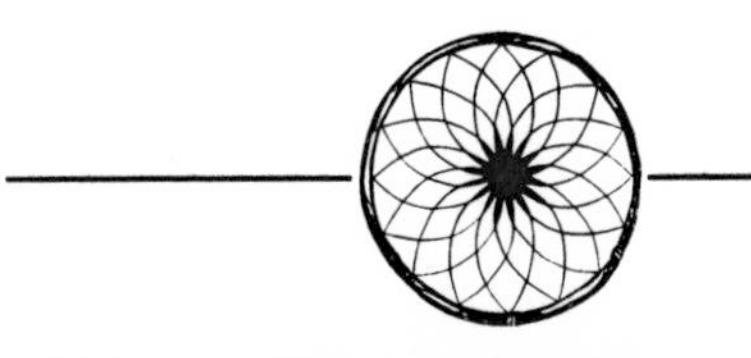

CHAPTER TWENTY-THREE

The heat came in waves. The air conditioning didn't work for shit, and you couldn't open the windows, so you were trapped in a fucking moving box, holding your breath until you passed the checkpoints.

Nothing was safe until the Land Rover pulled into the military base. For now, John drove them down the bleak desert road in a truck with bad shocks and worse brakes, the rest of their SEAL team trailing behind in a similar truck at a safe enough distance.

The rest of their team wasn't supposed to be following them. Backup wasn't provided, allowed, or necessary on this op, Prophet and John had been told. So Prophet, as he often did, listened, agreed, and then did exactly whatever the fuck he wanted to anyway.

He glanced down at his watch and he noted the time: 1652.

In one more minute, his entire life would change forever. A week and a day ago, he'd never even heard of Hal, and now, Hal was the reason why two armored trucks came barreling at them, the bullets hitting the front of their Rover, going through the grille and killing the engine. Prophet glanced behind him, saw the gas pouring out of their backup's truck and realized they'd been trapped from both directions.

He shouted for John to duck, pulled Hal down as glass shattered. And that pure, unmitigated instinct was maybe the most ridiculous thing he'd ever done. Even Hal knew it, stared at him, obviously wondering why Prophet had just saved his goddamned life.

John turned to him. "This isn't real, Proph."

You know that. Let this go.

But the movie kept playing out in front of him, no matter how badly he wanted to turn it off. This was the worst of it, and he'd known it would happen, should've prepared for it.

He could barely breathe, sure that at any second, he'd hyperventilate.

Buck up, Drews.

But panic was setting in inside the Land Rover, too. John had his semiautomatic and he was firing back out the window, trying to turn their truck over, from instinct more than anything, because the goddamned thing was dead.

Prophet looked out through the broken window using his rifle's scope. The enemy's trucks had paused about thirty feet away after the initial shooting, but now were once again rapidly approaching. Confident that the Land Rover wasn't going anywhere.

John was shooting to hold them off, trying to start the car but the engine was blown. A flame shot up and it was obvious they'd have to abandon the vehicle,

Hal was staring hard at John, who wasn't a casual ghost anymore. Then, "No one's supposed to know about this," Hal said to Prophet urgently. "No one's supposed to know where I am. There are decoys!"

There were. But obviously, they hadn't been enough. Prophet held his weapon pointed in front of him at the rapidly approaching enemy.

He was shaking. Sweating.

Because it was all happening in his fucking bedroom and he couldn't stop it at all, any more than he'd been able to then.

He refused to turn his head, didn't want to see the face of the man he was going to kill.

"Don't fucking do it, Proph!" John yelled, the anger and confusion in his voice unmistakable, and underneath it all was the fear.

And that was a worse enemy than any man coming toward them.

They were close.

No place to run.

"We're going to fight our way out of this," John yelled again.

Yes, they'd try.

At the last minute, Hal actually tried to wrestle his gun away from him. Grabbed his wrist, and for a second, Prophet considered not going through with it . . .

Until he turned and saw Hal staring at the men coming at them. John was watching the men too, then turned and looked at Hal. And then Prophet shot Hal twice in the head.

He would wear the man's blood for the entirety of his captivity.

"This isn't real, Proph," John told him now. He was standing on the opposite side of the bed from Prophet, looking down on a sleeping Tom as the desert faded away.

Prophet buried his head in his hands until he felt the cool sheets against his damp skin, until the softness brought him fully back into his bedroom.

Thank Christ Tom slept like a fucking log after sex, or else he'd see Prophet kneeling on the floor by the side of the bed, holding an invisible rifle, looking through a nonexistent scope at a target from the past.

He wasn't sure how long he'd been in that position, wasn't sure if a noise from outside had triggered him. But after twenty minutes of John telling him it wasn't real, after twenty minutes of reasoning to himself that *This isn't fucking real, dammit, so get up off your knees*, Prophet finally cleared his head enough to drag himself to the bathroom.

He could still smell the blood. And he ached in the places he'd been beaten during captivity, the way he always did after an episode like this. Blurred the line between real and imaginary. It would be fascinating to a shrink, because it was to Prophet, but would be more so if it wasn't actually happening to him.

He'd stopped sleeping for more than short naps because the dreams were worse since they'd partnered up. He'd been so desperate one night, he'd taken sleeping pills Doc had supplied. But those had simply locked him in a prison of his own making, paralyzing him. Suspended between flashback and the present, he'd relived what had happened long before the CIA caught up to him and made that goddamned videotape. Thinking about that always made his wrists ache with sympathy pains.

Prophet shouldn't have been surprised about the flashback, should've seen it coming after that kind of sex. He'd thought it more than worth it at the time, but now, with his cheek pressed to the bathroom tile, he wasn't so goddamned sure.

Then again, he'd been yanked into the past again after Tom had fought. Talk about a mindfuck.

And there were very few people he knew who were good—*that good*—at mindfucks.

One of them was dead for sure—Prophet had been covered in his blood for weeks. The other . . .

Prophet's blood ran cold as he thought about that evening Azar and his men had thrown the knockout gas into the Land Rover. He and John had killed at least ten of Azar's men when suddenly they'd been scrambling for the goddamned gas masks they always brought but never used.

When Prophet had woken, he'd been hanging by his wrists, Hal's body beneath him. Azar saying, "Tell me what you know about the man you killed or your teammate dies."

John's voice, yelling, "Don't you dare tell him shit."

A week and a day earlier, you didn't know Hal existed.

He jumped up and nearly fell. Grappled his way to his desk downstairs and paged through the datebook until he verified what he'd goddamned missed.

Meeting Hal. Ten years later, to the day, Chris was killed.

Sometimes a coincidence wasn't just a coincidence.

"I can't go back there," he said out loud. Thought about calling Mick, telling him he had to come in and deal with this. And Mick would, no questions asked. Mick owed him.

But he wouldn't do that. Because this was his battle, his war, and it had been since he'd shot Hal.

He'd been beaten and shocked so badly, most days he'd known that dying would be so much easier. *Too stubborn to die*, the man doing the torturing had told him every single day. Prophet hated that he'd been right, hated that the panic attack loomed over him now, threatening to sink its claws into him.

He curled his body up against the tiled wall of the bathroom, letting the cold keep him from fading away. Forced himself to breathe, to stay present and all that other new age crap he'd been forced to read about, thanks to Doc and his obsession with how the body needed the mind to heal first. Or something like that. He'd never paid close attention to any of it.

And maybe you should've, dumbass.

After the CIA released him, he went AWOL for two years. It had taken the better part of that to get over the panic attacks and the fear of small spaces, time spent traveling alone and relentlessly exposing himself to the very things that would terrify him. But he'd had no choice, because he'd needed to look for John. Because he'd asked to see his friend's body time and time again and was told no body had been recovered.

Not John's. Not Hal's.

Because, during his capture, the biggest mindfuck of all was Azar taunting him that John might be dead . . . but he also might be alive. Roaming the Middle East or Europe or who the hell knew where, alone, maybe drugged or suffering from amnesia.

By refusing to tell him if John was dead or alive, Azar had assumed Prophet wouldn't kill him, would need to keep him alive. Prophet rarely did what was expected of him. Killing Azar wouldn't have made John any more dead or alive than he already was.

He got up off the floor, grabbed some clothes and yanked them on as he walked to the computer and typed to Cillian, *Going on a job.*

Need some help?

Didn't realize you were for hire.

I'm not. But I wouldn't mind you owing me a favor.

Prophet considered this for a long moment, cursor blinking. Then he typed carefully, *Do you ever feel like you'll never shake your past?*

Past isn't meant to be shaken. It's meant to be dealt with and learned from.

"Aren't we philosophical," he grumbled. And that's when he saw that the phone he used for Gary and Gary alone was blinking red.

A voice mail message. And Gary never left him messages. He listened to Gary telling him, "Please come get me." He'd also texted Prophet the emergency code a minute after he'd left the voice mail, then another text with what must be his position.

Both messages had come in an hour ago. Maybe Prophet *had* heard the goddamned ring and that had triggered everything. But that didn't change the fact that he was an hour behind.

He sat for another few minutes, staring at the phone in his hand, replaying Gary's message in his mind.

He should refuse to go. There was nothing he could do for Gary but get them both killed. Because it felt like a trap, and even if it wasn't . . .

Was Gary a threat to national security?

That thought gnawed at him.

And what are your options?

Because he'd made a promise to Hal about his only son. But he'd never thought he'd actually have to follow through until he'd gotten Gary's message.

He blinked. Blinked again. Saw a flash of dark pass across his vision and fought the panic. He kept his eyes closed for a long time, seeking clarity in the dark.

When he finally opened them again, the darkness had lifted.

If you go now . . .

Better to burn out than to fade away.

Phil would kill him for thinking like that. Fuck, he'd hate himself if it were the only reason he was planning on walking into a trap.

But it wasn't. There was a promise involved. And the fact that he couldn't tell anyone else just made what he needed to do that much harder.

It was time to deal with this albatross from his past, and he was checking out before Phil could tell him no, and especially before Doc could cast his arms again.

As a concession, he wrapped them both tightly with splints and ACE bandages, which were much more forgiving and allowed better use of his hands.

Before he went to pack, he typed, *How long can someone survive as a prisoner?*

As long as they want to live, Cillian answered.

Prophet considered the truth in that. *How long would someone hold a prisoner for?*

Depends on his value. What his intel is. What he can do for the other team.

The guy I'm talking about would never turn.

Anyone can turn—don't bullshit me. A pause and then, *You're talking about someone specific.*

Yeah. He wouldn't go this long without getting in touch. I've been looking.

You're sure?

He didn't realize he'd paused until it was too late.

What can I do, Prophet?

His fingers paused about the keys. And then before he could stop himself, he typed in John's dog tag serial numbers and hit send.

Cillian responded, *I'll do what I can. Are you in trouble?*

Instead of answering Cillian's question, he just typed, *I'll be gone awhile*, and shut the computer before the guy could say anything else.

"Can you live through that torture again, or is this suicide by terrorist?" John asked.

Was hallucinating one of the signs that the disease was progressing? And did it matter when, fuck it all, the ghost might just be right? But Prophet owed Chris.

And what about you?

"What about me?" he asked aloud. He took all three of his phones, tucked them into various pockets of his cargoes, and went to make sure Tom left him the hell alone for this one.

Tom woke to Prophet packing.

"What's up?"

"Got called in," Prophet said, and the man was lying. And since he was usually good at it, this had to be a big goddamned lie for Tom to see it as clearly as a neon light in the dark. "You can hang out if you want."

Tom got out of bed and stood between Prophet and his gear. "What I want is to know what's really going on. Let me in, Proph."

"Like you did with me?"

Tom glared at him, hating him for his calm, cool, and collected bullshit. He wanted Prophet wild. Feral. Even angry. "I let you in."

"No, you didn't. Not really. You just think you did. You told me just enough to stop me from asking more questions."

"I know why you're doing this," Tom said quietly, and something inside Prophet stilled.

"Right. The voodoo."

"I knew it would happen before I fucked you like that, Proph. This is blowback from that. Don't . . . not after . . ."

"What? All the progress we've made?" Prophet gave him an easy smile. "I told you before, that's all just fucking. It's got nothing to do with our jobs. That's my livelihood."

Prophet hadn't been the only vulnerable one last night, and the anger Tom'd managed to quell and redirect then was now front and center. "I don't know what more I can do . . . I don't know what the fuck you want from me, Prophet."

"Nothing."

Tom felt that word like a physical slap, snarled, "You're too smart to lie to yourself like this."

"And you're too smart not to know when to back the fuck off."

"Which is exactly why I won't."

Prophet stilled, his eyes went cold, and his voice was steady and harsh when he spoke. "I can't afford any liability on this one."

That cut Tom, deeper than he'd thought it would, deeper than it should. It meant that all of Prophet's cheerleading about what a good job Tom had been doing was bullshit.

"You want *nothing*? Then that's what you'll get." Tom yanked his jeans on, grabbed his shirt and shoes and was down the stairs and out the door in under a minute. He put his shoes on outside, shoved his shirt on angrily. Tried his best not to look behind him because he knew Prophet wouldn't follow him.

The man was possibly more stubborn than he was. And that was saying something.

He got onto his bike, slammed his hands on the handlebars, then blew out a frustrated breath.

What did you think, that things would all be smoothed over? That Prophet would treat you like a real partner?

He revved his bike, the familiar pop-pop sounding too close to the machine gun fire he'd gotten intimate with in Somalia, and Prophet's words crashed through him. *"Maybe they were just trying to warn you that partnering with me was a bad idea."*

"Since when did you want a partner anyway?" he asked Prophet's echo and took off.

He was several blocks away, idling at a light, when he shoved his shirtsleeves up and caught sight of the leather bracelet. And that's when he realized he'd been played.

". . . we can't go back out because I can't protect you."

"I already almost got you killed."

Prophet was just as much of a liability to Tom as Tom was to him. And that wasn't an accusation, but rather an inescapable fact.

His gut screamed at him to go back, which he did, swerving into an illegal U-turn in the middle of oncoming traffic, but it was too late. Prophet's truck was gone from the alleyway his building used for its driveway.

He grabbed for his phone, thankful the back-up tracker he'd planted in Prophet's had gone unnoticed.

What the hell are you doing? He's not your problem.

But something was wrong. Really wrong.

And you promised Prophet you'd follow your instincts.

And why the hell should he make promises to that asshole? Ever?

He stood in the street like a lovesick idiot, worrying. The unease turned quickly to an overwhelming panic as he watched the tracker for ten minutes. He was on the parkway, headed south.

And then the tracker cut off.

"Dammit."

The only thing that could take that tracker out was human tampering. Seemed Prophet didn't trust him after all.

He called the phone, and of course, it went straight to voice mail. "Prophet, it's me. Tell me where the fuck you're going."

Three hours and much cursing, pacing, and riding around aimlessly later, Prophet texted him an address. He stared at it for a long moment before getting into his car and setting the GPS.

Something was very wrong. The only thing he knew for sure was that Prophet was at that address. He was also pretty certain that Prophet hadn't been the one to send the message.

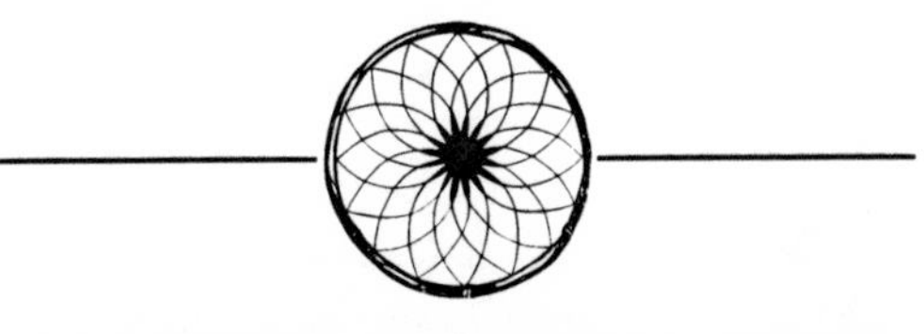

CHAPTER TWENTY-FOUR

The coordinates Prophet had been texted put Gary twenty-five miles from the last place he'd moved, post-college. After the death of Gary's mother, it had been more challenging to keep track of him. But with Prophet's encouragement, Gary had been dutiful about checking in—albeit grudgingly so. Prophet made it simple—a weekly text utilizing a simple code. If the code didn't change weekly or the amount of numbers varied by one, Prophet would know Gary was in trouble.

They'd never talked about what Gary's father had actually done for a living. But as far as Prophet knew, Gary's mother had told him everything. The kid was brilliant, would've had a future with an agency, if not for the fact that there was a target on his back because of what he may or may not have known about his father's work. And if not for the fact that no agency would ever trust him, a fact Hal drilled home to Prophet when he made him promise to keep Gary safe no matter what. And Prophet couldn't argue with Hal on that one, because Hal had lived it for years—being needed and yet considered dangerous enough to terminate was a burden Prophet couldn't imagine bearing for long.

"You have to make sure he's hidden. At all costs. No matter how much he hates you for it," Hal had emphasized. "And he will hate you. That's how you'll know you're doing the right thing."

There was so much more to that promise, though. He didn't know how a father could make those decisions for a son, but he hoped he'd never have to find out.

The abandoned warehouse was in the middle of goddamned nowhere. There were woods to one side, a giant open field to the other that went on for miles. There were no cars parked around the area, but hell, they knew he was coming, so he pulled up about ten feet from the building and went toward it, scanning for danger in the form of snipers or bombs. He could practically be a ghost if he needed to, but this time, he knew someone was waiting for him. The longer he'd driven, the more sure he'd become that this was all a trap, but there was no turning back.

No ransom. No demands for anything. Just Gary, asking him to come get him and using the emergency code for the first time in ten years, all on the heels of Chris's death.

The door to the back of the abandoned building was unlocked. He moved inside cautiously. The place was like a maze of tunnels and he didn't know where any of them led.

He went inside already braced for the worst. He remained still in the middle of a darkened room, unable to see but sensing everything.

This is what it'll be like. Can you handle it?

If he got out of this alive, he supposed he could handle anything.

Then a sound blared. He put his arms up over his ears in a futile attempt to soften the blow of the racket and sank to his knees. After a minute, it went away, but his ears rang—almost like a flashbang grenade, which temporarily deafened anyone in range. It also caused temporary blindness, so Prophet figured he should be grateful for small miracles.

Speaking of which, a screen on the wall in front of him flashed. Prophet blinked rapidly, put a hand up to his eyes to help him adjust to the sudden barrage of light. He recognized Azar's brother Sadiq immediately; he'd been tracking him for years. Sadiq's suit-and-tie refinement was a far cry from Azar's love of BDUs and heavy beards.

The whole mission had been a setup. One big mindfuck trip down memory lane, and Prophet had fallen for it, jumped in with both feet into a pit of melancholy and sentimentality that had left him circling the fucking drain.

"How'd you find him?" Prophet asked.

Sadiq's expression was unreadable, as always. "That's what your concern is? That you *screwed up*, as you'd say."

Prophet gritted his teeth and nodded, tried to stop his eyes from watering against the painful lights. "Yes."

"You didn't. Gary found us."

His worst fear, confirmed, because Gary had always been the wild card in this situation. And yet, he couldn't bring himself to believe that was true. "And what did you tell him?"

Sadiq smiled. In all the years he'd hunted the bastard from afar, Prophet had never seen him smile, had never seen him captured in a picture looking anything except stoic. It made his next word especially chilling. "Everything."

Tom drove like a maniac, made a three-hour drive in two, nearly killing himself several times in the process. He'd thought about calling Phil, even Cope, but decided against it.

This was between partners. And he owed Prophet, even if he wanted to kill him.

He'd overestimated everything except his want and his willingness to help his partner. This was life or death. This was the mission. He could feel it.

He could also feel the gun at the back of his head as he moved through the parking lot, weapon drawn. He stopped dead in his tracks and waited, knew he could grab it easily, but he didn't know how many others there were.

"Glad you could join us."

"I'm thrilled," Tom said through clenched teeth.

"Put the safety on your weapon and slowly bend down and put it on the ground. Kick it away from you, please. Any tricks you pull will be taken out on your partner," the man said.

Tom wanted a look at his face, wanted to know how all of this connected to Christopher, but he wasn't in the position to be asking questions. Yet. He did what the guy asked.

"Any other weapons?"

"Yes."

"Where?"

Tom listed the places he was carrying, and another man came forward and stripped him of every last weapon, patting him down more thoroughly than the TSA agent at the airport. By that point, he was inside the old warehouse, with who knew how many floors.

There was heat and electricity, which meant it wasn't abandoned. They led him into a large, empty room with concrete walls and dirty floors, bound with his hands above his head, his ankles chained to the ground. His weaponry created a little pile in front of him.

The dark haired man dressed in all black BDUs looked at him impassively. "Impressive, Mr. Boudreaux."

"Please, call me Tom. And you are . . .?"

"And you're as much of a wiseass as your partner is," Black BDUs said, and he wasn't happy about it.

Tom's shirt hung open, but at least his pants were pulled back up. "Where's my partner?" he asked, and was rewarded with a punch to the face.

"Shut up," the man hissed. "We're making sure your partner's having a lot of fun. Now it's time for you to have some fun of your own."

As soon as the screen went black, so had Prophet. When he woke, he felt woozy and sick from the knockout gas they must have used. He was also half-hanging by his wrists, which were handcuffed around an overhead pipe. As a concession, his feet were on a flat chair, but it was replaced as soon as he opened his eyes by a stool that barely kept him upright. He had to balance on his toes in order not to break his wrists. Again.

Nice to know they hadn't expected him to balance in his sleep.

The screen flashed again, hurting his eyes, and Sadiq was framed in the center, the background a painted wall with a picture Prophet recognized from the man's house in Khartoum. "Did you have a nice sleep?"

"Fuck off, Sadiq."

"Still the same."

"So are you," Prophet bit out. While he had been hunting Sadiq, Sadiq had spent those same ten years haunting him . . . taunting him, giving him just enough of a lead on the possibility of John's whereabouts and then pulling back.

He supposed he'd get some answers now. "Just tell me, Sadiq—why Chris? The rest of us were involved in this, we signed up for it. We fucking knew what we were in for—Azar included. But Chris was innocent. I'd pegged you for better than that."

Sadiq shrugged. "He wouldn't play his part. Would've been so easy. All he had to do was call you to come rescue him. He refused. I gave him an option—told him he could fight my men. I told him that if he won, I'd let him go."

Prophet's chest tightened with guilt. Even after all that time, even if it meant risking his life, Chris had been loyal to his brother's best friend. "And you drugged him."

"After a while. It got boring watching him win."

"You were the one calling him . . . before you took him."

"Yes. I told him I had some very interesting information on his brother and the circumstances surrounding his capture. From what I understand, your military refuses to release that information to the family. But Christopher said that he didn't need to know any of that. Since he wouldn't come to us, we had to resort to other measures."

I told him that, if he won, I'd let him go.

Chris, beaten to death and too drugged to do anything about it. And Prophet had no doubt he'd been smart enough to know that, once he'd realized he'd been drugged, he was probably fighting his final fight.

Goddammit. He closed his eyes for a second, the pain of the guilt overriding any physical pain.

"I also mentioned to Chris that you refused to give my brother information that would've kept John from being hurt." Sadiq paused and then said, "Of course, I had to share the fact that no one had ever seen his brother's body, and that you knew that as well."

Jesus Christ. "You motherfucker. Knew you wouldn't win a fair fight."

"I don't like fair. I like to win. So does your partner, Tom."

Mindfuck alert. Prophet wouldn't go there, asked instead, "Where's Gary?"

"He's busy."

"If you hurt him . . ."

"I thought you were smarter than that, Petty Officer Drews."

"Let's pretend I'm not."

"But you are. The Navy doesn't recruit men into such a rigorous role unless they are exceptional. And exceptional men are given special jobs. You were picked—handpicked—because of your leadership qualities, your uncanny ability to assess, analyze, and take necessary action without losing sight of the objective." Sadiq ticked off phrases that Prophet knew were in his original military file, which was supposed to be buried deep.

This was like the most fucked-up version of *This is Your Life* ever.

"But do you wonder why you were given such an important role so early in your career? Why did they trust *you* with Hal Jones's life—or death?"

"Do you?" Prophet bit out.

"It's because they felt you were able to carry out the job efficiently, without emotional attachment. Another way of saying that your conscience was, perhaps, faulty?"

Prophet stared at him, refusing to let his expression change, even as a ball formed in the pit of his stomach.

"But you and I both know that only a man with more compassion and empathy than most could actually do a job like that." Sadiq nodded, obviously pleased with himself, the bastard. "I counted on that empathy to bring you to my door."

"I wasn't being empathetic when I broke your brother's neck," Prophet told him, saw the men in his periphery rush to him and braced himself for the blows.

"No!" Sadiq said, and the men backed off. "We are not done talking." He tilted his head and stared at Prophet. "You remind me of him. Of Azar. Hotheaded. Angry. Willing to take on the world."

"I'm nothing like that asshole."

Sadiq's eyes burned with a dark anger, but his voice was calm when he said, "Every action has a consequence. You'll have to live with the consequences of taking my brother from me. Now, I get to continue to take things from you. Gary was more than happy to share his father's intel with us. I knew it would take years, but fortunately, I'm patient. Especially when it comes to avenging the people I love."

"Me too. Especially when I have help."

Sadiq's expression changed slightly. It was almost imperceptible, but there was a falter there, because he knew Prophet's reputation well enough to believe it could be true.

I might be hanging, but I can still fucking con the shit out of you. One of Joe Drews's favorite sayings.

Prophet hadn't actively thought about the old man in years. But he supposed the guy was always there, the way Prophet preferred to remember him, the young soldier slash con artist who'd left when Prophet was ten and who'd lost his sight and killed himself six years later. He'd heard that through the grapevine of cons who knew and worked with him, who'd check in on Prophet and his mom from time to time.

Conning was what had helped Prophet stay alive until he could make an honest living. And conning had often helped keep him alive during that honest living thing.

But now, *What would Joe Drews do?* seemed like a saying on a banner in front of him. Because it might be the only way out. "If you kill me, Gary can't get the nuke off the ground."

But Sadiq wasn't looking directly at him any longer. Rather, he was looking past Prophet, who couldn't turn around without major pain. He waited patiently to see what kind of torture was coming next.

When Tom was dragged in and dropped in front of him, bound, gagged, and staring up at him from the foot of his stool, Prophet flinched.

Dammit.

He schooled his expression quickly, but both Sadiq and the man who'd brought Tom in caught it. They both smiled at Prophet.

Prophet did *not* like it when Sadiq smiled.

"Did he sign up for this?" Sadiq asked, pointing to Tom. "I can safely say that Gary did."

Prophet closed his eyes and thought about a phone call he'd had with Gary, maybe five years ago when he was just entering his senior year of college, right before his mom died.

"I want normal."

"You have a mom. A roof over your head. You're getting a good education," Prophet had shot back. "You should've been able to see that shit by now."

"You're telling me to grow up?"

"Hal told you the same thing."

"Because you knew him so well."

"Yeah, I knew him well." One week, twenty-four seven. Prophet had been Hal's confessor. It was like he'd known he wouldn't survive the trip, and no matter how Prophet had tried to tell him that it was bad luck, Hal wouldn't shut up.

"You want to turn back?" John had asked in the early afternoon hours, before they'd set out to drive Hal to his next location, the day it all ended.

"I want to. But it's already been put into motion. Turning back's not going to change shit."

He believed that one hundred percent, then and now. He hadn't been wrong—and that's probably what was the hardest to accept.

When wheels are set into motion, there's no way to shut the machine down without causing major blowback. It just makes things worse.

And when he'd killed Hal, all of the man's burdens had fallen on Prophet's shoulders. And Hal had known that would happen.

A part of Prophet—a not so small part—hated Hal for that.

Now, he looked at the image of Sadiq on the screen in front of him. "You killed Chris on the anniversary of my meeting Hal. How fucking sentimental of you."

Sadiq smiled. "Very. And that's why you'll receive the same torture you received under Azar. Why your friend will receive the same punishment as John did. You Americans are very into symbolism, yes. I find it . . . fun."

"You're going to take Tom and not let me know if he's dead or alive?" Prophet challenged him, and that fucking bastard smiled, because yes, that was exactly his fucking plan.

Fuck. *Fuck.* He hung his head, more pissed at himself than at Sadiq for winning that round. Pissed at himself for panicking and revealing his worst goddamned nightmare.

God, if Tommy was taken and Prophet didn't know where he was . . .

He stared down at Tom, who'd been watching him the whole time, and willed him to not let himself get taken. To somehow beat the shit out of anyone and everyone who came near him. Most of all, he willed Tom to believe that Prophet could—would—save him, no matter the cost.

And Tom . . . he fucking nodded. Imperceptible to most, but not to Prophet.

Sadiq shut off the video feed, and the guard dragged Tommy away.

After that, the torture began. He kept track of the hours by counting minutes, even when they all began to blend. It was the only way to keep himself from blanking out or blacking out. He did the latter several times anyway, despite his best efforts. He figured he lost about five hours tops, which still put him under forty-eight hours since being captured, and he was still in the States. Wasn't sure why, but that would change sooner than later.

He'd been training his other senses since he joined the military—it had saved his ass numerous times, but also made things far more torturous for him during times like this. He kept his eyes closed purposely, had no doubt they hit him harder and more often because of that.

He counted. Hummed. Sang. Laughed when they wanted him to scream. Tried to drive them crazy, because that would give him something to do besides focus on the pain.

Tom couldn't get the image of Prophet hanging by handcuffed wrists out of his head. They knew the man's weakness, an Achilles heel he'd actually given himself. And he'd heard everything, first strung up against the wall, listening to Prophet's words through a speaker, then the rest when they'd dragged him in front of Prophet.

Now he was in a cell-like room. One steel door with no lock on the inside. Bolted from outside. Windowless. Alarmed. A big screen on the wall, like the one in the cell where Prophet was being held.

The screen remained dark, but they'd made sure to turn on the sound, so Tom *still* heard everything.

Tom knew it was important to pretend he didn't give a shit about what was happening with Prophet—if Sadiq didn't think they were close, it would be harder to pit them against each other. But Tom had seen the look on Proph's face when they'd brought him in, and if he'd seen it . . .

Fuck. And he understood, because it was next to impossible to remain expressionless while hearing the heavy rain of punches on a body. Once in a while, he heard an involuntary grunt from Prophet, but for the most part he was eerily silent when they were actually hitting him. When they stopped, that's when Prophet would begin to mumble, sing, and hum. Which seemed to make the men hit him harder the next time. He could imagine the look on Prophet's face, and that made him continue his attempts to free himself from the heavy ropes around his wrists.

Suddenly, the screen hanging above him flickered to life, and he was looking at a dark-haired man he'd never seen before, but he recognized the voice immediately. He'd been the one talking with Prophet. The one Prophet called Sadiq.

"Let's talk, Mr. Boudreaux," Sadiq said.

"Sure. How about, fuck you?"

"I see you're learning from Petty Officer Drews. That never seems to work out for his friends."

Sadiq had to be referring to John. "This time, it's not going to work out well for you."

"I like your confidence. It will be short lived." The man paused. "How well do you really know Petty Officer Drews? Enough to die for him?"

Tom stared at the man. "Enough to kill you for him."

The man shook his head sadly, like that was the wrong answer. As the screen went dark, the door in front of him clanked open. He watched two guards drag Prophet in. He was shirtless, his wrists were tied together behind his back, his head was down, and it took everything Tom had to pretend he didn't give a shit.

The guards threw him to the ground with enough force that he rolled over twice before hitting Tom's body.

Prophet ended up on his chest. He raised his head, and Tom got a look at his beaten face. His left cheekbone was swollen, his eyes black, but his face hadn't taken the brunt of this beating.

"Your friend," one of the guards said to Tom. Tom spit in Prophet's direction and aimed the next at the guard, who scowled. He took a step toward Tom, but the other man grabbed him.

"No touching the merchandise. Only Sadiq can do that," he reminded him.

Tom smiled and spit again, and then the two men left the cell with the clang of the door.

Tom had little doubt that this meeting was orchestrated to make it tougher on Prophet. As if that were possible.

Prophet blinked, rolled on his side so his back was to the camera next to the screen. "I'm seeing several of you right now."

"Better than not seeing me at all."

For some reason, that made Prophet laugh slightly. "You have no goddamned idea."

Tom didn't ask what he meant, figured he should be grateful that Prophet was semi-coherent.

"You've got to make a break for it," Prophet mumbled, his face turned toward Tom so the cameras couldn't see it, the words barely audible.

"Both."

"Not happening."

"Fight?"

"Can't shoot me. He wants me alive."

Tom stared at the floor, spoke without moving his lips. "Guy on screen—killed John?"

"Sadiq's the brother of the guy who tortured me and John." He paused. "The video you saw wasn't made by him. That was the aftermath. The CIA."

Tom stared straight ahead, schooling his features. Anyone watching would think he and Prophet hated one another, and that was the way he wanted this to go. Prophet spoke so quietly, Tom doubted audio would pick it up.

"They're going to keep torturing me, for old time's sake."

Tom wanted to touch Prophet, hold his damned hand at the very least, but showing any weakness or affection to their captors would make things worse for both of them. And things were pretty bad already. "Why?"

Prophet shook his head, and Tom's anger rose that, even now, he wouldn't tell Tom why he was risking everything.

"My shit, not yours."

"A little late for that now."

Prophet just stared at Tom. Was he accepting his fate, surrendering to the inevitable . . . or was there something else going on that Tom was missing?

"Why not just kill you?"

"He will, eventually. But this . . . this is a taunt. He won't have to look for me anymore. He knows I'll spend however long it takes hunting him down. He knows I'll find him, so I can find you. Just like I hunted for John."

"Fuck me," Tom muttered.

"Just get the fuck out. Any way you can," Prophet told him as the door opened and the guards came back. They tossed freezing cold water on both men, even as Tom lurched to his feet to fight.

"Don't, Tommy," he heard Prophet say as one of the men dragged him off.

But he'd already seen red and Prophet had to know it was a matter of time before his temper flared, hot and uncontrollable. And the only thing that mattered was getting the hell out of here and taking Prophet with him.

Minutes later, the black BDUs guy and another man came in with cuffs and chains, and he heard one of them say, "Get the plane ready."

They're moving us. And he thought about what was always taught, from basic self-defense classes to the FBI's training camp: if you let yourself be moved to a second location, you're as good as dead.

Whether they planned on taking both him and Prophet, he didn't have a goddamned clue.

He was in pain, but he had learned long ago to ignore that, push it down so he could function and continue saving himself. This was no different than what he'd survived as a kid.

He charged the men head-on, prepared to fight to stay alive.

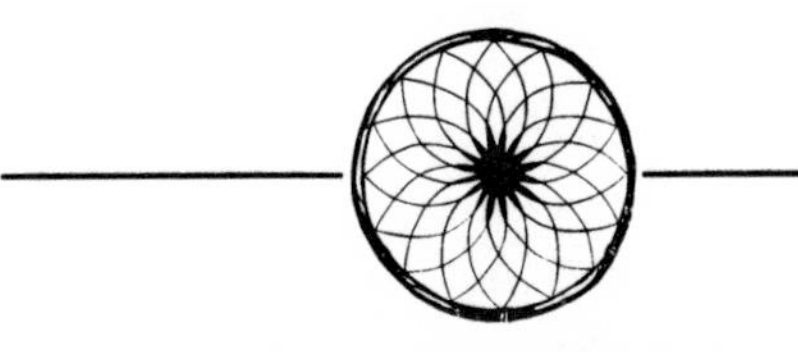

CHAPTER TWENTY-FIVE

"Gary, are you okay?" Prophet asked as Gary was escorted into the room. Although he hadn't seen Gary since just after his sixteenth birthday, he'd have been able to pick him out of a lineup. The resemblance to Hal was everywhere, from his dark eyes and curly, dark hair to the set of his shoulders, the slight build, and the smile that pulled too much to the left. Gary paled when he saw Prophet suspended from another set of piping by his wrists, balancing on his toes on a too-short stool. He opened his mouth and took a step forward before being pulled back by one of the guards.

The look on Gary's face—regret and fear, pride and anger—was all it took for Prophet to know that Sadiq had told the truth about Gary betraying him—and his country. Prophet knew that whatever promises he'd kept until now would ultimately turn darker before it was all said and done.

"Don't say anything," he warned Gary.

"You still think you make the rules," Gary said furiously. He moved toward Prophet, and this time, the guards didn't stop him. They all knew any pretense was gone. "You don't have any control anymore."

"Control's in the mind as much as the body, Gary. I'm more in control tied up than you are standing there free. And you are free, aren't you?" He kept his voice quiet, tone measured. It was the way he'd always spoken to Gary.

"My son's skittish," Hal had explained to him in the tent that afternoon before the capture. "Brilliant. Easily swayed. Kindness goes a long way with him." Hal's words about his son as they'd driven down that dusty road. As the miles unfolded, he'd laid out his life's story as if he'd known his time was ending. He'd needed a witness, had used Prophet like a priest for his confession.

It had been the least Prophet could do. Now he was forced to face another obligation that had come out of his conversations with Hal. "Gary—"

"Is not my real name," the younger man shouted. He seemed surprised when his voice boomed around them in a mournful echo.

"Your name's not the most important thing here."

"You're right. It's my knowledge. And I'm finally able to put it to good use."

"You can't."

"Can't?" Gary's laugh was bitter. "After all this time, you're still not ready to admit that the United States government killed my father because it refused to rescue him. That whole 'we don't negotiate with terrorist thing' sounds great, until it's your father who's in danger."

Gary paced in a circle, looking a little bit like that gangly teenager he'd hidden away. The anger had no doubt been building inside of him all this time, festering, until he'd done what Prophet supposed was inevitable.

"The government takes a hard line with terrorists for a reason, Gary."

"Well, fuck them and fuck you. I hold you and them responsible for the slow, painful death of my mother too. And it took away any chance I had at the life I wanted. Or should I say, it almost took away that chance. I had an opportunity to seize it back, so I took it."

"I can't let that happen."

"What are you going to do? Kill me like you did my father?" Gary bit out.

Prophet stared at him, then exhaled, like the whole story being out in the open freed something in him.

"Yeah, I know," Gary told him. "I finally know the whole truth."

"If you're working with Sadiq, you don't know shit." Prophet paused. "You're going to have to work with him, Gary. Against the United States."

"He said I could leave after I talked to you," Gary said, trying to be smug, but a glimmer of doubt shone through. It got stronger as the guards circled him. "I'm done talking," he told them, apparently trying to take back his tenuous control. "I want to go."

One of the men smiled. Nodded. Another grabbed Gary's arms and hoisted them up behind him.

Gary began to struggle in earnest, apparently realizing the finality—the stupidity—of his lifelong temper tantrum. "I can't do this."

"But you already have."

"You can't make me build you the triggers!" Gary yelled, but Sadiq's quiet laugh across the computer speakers, across the ocean, rolled over them like an eerie fog.

Gary stilled when Sadiq said, "There are so many ways that I can and will make you do just that. You have no idea, Gary. But you will."

"Let him go," Prophet said through gritted teeth. "You've got me instead."

"How noble of you," Sadiq said dryly. "What knowledge do you have for me?"

"Plenty."

Sadiq studied him. "I believe you do. But I have a specific use for you, and it involves plenty of pain. A quick death is too good for you."

That Prophet believed. It was too late to get Sadiq to let Gary go. The kid knew too much. The second he'd stepped foot into Sadiq's world, he'd sold his soul. There was no going back.

"Prophet?" Gary looked uncertain, the way he had when Prophet had first moved him and his mother on that snowy day in the middle of February. Gary had refused to leave his father's picture and Prophet had to pry it out of his hands, because Hal's wife hadn't been able to force herself to do it.

"Just do what they say, Gary, okay? I'll find you."

"You want me to help them?"

"I don't want you to get hurt, kiddo." Hal's name for him. Code between Prophet and Gary for, *I'll find you if it takes the rest of my life.*

Gary stilled for a second, but Sadiq didn't catch it. He was too busy watching Prophet's reaction.

"Here's your chance, Petty Officer Drews," Sadiq said. "Your morality question. What do they call it? A trolley question? Anyway, you have time to get to only one of two men. One can cause massive destruction for your country. The other? A simple mercenary, dying in a room somewhere down this hallway. One life for untold millions. Who will you choose, Petty Officer Drews? Oh, and I've left you a little something to help you actually follow through on your choice."

The screen went black. The man in the black BDUs took the stool out from under Prophet as he dragged Gary out of the room. Gary kept looking back over his shoulder the entire time. But until the door closed, Prophet didn't allow himself to scream his agony.

He'd tried to grab the pipe, to stop himself from dangling, but there was no way to do that. He was able to grip the pipe with his hand, and slide his fingers along it until he felt the sharp metal. His *little something* from Sadiq.

No matter how he did this, it was going to hurt like hell, so he swung his legs to help the rope forward. The sharp metal had been left in the perfect position to slide and cut through the ropes that held him bound, hands over his head. But the ride down would be a bitch. As he worked, he stared at the black screen until it flickered back to life. It wasn't Sadiq anymore. Instead, half the screen showed footage of Gary, outside, being bound and dragged away by the guards. A helo waited in the background. The other half came to life seconds later. Through a thick fog of gas, he saw Tom, passed out on the floor of a cell.

Who will you choose?

As if there were really a choice. This was about the mindfuck, not choices, and Prophet screamed again into the empty room just to hear his own voice bounce off the walls.

As the rope began to fray, his wrists pulled apart, and for a second there was blinding pain before the rope mercifully broke. He slammed to the ground, tried to push up on his wrists and nearly screamed. They were, of course, broken again. Barely functioning, but he'd lived with—fought with—worse.

He didn't even have to second-guess his choice. He slammed the locked door with his foot, which splintered it enough that a second kick got him free. He then did the same thing to each locked room down the hallway from where he'd been kept because he couldn't grip the doorknobs, yelling in case Tom could hear him.

If he knew what kind of gas it was, if he'd had any time to play with, to get Gary and then detox Tom, he would have. It's what Tom would want. Beyond that, it's what Tom would expect.

But time had run out. He kicked open the second to last room and didn't even give himself time to note that his heart started fucking beating again, because Tom was barely breathing. He pulled his T-shirt up over his mouth and nose, held his breath until he kicked out the two back windows to allow enough gas to escape. A quick breath of fresh air, and he turned back to Tom.

The screen in Tom's room flickered, allowing Prophet to see the men dragging Gary onto the helo. The last thing he saw was Gary's face, the frightened look of a young boy still frozen in his expression, before the guards pulled him away.

You failed him. Again.

Prophet pushed those thoughts from his brain impatiently as he shoved his arms under Tom's arms, bent his own at the elbows despite the screaming fucking pain, and dragged Tommy out of the room before he passed out from the gasses too. The entire time he was dragging Tommy, the slowest fucking moments of his life, he couldn't help but think that they weren't going to let Tom live, even if they did allow Prophet to save him.

He got Tom out of the room, shut the billowing gas behind the door, and nearly collapsed in front of it, sweating and shaking.

A shadow fell across him. He looked up, vision hazy from the gas he'd inhaled, to see one of the guards. He forced himself to his feet and tackled the man to the ground with a head to the guy's stomach.

Even so, his head began to spin, and then the world went dark.

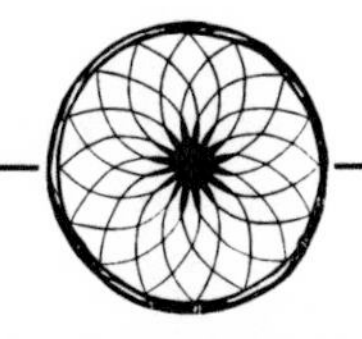

CHAPTER TWENTY-SIX

Prophet roused. He was still in the hallway, but Tom was gone. *Fuck.*

He stilled when he heard footsteps. Braced for a fight and found one. Maneuvered onto his knees and used his legs to propel himself forward so he slammed into the man who came around the corner. Fought for his goddamned life, because he wasn't going down. Didn't matter that his shoulder was dislocated or his wrists were fractured.

He slammed the man to the ground, his elbow pinning him. Immediately, he was thrown aside and found himself with his cheek on the floor.

"You might not want to kill your rescuer."

That voice, murmured in his ear, didn't sound familiar, but the British accent was enough to make Prophet ask, "Cillian?"

"Tom's safe. Stop fighting me and pretend to be unconscious. I'll carry you out. There are still guards left here."

Prophet had figured it wouldn't be that easy for him to escape with Tom—and it was just as he'd feared. If Cillian hadn't been here . . .

But he was. And Prophet would take any help as long as it meant Tommy was safe. He closed his eyes, went limp and allowed Cillian to pick him up and carry him along.

He heard another guard call out to Cillian, who answered, "I've got him—he was passed out in the hall. Why the hell did you let him get this far?" He did an American accent well.

The other guard argued back, and then Prophet heard a familiar gurgle and then silence.

"The rest of them are on the helo," Cillian said as he lowered Prophet gingerly to his feet near the guard lying on the floor with his throat slit. "They've got Gary."

He stared into the face of the dark-haired, dark-eyed man who was taller than he'd expected, and just as handsome as he'd dreamed. "Get me to the tarmac."

Cillian held him in place. "Forget it."

"Come on, man, you and me, we can stop this."

"It's already done."

That's when Prophet knew that Cillian wasn't just here on a mission of mercy. "You rigged the helo to blow."

"Yes.

"You can't fucking do this."

"I have to. I make the same hard choices as you."

"It's not his fucking fault," Prophet growled. And yet he knew this was the right outcome. After all, he'd sold his soul twice, making the same promise to Hal about Gary that he'd made to his country about Hal.

Cillian shook his head, but the guy understood. Maybe a little too well. "That doesn't matter and you know it. I'm not letting go of you. It's too late."

Prophet didn't want to believe that was ever the truth. He knew fighting Cillian wouldn't get him anywhere. He leaned against the wall, but Cillian still didn't let him go. Said, "You know this is the right thing."

"It would be, but Gary knows he's done the wrong thing. He's being forced now."

"Sometimes you can't take back your choices," Cillian told him.

"I don't believe that. I don't think you do either, no matter how cynical you try to be."

Cillian countered with, "*You* don't want to believe that," in a voice that was oddly gentle, as was the hand that brushed the hair out of Prophet's eyes. Cillian stared at his bruised and swollen face, then said, "I'm sorry, Prophet," as the explosion rocked the building.

Prophet closed his eyes, and Cillian's ironclad grip loosened, but the man was still the only thing holding him up. "Not his fault," he repeated.

Cillian shook him a little, forcing Prophet to open his eyes. "It *is* his fault. And you live to fight another day."

"How'd you find me?"

"Trackers."

Fuck, why the hell was every guy in his life tracking him? "Invasion of privacy," he croaked.

"And here I'd have thought I'd at least get a thanks for saving your ass."

He encouraged Prophet to lean on him as they started to walk through the hall. The guy smelled good, even through the metallic tang of blood in his nostrils. "Where's Tommy?"

Cillian stared at him. "I told you, your partner's fine. He's with medics. He's conscious. I got him out first because I figured you'd insist on it."

Prophet didn't argue, concentrated on moving one foot in front of the other, trying to pretend Cillian wasn't the only thing stopping him from meeting the floor headfirst.

"For the record, he refused to leave until I got you out first," Cillian told him.

"How'd you get him to change his mind?"

A small, satisfied smile played on Cillian's lips. "I punched him out."

"You what?"

"Relax. I'm almost positive there won't be any permanent damage."

"He's going to kill you."

"Like I don't hear that every day of my life." Cillian lowered Prophet into an old metal folding chair by the front door. "Another helo's coming soon. I don't think you're in any condition to drive, so I'll make sure your truck makes it home."

Prophet watched the man's face as he checked Prophet over, fingers running along his face and neck . . . feeling the dislocated shoulder. "I can take care of that now."

He'd had this done before. He braced himself as best he could. The excruciating pain made him stop breathing temporarily. He was aware of Cillian steadying him, talking to him . . . Finally, he whooshed in a breath, and the pain went from level holy fuck to an ache.

Gingerly, he moved his shoulder up and down. He'd be sore, but better than the alternative. Cillian held up a syringe. "Pain meds?"

"Fine."

Cillian paused before giving him the shot. "You didn't think you were getting out."

It wasn't a question.

"Didn't realize you'd graduated from spook to mind reader." Fuck, it was so much easier talking to Cillian on IM without the prying, all-knowing eyes.

"Why the suicide mission? And don't tell me I wouldn't understand. Your partner might not—"

"He's a good guy."

"I believe that."

"Then what's the problem?"

"Good guys don't always make good partners, Prophet."

"What happened is just another chapter."

"And it's not over yet."

"No."

"So why die now?" Cillian prodded as Prophet heard the whir of the helo's blades in the distance.

"I wasn't trying to die," was all he said. "And no one asked you to come here after me. This mission was obviously on your radar already, so don't pull your hero shit with me, you fucker. It wasn't *about* me."

Cillian's eyebrows shot up, but his face still wore a slightly amused expression. And if Prophet's could've punched him, he would've, especially when Cillian said, "Believe what you want, but you're wrong. Do you think it was easy for me to break into your computer and all your phones?"

"Probably."

"Fine. But that's not the point. I risked life and limb."

"You love it. Live for this shit."

"Again, beside the point."

"Angling for a job at EE?"

"I don't think so. I have employment." Cillian stared at him. "I want my couch back."

"Bastard. Fuck, I hate owing people."

"I know. And you owe me twice."

"You'd better hurry and collect. I'm not letting this shit hang over my head forever."

Cillian laughed softly, stared straight ahead. Bastard wasn't committing to a damned thing. "You can close your eyes now," he told Prophet.

He wanted to, but a lifetime of experience refused to allow him. Doc would have sedated him further; Prophet was pretty sure of that. His body was one big throb—not the good kind.

Cillian watched him carefully, finally asking, "Do you want to tell me what this is really all about?"

"Can't."

Cillian accepted that with an ease that Tom probably never could. Prophet's brain was too rattled to figure out which way was actually better, but for sure, Cillian made things easier. The spook understood that this wasn't his mission, his fight.

"I'll take care of it," he told Cillian. "All of it."

"I have no doubt." Cillian stood. "Wait here—I'm getting you a stretcher."

He didn't bother arguing. He was already swaying in his chair.

"Just because he makes things easy on you doesn't make it better," John said from his usual leaning pose. This time, he was close, propped against the wall, surveying the situation and shaking his head. "You always fuck up the trolley questions. This was a big fuck-up."

"Takes one to know one," Prophet said.

"That's all you got?"

"You . . . need to shut the fuck up," Prophet told John. He blinked and he was alone again. And he was going goddamned nuts. Completely certifiable, and he hoped the drugs Cillian gave him were to blame.

After he was ushered onto a helo, Tom watched with clenched teeth as Cillian tended to Prophet. His partner looked like hell, although Tom wasn't surprised he was still fighting unconsciousness with everything he had. He'd crash soon. And then maybe Tom would kill Cillian. Or at least return the favor of a knockout punch.

He rubbed his jaw—it would ache for weeks, although it wasn't broken. But that wasn't actually what had made him go out. While he was down, Cillian had used pressure points to put him to sleep. The punch had been unnecessary.

Asshole.

"All you had to do was follow my order," Cillian called to him over his shoulder, no doubt because he felt Tom's scathing look on him.

"I don't have to follow any order of yours or any of your fucking people. I don't know who the fuck you are," Tom yelled back.

Cillian turned around then, his eyes flashing. "I'm the one Prophet was talking to when you were in his bed. Do we need a further introduction?"

"You need to leave him the fuck alone."

"I didn't realize you'd marked him as yours," Cillian commented.

"He's my partner," Tom ground out as Prophet opened his eyes, stared straight at him and said, "Tommy?"

Tom couldn't help but smirk. Cillian walked away, off the helo, which was just fucking fine with Tom. He moved over to Prophet, bent close so he could hear him clearly over the roar of the chopper. "Hey, we're headed back to EE now."

"Good." His eyes looked unfocused. "Fucking drugs again."

"Yeah, they gave them to me too."

The helo lifted. Tom braced himself next to Prophet, held on as the bird rose and took flight away from the warehouse. He put a hand over Prophet's, and they remained silent through the hour's ride to EE's helo pad. When they touched down, Prophet refused the waiting stretcher, instead asking for Tom to help him out of the bird and into the infirmary.

As they limped along the tarmac and across the grass toward the EE building, Tom finally said, "Sadiq said you'd choose wrong. He said you'd choose wrong every time."

"*He's* wrong. It was all a trap anyway. They wouldn't have let any of us go."

Tom didn't say anything for several more feet, trying to figure out what Prophet's choice had cost him. He knew Prophet had made the wrong choice, but he also knew neither one of them regretted it. "So that's the only reason you saved me?"

"Double trap. No matter which way I moved, I was screwing someone."

"Now what?"

"Now we both have bounties on our heads. Welcome to my world, T. Float down the river of crap that runs through it with me."

Somehow, that ended up being the most comforting thought of the day.

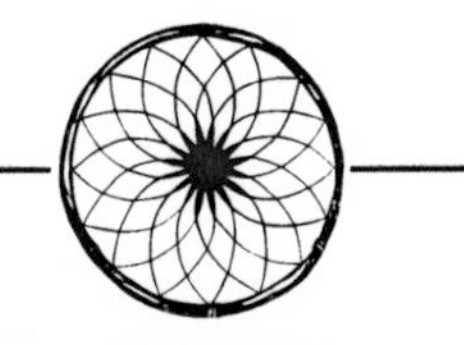

CHAPTER TWENTY-SEVEN

Doc cleared Tom after twenty-four hours.

"Prophet's staying," was all Doc would tell him. "Go home. Rest. You'll hear from Phil about your next job soon. I'll let you travel in a week."

A week to sit around and think. "I want to go sooner."

"And I want a million unlimited blowjobs, but we can't all have the perfect life."

"Fuck you."

Doc laughed. "They say you're not officially part of the EE team until you say that to me."

Tom had been wondering if Phil would keep him after all of this. It was one thing for Prophet to disobey a direct order, but Tom was new and unproven. Didn't expect to have the same kind of leeway, or any, for that matter. He'd gotten more than he'd ever thought from this company autonomy-wise, and he knew he'd gotten lucky for maybe the first time ever with a partner.

"You've still got a job."

"What, does everyone around here read minds?" Tom asked, exasperated.

"Yes. Now go home. Watch a movie. Stop brooding." Doc paused. "He'll be all right."

"He took the brunt of the beating."

"He doesn't want to see anyone."

"Anyone . . . or me?" Doc's nonanswer was the only one Tom needed. "I don't give a fuck what he wants."

He pushed past Doc, surprised and relieved when the broad mountain of a man let him. Prophet didn't look surprised when Tom stormed into his room. He looked a hell of a lot better than the last time Tom had seen him.

"Heard you're going home," Prophet said.

"Yeah." Tom moved closer to the bed. "What about you?"

"Another week, I'm told. Sucks."

Tom nodded, then asked, "Was John killed before the video was made?"

Prophet stared at him steadily. For a moment, Tom was sure he was going to lie, but then he said, "I don't know that John's dead. I never saw a body. I was told he died during the torture."

"And because you survived, you think he might've."

"I spent two straight years AWOL, looking for him. No trace. No one could give me an answer."

"You stopped looking?"

"I kept feelers out there. I sweep when I can. But if he's there, until I find a body . . ." Prophet paused. "He'd never leave me behind."

"Ah, Proph." Tom would've pulled him in for a hug if he'd thought the man would let him. But Prophet wouldn't, not now.

"Thanks for not giving me the *It's not your fault* bullshit."

"I'd rather just get you a step closer to finding out what happened to John."

Prophet nodded. "Cillian's looking into it for me. Off the record."

He glanced down at Tom's hands, which he'd inadvertently fisted at the mention of the spook's name. "You sure it's a good idea to involve that guy and his team?"

"Cill works alone."

"You know him that well?" Tom asked, then sighed. "He wasn't working alone when he grabbed me."

"Yeah, he said there were medics with you in the warehouse."

"There were at first. I woke a little while they were giving me oxygen and an IV of something, then I went back out. When I woke up the second time, there was another guy in there with me."

Prophet's brow furrowed. "What'd he look like?"

"It was a little bit of a blur. He had a black skullcap, so I couldn't see his hair. Green eyes. Caucasian. Not as tall as me, but not much shorter. He had this big watch on too. Looked expensive but sturdy. He didn't say anything, but he was watching me. Like a fucking prison warden."

"Not bad for being blurry," Prophet said wryly. "You say anything to Phil about it?"

"It's in my report, yes."

Prophet closed his eyes. "Wouldn't worry about it."

Tom wasn't. Because there were too many other things to worry about, including Prophet. "Do you know where Sadiq is?"

"I have an idea."

"Then we'll go when you're out."

Prophet shook his head. "It's not an EE mission. It's mine. Because it's not over, T. Won't ever be, but at least I know what happened to Chris, and it had nothing to do with the fighting and everything to do with me." Prophet's face looked fierce and somehow beautiful, etched in all that anger.

Tom ran his palm across the crisp white sheet, wishing he could just take Prophet's hand in his instead. But he didn't. "Secrets are necessary. I believe that more than anyone. But you're still going to pull that shit on me, even now? What, is Cillian the only one allowed to help you? What do I have to do, Prophet? What the hell do I have to do to—" He choked back the last word. "Forget it. Fuck it."

Prophet's brow furrowed and his jaw clenched a little before he asked almost reluctantly, "Do you want me more because you don't want him to want me?" He paused as Tom stared at him. "I don't think you can answer that honestly."

"Fuck you, Prophet. Don't you tell me how I can answer. You don't know enough about me. You think you do, but you're wrong."

Prophet pressed his lips together, brow furrowed. "I don't goddamned want what I asked to be true, Tommy."

"Believe what you want." Because Tom wasn't only competing with a ghost that might not be a ghost, but also a very not-dead spook. "You're blind if you can't see what's happening here . . ." He stopped talking when he saw the odd look in Prophet's eyes and had a flash of memory he just couldn't see clearly, like an underexposed photo. "What?"

"Nothing. Just gonna keep on being blind. That's all."

"Fuck you, Prophet." *And why did it always come back to that?*

"And fuck you harder, Tommy."

"You're going to be alone for the rest of your life."

"I know," Prophet said, with no emotion behind his words.

"And you fucking deserve it, because it's no one's fault but yours."

"I know that too. Can you shut the door on your way out?" he asked mildly.

Tom did more than that. He slammed it so hard it cracked. The EE office staff stopped to stare for 0.5 seconds, but then went right back to work.

Tom knew it was par for the course for anyone who'd worked with Prophet.

He didn't leave, though. He stayed in one of the empty rooms until he'd calmed down. Because if Prophet was purposely trying to push him away—again—why the fuck did he keep falling for it?

He moved to go back into Prophet's room, looked through the small glass pane and saw Prophet sitting on the edge of the bed, getting his casts redone. The door was partially opened, and Prophet was really fucking quiet. Not sulky quiet, but dark place quiet. Tom could already recognize the difference.

Prophet's arms were in front of him, one partially wrapped already. Doc stopped, put his hand on the back of Prophet's neck. Prophet's head hung down, and Tom heard Doc saying, "Breathe," then "I'll leave as much free as I can and I'll make sure you can cut it off if you have to." And finally, "No one can hold you down again."

He had no idea what Doc was talking about, but obviously, Prophet had bigger issues than he'd realized. Mainly because Prophet had spent so much time taking care of him that Tom had only just began to realize how deeply Prophet's wounds ran. After a few minutes, and just when Tom was going to walk into the room, Doc gave Prophet a one armed hug, and Tom's belly tightened with jealousy.

But it was more than that. Prophet only let a few people get close to him, and those men were his walls, his fortress. He used them to keep people out, and that wasn't changing anytime soon.

Tom walked away, and he didn't look back.

Doc was babying him again and Prophet let him, because he couldn't get through the casting without it. The fact that the panic attack he should've had during his capture had happened here instead was good news to Prophet. Better news for Tom.

"Your partner's worried about you," Doc said.

"Good for him." Prophet turned and winced. The IV was tangled around his chest, it was hard to move with the cast and the bullet wound on the same side of his body—and all of it was for nothing.

He'd failed in his promise to Hal. And that promise had meant everything. At times it felt as if it was all he'd had left.

"You're really fucking dangerous when you're quiet. You know that, right?"

"Yeah."

He'd known Doc since their Navy days. Even though they'd never worked together as operatives, Prophet had a great deal of respect for someone who recognized that his own injuries (arm and shoulder) were extensive enough to put his teammates at risk and quit. Now Doc ministered to operatives, telling them how and when their injuries might affect them. Urging them to think of options, ways to use their expertise instead of getting hurt beyond repair.

"You know he saw us, right?" Doc asked.

"Yeah."

"And you want to leave him with the impression that you and I are fucking?"

Prophet shrugged. The whole thing had taken too much from him—even Doc knew that, which was why he stopped pushing the issue.

"I let him in."

Doc didn't require any further information. For most, letting someone in was good. For Prophet, not so much. He closed his eyes and saw them together, tangled in the sheets. Tom's weight on him. Tom, whispering his name, then shouting it.

"You've got it bad," Doc said.

"Shut up."

And Doc did, until the casts were finished. "I'll give you a minute. Then Phil wants to see you."

He nodded. Put his head back on the pillow, felt like he was shattering, the way he had when he was with Tommy in bed, with breath forced out of him, eyes rolling back, everything breaking apart until he knew he'd never be able to put himself together again. Not the way he'd been, anyway.

Had that way really been so great? Comfortable? Not really.

But he wasn't going to be that shattered man for much longer. He had no choice in the matter.

You could give up your quest now. Take your choice back.

But it wasn't only his decision to make.

Phil marched in, looking grim. "You okay?"

"I will be."

"Good."

Prophet waited for more, because he knew he'd disobeyed Phil's orders once too often—and had gotten away with it more often than anyone had a right to. At least the clean-up of the warehouse and the exploded helo were on Cillian, so it wouldn't blow back onto EE. But somehow, Prophet knew that wouldn't comfort his boss much.

Phil was staring at him. He did his best not to shift under the gaze, wondered how many young Marines had cracked and cried for their momma in Phil's lifetime.

When the man spoke again, his tone was harder than it had been moments earlier. "You almost got an operative killed."

"He followed me."

"On an unauthorized mission."

"It was part of Chris's mission," Prophet told him. "There's no way to trace what happened at that warehouse to EE."

"That you know of."

"What do you want, Phil? My balls on a platter?"

"I want you to keep me in the goddamned loop."

He nodded instead of making promises he couldn't keep.

"And you were on medical leave. I expect you not to take on other jobs during the time you're under medical care."

Prophet nodded again.

"And now, you're officially on medical leave. Again."

Prophet gritted his teeth and nodded, because it was infinitely safer than opening his mouth.

Phil lowered his voice. "What the fuck really happened, Prophet? What's really going on?"

"A lot of shit."

"You know who killed Chris."

"Yeah." He winced internally as he said, "Collateral damage." Knew that Phil would understand he didn't mean that callously.

Phil did understand, but he was probably the most fed up Prophet had ever seen him. And when Prophet opened his eyes, he noticed that the muscles in Phil's neck were corded, like he was trying very hard to stay under control.

"I don't know what the fuck's going on, Prophet, but if I'm ever going to trust you to take this place over, you're going to need to put your head on a lot straighter than this."

Prophet didn't trust his voice, but Phil didn't seem to want an answer.

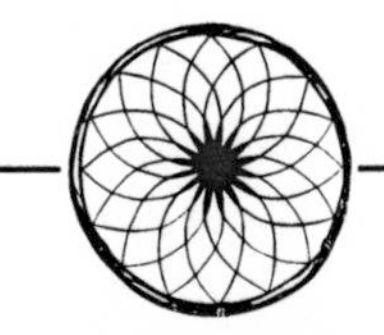

CHAPTER TWENTY-EIGHT

Prophet remained in the infirmary for two more days. Doc reluctantly released him, with new casts on his wrists, more involved, and his arms ached like a mother. So did his ribs and head, but he pretended he was completely fine just to get the hell home.

It was all quiet here. The coding of lights on Cillian's surveillance system let him know that the spook had left the building again.

He was both relieved and slightly disappointed.

He got on IM and found a message from days earlier.

I've got the intel you needed.

Prophet's fingers froze above the keys. He lowered himself into the chair and just stared at those words until they got blurry. Finally, he typed, *Tell me.*

He only had to wait half an hour for the reply.

Sorry—on the road. I've got DNA evidence.

You found a body?

There was no answer to that. Prophet typed, *How long?*

As far as the coroner can tell, he died in that prison when they told you he did. You can stop beating yourself up now.

Yeah, like that would ever happen. *Who covered it up?*

You're asking questions you know I can't answer. Stop.

Prophet snorted. Telling him to stop made his stubborn streak go into overdrive. He would dig to the bottom of this. He had no choice.

He also had no way of knowing if Cillian was telling the truth, but what would the guy have to gain by lying?

Everyone has something to gain by lying, Proph. John's words, echoing in his ears. And for once, John's ghost was fucking spot on.

Prophet would play along. He typed to Cillian, *I owe you.*

I know. And I like collecting favors.

It was only then that Prophet noticed the couch was back in the middle of his living room. Son of a— *Why the hell did you fight so hard at the warehouse instead of telling me it was you from the start?*

Wanted to see what you were made of.

Anything surprise you?

You're exactly what I expected.

And that's good or bad?

There was a long pause, and then Cillian typed, *Better.*

Prophet laughed out loud until he realized the guy was serious. He drummed his fingers on the table on front of him, not sure what to say next.

As though Cillian sensed that, he continued, *I figure we'll put the couch to good use when we're in town at the same time.*

Prophet's thoughts turned to Tommy, and he cursed under his breath. And then he typed, *I'll take you up on it,* and closed the lid like that would erase the evidence. Or the fact that Cillian intrigued him more than he wanted to admit.

For someone who didn't want to get involved with anyone, he was certainly involved as hell. And he still didn't know Tom's decision about partners. Not that he was going anywhere soon—not that it mattered. Not after what had just happened . . .

He squeezed his fists around his casts as he thought about this morning. He'd finished with Doc, then met up with the company shrink, who asked him about how he would handle the time off.

"How you'll handle it differently from your last medical leave," Sarah had corrected. "For instance, you could take this time to catch up on your paperwork."

"Why you gotta hurt me so?"

"It's so much fun." She'd grinned, then sobered. "Prophet, this is serious. Phil wants you back out there but—"

"Let me guess, you can't clear me."

"Won't, not can't."

"Why's that?"

She'd sat back and stared at him. "Until you can tell me that, you're definitely not going back out there."

"Dealing with a shrink's worse than a hostage negotiation," he'd told her, then he'd stopped by Phil's office to see if he could cajole his way out of this leave shit. And that had probably been his biggest mistake.

"Thought you said there were no mistakes in life, only opportunities." John's ghost mocked him now from across the room.

Prophet closed his eyes to block him out, and his last conversation with Phil replayed itself instead, the way it had been doing all damned day.

"You're on medical leave until I say differently," Phil had started the second Prophet had walked in. "And just to be clear—you'll be getting a new partner not because you asked or forced the issue, but because Tom shouldn't have to deal with your utterly unprofessional ass for one more day."

Prophet had smiled like he didn't give a shit, but Butler's words cut him to the quick. Plus, they came on top of his already very guilty conscience.

"Don't necessarily want anyone else," he'd said carefully.

"What are you saying?"

He'd wanted Phil to make the choice for him, but Phil was too smart for that, wouldn't give Prophet that satisfaction. "I'm saying, I'm tired of it always being my choice."

Phil had nodded slowly. "Well, then, even though I'm not giving you one, I'll let you know what Tom's choice is."

"Yeah, you do that," Prophet had muttered with a dismissive shrug. As soon as he did so, he knew he'd gone a touch too far. And the worst part was, he didn't think he gave a fuck.

The air in the room changed in a split second. Phil was on his feet, holding onto the desk so hard Prophet thought either the wood or the man's fingers would break.

"Always have to push it, right, Prophet?"

"S'what I do."

"You think I don't know you're doing everything possible to avoid running this place? Because we both know the circumstances under which you would be. I've come to terms with it."

"Good for fucking you, Phil." Prophet hadn't realized how much venom his tone held until Phil took a step backward, like he'd been slapped. But Prophet hadn't been able to stop. "I'm thrilled you've come to terms with my disease. With something that's going to take me off the playing field. But until then, I have jobs to do."

"Not here, you don't."

Prophet had stared at him.

"You go. You get your shit together, and then you come back. This last mission, you won't tell me what it was about, your report's shitty and incomplete, and Tom's story's worse. And yes, I know who else showed at that warehouse—Tom might not know who it was, but I goddamned do."

"I didn't ask King to come there—that had nothing to do with me."

"Never does, Prophet," Phil had said, and yeah, that had fucking hurt. "Whatever happened, it's not over. But your job here is. Forget what I said before and consider this an indefinite leave."

"Fuck you, Phil," was what he'd wanted to say, but the look on his face must've said it all, because Phil had softened.

"Prophet . . ."

But Prophet had been done. He'd given everything to Phil. Everything. Once again, he'd proven that he was too much for anyone to handle, at least for long periods of time.

He'd put his hand up to stop Phil from saying anything further, yanked his EE ID out of his wallet, and held it out to the man, daring him to take it. "I'm done."

After what had seemed like forever, Phil had taken the card from him, but then said, "Prophet, wait— "

But Prophet had been out the door before he could hear anything else.

Phil Butler called Tom in five days after he'd left the infirmary. Every single minute of those five fucking endless, boring days, he'd had to force himself not to call Prophet. Now, standing in Phil's office, his stomach was tight. He'd half expected—hoped—to see Prophet here.

"Please, sit."

Tom did.

"Prophet's home."

"Okay."

Butler stared at him. "You got attached."

"You sound surprised."

"While most agree that he's a good man to have at their side and have never requested a reassignment, they're always relieved when he moves on."

Tom digested that for a second. "He doesn't want any long-term attachments."

"No."

"Any particular reason?"

"You'd have to ask him."

Which meant there was a reason. There always was. Tom had to decide how deeply to dig. "When you put me with Cope, that was a test, right?"

Phil nodded. "Wanted to make sure you two got along."

"Didn't matter with Prophet."

"No one gets along with Prophet."

"Then why bother trying?"

"It's a matter of survival."

Tom knew Phil wouldn't elaborate on his cryptic statement, so he didn't bother asking. Because the question in Tom's mind was, whose survival, his or Prophet's? And in the end, did it really matter?

Walk away while you can. While Prophet still could.

Maybe Prophet had it right—don't stick with any one partner long enough to do any damage.

Permanent damage. He'd gotten lucky, and he'd never thought about himself and lucky in the same sentence, but when he was looking at Prophet, he couldn't help but wonder if his luck was about to change.

Phil put two folders on the desk in front of Tom. "Two missions," he said.

Tom looked at the names on the folders. One was Prophet, the other Cope. And here was the choice Phil had wanted him to make weeks ago, before he'd run off, half-cocked, back to Prophet and the mission that wasn't sanctioned.

"I understand why you went to Prophet," Phil had told him when he'd first stepped foot into EE's infirmary with Prophet's stretcher next to him. "I understand loyalty. I look for it in every operative I employ."

Now, Tom swallowed hard at the thought of Prophet, pictured him hanging by his wrists, interspersed with flashes of him from the video, the feral grin. The way he said Tom's name when he came.

It's not like you're never going to see him again. You're just not partnering, which means Prophet will be safe.

And after a moment's deliberation, he picked up Cope's folder. Phil nodded, like he understood. "Good choice."

It was, for Prophet's sake.

Because you couldn't make your own luck. You were either born with it or you weren't.

Explore more of
SE Jakes's *Hell or High Water* series at:
riptidepublishing.com/titles/series/hell-or-high-water

Dear Reader,

Thank you for reading SE Jakes's *Catch a Ghost*!

We know your time is precious and you have many, many entertainment options, so it means a lot that you've chosen to spend your time reading. We really hope you enjoyed it.

We'd be honored if you'd consider posting a review—good or bad—on sites like **Amazon, Barnes & Noble, Kobo, Goodreads, Twitter, Facebook**, **Tumblr,** and your blog or website. We'd also be honored if you told your friends and family about this book. Word of mouth is a book's lifeblood!

For more information on upcoming releases, author interviews, blog tours, contests, giveaways, and more, please sign up for our weekly, spam-free newsletter and visit us around the web:

Newsletter: tinyurl.com/RiptideSignup
Twitter: twitter.com/RiptideBooks
Facebook: facebook.com/RiptidePublishing
Goodreads: tinyurl.com/RiptideOnGoodreads
Tumblr: riptidepublishing.tumblr.com

Thank you so much for Reading the Rainbow!

RiptidePublishing.com

ACKNOWLEDGMENTS

I'm having such a great time working on this series with Riptide, so first and foremost I have to thank the fabulous Sarah Frantz for her kick-ass (and yes, there is a double meaning there) editing, her brilliant insights and infinite patience, and for loving the book as much as I do. Ditto for Rachel Haimowitz and the rest of the Riptide team—I'm a lucky author to be working for such great, dedicated publishers, authors, and artists.

As always, for my amazing readers, for coming along for the ride, for giving me your time, trust, and enthusiasm for each new release. The Hell or High Water series began with Prophet, a character who wouldn't stop showing up in my head, and in my other books. When I introduced him to Tommy, I realized that these men—and their relationship—were far bigger than any one book could do justice to. It wouldn't have been fair to them, or to my readers, to even try. The series is going to be a wild ride, but please, keep one thing in mind—I write romance. I write this particular genre for many reasons, the most important of which is that I think everyone deserves a happy ending, no matter how rough the path there might be.

And for my family, for always supporting my wildest dreams. I can't ever thank you enough.

ALSO BY

SE JAKES

Havoc Motorcycle Club
Running Wild

Hell or High Water (EE, Ltd.) Series
Long Time Gone
Daylight Again
Not Fade Away
If I Ever (Coming soon)

Men of Honor Series
Bound by Honor
Bound by Law
Ties That Bind
Bound by Danger
Bound for Keeps (EE, Ltd.)
Bound to Break

Standalone
Free Falling (EE, Ltd.)

Dirty Deeds Series (EE, Ltd.) Series
Dirty Deeds

ABOUT THE AUTHOR

SE Jakes writes m/m romance. She believes in happy endings and fighting for what you want in both fiction and real life. She lives in New York with her family and most days, she can be found happily writing (in bed). No really . . .

SE Jakes is the pen name of *New York Times* best-selling author Stephanie Tyler (and half of Sydney Croft).

You can contact her the following ways:

Email: authorsejakes@gmail.com

Website: sejakes.com

Tumblr: sejakes.tumblr.com

Facebook: Facebook.com/SEJakes

Twitter: Twitter.com/authorsejakes

Instagram: instagram.com/authorsejakes

Goodreads Group: Ask SE Jakes

Truth be told, the best way to contact her is by email or in blog comments. She spends most of her time writing but she loves to hear from readers!

CPSIA information can be obtained at www.ICGtesting.com
Printed in the USA
LVOW08s0920150516

488338LV00001B/72/P